LAWFUL
DEATH

By

Katherine Pathak

For Mum and Dad,

who introduced us to the wonderful east Essex
landscape

THE GARANSAY PRESS

**The Imogen and Hugh Croft Mysteries
Series:**

Aoife's Chariot

The Only Survivor

Lawful Death

Coming Soon:

The Woman Who Vanished

Short Stories:

Full Beam

THE GARANSAY PRESS

Prologue

It is just after midnight. The sky remains light due to the brightness of a full moon which hangs ominously over Langley Farm. The glow illuminates the numerous pieces of broken down machinery lying strewn about the yard surrounding Thomas Langley's old cottage.

The farm covers roughly ten acres of land, most of which is arable. It sits next to a thick, dark copse of oak and ash trees, within the gently undulating landscape of east Essex. The Langley small-holding is situated between the villages of Cold Norton and Mundon, only a few miles from the muddy banks of the River Blackwater. On this cold and clear night, there is a disconcerting quietness to the place.

From somewhere within the blackness of the nearby woods, comes the unmistakable sound of movement. It is impossible to progress silently amidst the fallen twigs and foliage which coat the forest floor. Three tall, well-built figures finally emerge from within the dense, crackling thicket; their widened eyes peering out across the open fields beyond.

'Do you think anyone heard us?' one of the men asks the other two in a loud whisper.

'How should I know? We'll wait here for a few minutes. If the coast's clear we can move in,' another replies.

The men are dressed in dark green camouflage gear, like soldiers on a night-time training exercise. Their faces are blackened with a cosmetic paint of some kind. Two of them have their woollen hats deliberately pulled down low. It is only possible to make out the colouring of one member of the gang, who has left his mane of shaggy, blondish hair uncovered.

When they have waited for what seems to be an appropriate length of time, the three men make their way, more quietly than before, towards a large barn lying between the woods and the old cottage. The tallest of the three attempts to open the barn doors but finds them to be firmly secured with a padlock.

'Shit. He doesn't normally lock up the sheds.' The man looks frantically around him for an implement he can use to prise open the wooden panels.

'Maybe we should look for stuff we can take without having to break into anything? There must be some half-decent tools lying around the yard - it's a mess,' suggests the intruder with the long hair.

'But he keeps the lead in this barn. I've seen it myself. It'll be worth thousands. Come on, we've made a big effort planning this, we won't get another chance,' the tall man replies, as he scans the nearby ground, suddenly bending down to pick up a rusty old crow-bar. 'Gotcha!' he grins, showing a set of yellowish teeth which glow oddly in the pale moonlight and contrast starkly with his darkened face.

It takes several attempts to lever open the huge set of doors. They finally break apart with the loud crack of splitting wood. Once inside the dank building, the three men move quickly and quietly, packing as much of the heavy dark metal into their rucksacks as possible before turning back towards the entrance. The gang stop dead in their tracks. Standing, silhouetted against the moonlight, is a man. He is cradling something large in his arms. From within the blackness of the barn, it is impossible to make out what it is.

'Who's there?' The figure calls into the shadows. It immediately becomes clear to the three men that Thomas Langley cannot see them inside the dark shed. He must have come out of his cottage simply looking for the source of all the noise. Acting instinctively, like a pack of wild animals cornered by a predator, the gang move in unison.

6

They run towards the old man, barging into him with all their strength and knocking him off his feet. Then, the tallest of the three brings down a hard blow on Langley's temple with the crow-bar and they make a dash for the trees.

'What the hell did you do that for?' shouts the blond man, as they stumble across the uneven soil, their heavily laden backpacks slowing them down. 'You might have bloody-well killed him!'

The tall man doesn't reply but the third member of the group starts to whimper, 'Oh Christ, what have we done? It wasn't supposed to be like this.'

'Shut up and head for the woods, you idiot,' the other man spits out.

They don't manage to reach the protection of the undergrowth. Half way across the field they hear the sound of a single gunshot, aimed somewhere in their general direction. All three men automatically drop to the ground.

'Empty your bags and give me back what you've taken,' calls a voice from not very far behind them.

The intruders continue to lie perfectly still on top of the cold earth, frozen in fear and with none of them daring to utter a word.

'I said, tip out your bags and then you can leave - I just want my property returned - okay?'

A few more seconds of complete silence tick by and then one of the men slowly lifts himself up onto his hands. He turns to face the old farmer. 'If I leave the bag here, will you let me go?'

'Yes,' Langley replies and gestures towards the ground in front of him with the barrel of his shotgun.

The intruder tentatively stands up and tosses his weighty rucksack over to Thomas Langley. The farmer responds with a small nod of acknowledgement. The lad turns and sprints off towards the trees, without even pausing to glance at his two companions. The other men remain stock-still and prone, somewhere within the damp grass and mud of the overgrown field.

Expecting his mates to follow on close behind, the dark figure reaches the edge of the copse and then slows down his pace a little. He continues to jog along, weaving carefully through the dense pattern of trees, occasionally looking over his shoulder, waiting for his partners-in-crime to finally catch him up. Stopping by the trunk of an old oak tree to take a breather, his body abruptly jerks to attention as he hears the clear sound of a gunshot. The noise simultaneously disturbs a group of birds nesting in the branches above, sending them momentarily flapping in all directions. They soon settle once again, leaving nothing in the isolated forest but an absolute and terrifying silence.

Two Months Later.
Chapter One

The Carlisle Rooms, located at the west-end of London's Regent Street, are a set of grand Georgian reception halls, catering for all manner of special events. Tonight, the occasion happens to be the launch of a new book by the revered psychologist and lecturer, Professor Hugh Croft.

Professor Croft has penned a good number of academic tomes over the past two decades, but this is his first attempt to introduce those theories in a more popularised form. His publishers have decided they will promote this new title with a little more gusto than they have done with his previous releases.

Hugh was initially reluctant to agree to such a lavish venue for the launch. His agent had to work hard to persuade him. Apparently, it was the best way to introduce his work to all of the appropriate people and was essential if he wanted his book to be successful.

Now the evening has got under way, Hugh is forced to concede it is quite an exhilarating experience. The main drawing room is tastefully lit by three enormous chandeliers and the long central table supports a large, pyramid-like formation. This bizarre centre-piece is constructed out of several dozen hardback editions of his new book: 'Beyond PTSD: how to live with the past and move forward'. Waiting staff are milling about the crowded venue with trays of champagne and canapés. Hugh grabs a fresh flute as one of the smart waiters passes him by.

The middle-aged author stands a little awkwardly. He is sipping steadily from his glass of bubbly and wishing his wife, Imogen, was here with him. Hugh's parents were primed to keep an eye on their teenage children for the evening. Imogen was just about to slip into her little black dress, when their daughter, Bridie, started throwing up loudly in the downstairs toilet. The poor girl didn't look any better half an hour later. Imogen reluctantly decided to stay at home, persuading her husband to go to the event without her. Despite, in theory, playing host to the proceedings, Hugh finds himself without anyone to talk to.

He notices how his agent is expertly 'working' the room; speaking in turn to publishers, editors and book retailers. It would not be worth Martin's while to spend the evening making small-talk with his own client. Imogen's brother, Allan, is here with his girlfriend, but since they arrived, Hugh hasn't been able to spot them anywhere within the lively, chattering crowd.

Just as he is wondering if he can sneak away early from his own party, Hugh sees someone he recognises. Making her elegant way towards him is Penny Mills. She was a contemporary of his at the private school they had both attended near Colchester in Essex. Hugh seems to recall she is a lawyer of some kind and notes how well she is looking. Penny's dark green velvet dress is figure-hugging and shows off her slim, athletic build perfectly.

'Hugh!' Penny cries out, as she plants a kiss on each of his cheeks, continental style. Her immaculately cut blond bob barely shifting out of place. 'Congratulations on your wonderful book!'

'Thank you, Penny, how lovely to see you again.'

'You don't look any different! Perhaps a little more 'filled out', but basically the same dark and brooding intellectual you always were!'

Hugh returns the compliment, as he knows he is expected to do. They chat for a while about how life has been treating them over the past few years. Their paths have crossed several times since school but they have never kept in regular contact during the intervening years. It turns out Penny is a defence lawyer for a prestigious Legal Chambers in Lincoln's Inn. He remembers now that she had studied Law at Oxford. Hugh is sure he heard she'd got married at some point.

Without him having to enquire, Penny suddenly says, 'sadly, I'm on my own again. James and I divorced last year. There's no bad feeling between us. We just couldn't make our busy jobs work alongside our marriage. It must help that Imogen is a housewife, without all of those conflicting priorities us 'career women' bring to the table.'

'Well, she keeps herself pretty busy,' Hugh responds weakly, somehow knowing his wife would not appreciate Penny's assessment of her and feeling he should put forward a qualification.

'Oh yes, I'm sure she does,' Penny replies, a little dismissively. In a change of topic she adds, 'have you heard about the Langley Farm case at all Hugh?'

'I could hardly have avoided knowing about it, living in my neck of the woods. The local community are completely divided over the incident.'

'I see. Because my chambers are defending the old man, Thomas Langley. Actually, I would very much appreciate it if you could give us an assessment of him - in the capacity of an expert witness, of course.'

Caught totally off-guard by this unexpected request, Hugh takes a few seconds to answer. 'Look, I'm not sure if that would be such a good idea. My son is quite friendly with one of the victim's families. I've probably got a vested interest.'

'Would this connection affect your impartiality as a psychologist, Hugh? You are the leading specialist in the field with regards to PTSD. We would rather have you than anyone else,' Penny presses.

He considers this for a moment. 'My clinical assessments are always totally unbiased, Penny, you know that. I only look at the evidence I am presented with. Is this a key part of your defence case - that Langley was suffering from PTSD? I know he's an ex-army man, but he must have retired decades ago.'

Penny shrugs her shoulders. 'It's an avenue we are exploring. The counsellor who has been working with him felt Thomas might benefit from more specialist treatment. She believed some of the things he told her suggested Langley had experienced traumatic events during his time as a soldier. She thought this might have triggered a 'disproportionate' response to the break-in. We just want to investigate it further, that's all.'

Hugh takes a gulp from his glass, finishing off the last few dregs of champagne. He has to admit he is very tempted to get involved in the case. Thomas Langley has been front page news for the past couple of months. Not least because the 'The Daily Informer' are running a high profile campaign to have all criminal charges against the elderly farmer dropped. Within Hugh's local community, in the rural east Essex countryside near to the Langley property, the case is not being viewed as quite so clear cut.

Back in August, Thomas Langley shot two young intruders who had stolen some lead flashing from one of his sheds. Twenty year old Darren Beck was hit in the shoulder by shotgun pellets and has recovered reasonably well from his injury. The twenty two year old Danny Carlow wasn't so lucky. He took the full force of the shot to the side of his head and died a few days later in hospital.

There was another intruder on the Langleys' farm that night too; a nineteen year old lad called Joshua Nash. He was the one who raised the alarm. It was his testimony which had resulted in Thomas Langley being charged with murder.

Nash claimed Langley held him at gunpoint, only 'allowing' him to flee after he had returned the stolen property. Nash described how he dumped his bag and left the other two boys behind, expecting them to do the same and catch him up at a nearby copse of trees. Nash made it absolutely clear that when he left Carlow and Beck, they were completely at the mercy of Thomas Langley, who was armed with his shotgun. The lads had been lying face down on the ground, posing no threat whatsoever to the old farmer.

Despite recent changes in legislation to allow property owners more freedom to defend themselves and their possessions, the law does not extend to allowing young men to be shot dead whilst running away from the scene. Joshua Nash's evidence became a crucial part of the case against Langley.

However, there were other mitigating circumstances involved. It is the knowledge of this which tempts Hugh to assist the defence team.

Danny Carlow had armed himself with a crow-bar whilst they were pilfering from the farm. He used it to strike Thomas Langley down just minutes before the gang made their escape. At the time of the shooting, the seventy-eight year old had a heavily bleeding gash across his forehead and was suffering from a severe concussion.

Added to this, Carlow appeared to still have been holding onto the crow-bar when he was shot by Langley. Indeed, Darren Beck's testimony had proved extremely interesting. He said that after Nash ran off into the woods, Carlow slowly manoeuvred himself backwards along the ground and made a lunge for the old man again with his rusty weapon. Beck said it was amidst the confusion and panic of Carlow's second attack on Thomas Langley that the gun had been fired.

Hugh is just about to give Penny Mills his answer when their discussion is interrupted by the unsteady arrival of his brother-in-law. Allan looks as if he has had a little too much to drink.

'Good evening, Hugh. I hope I'm not butting in on anything I shouldn't be, old man,' Allan slurs, with a mischievous glint in his eye. 'Should I be letting my little sister know you're chatting up a glamorous blonde, whilst she is at home, performing a vigil by your daughter's bedside?' He then proceeds to introduce himself with a flourish to the stylish lawyer.

Hugh is fond of Allan, but sometimes he has to work very hard to remind himself that Imogen's brother takes great pleasure in trying to push people's buttons. He simply draws in a deep breath and replies, 'it's purely business, Allan, so you can climb down off your white charger. Penny has asked me if I would act as an expert witness in her latest case. Before you rode up my good fellow, I was about to agree.'

Penny breaks into a broad smile and for a brief moment, Hugh senses it is prompted by relief. Allan begins to totter about dangerously, causing Hugh to put out an arm to steady him. Thankfully, his brother-in-law's partner, Abigail, joins them at this moment and moves in to support Allan on his other side. There is a look of what can only be described as affectionate exasperation on her pretty face.

'There you are!' she gushes. 'Good, you've found Hugh at last. Now we can say our goodbyes and I can get you straight back home - we've both got work tomorrow morning, for heaven's sake.'

'Come on, Abigail, I'll help you,' Hugh says kindly. 'I was just thinking it was time to leave myself.'

14

The three of them slip away from the party as inconspicuously as they possibly can, climbing straight into an awaiting taxi and out of the busy night-time streets of London's west-end.

Chapter Two

Hugh has been dreading telling Imogen about his decision to assist Thomas Langley's defence team. Their middle child is closely involved with the Carlow family. Hugh is worried his association with the case might cause problems for their son. As it turns out, his wife's reaction to the news surprises him.

The Crofts live in a relatively modern house which sits half-way along a single track lane, near the pretty little hamlet of Cooper's End. It is in a remote part of the east Essex peninsula that stretches out into the sleepy and meandering River Blackwater. The area is low-lying and full of rivers and creeks, making it marshy and occasionally prone to flooding. The potentially isolated nature of the location is tempered by its close proximity to the bustling town of Maldon, which is just a mile or so up the coast from here. This is where Ian and Bridie Croft attend secondary school. It provides all the necessary services and amenities for the many little village communities which lie within its environs.

It is on the outskirts of one of these tiny communities that the Langleys' Farm is situated; close to the village of Cold Norton. When the burglary and shooting occurred in the summer, it sent shock waves out across the surrounding area.

The Carlow family live in Maldon itself and are well known there. The uncle of the dead boy runs a small chain of hardware stores of which there is a branch in the town's busy High Street. There was a huge outpouring of sympathy for the whole family in the aftermath of Danny's tragic death.

On the other hand, this largely rural landscape is dominated by farming. There was a considerable amount of understanding and support for Thomas Langley and the manner in which he had been forced to defend his property. The case had very much divided opinion within the area. At one stage, a week or so after the incident took place, emotions were running very high. Angry letters were being written to the local papers on a daily basis, fiercely representing both sides of the argument. There was even a suggestion amongst local farmers they should boycott the Carlows' shop. This campaign was sparked by the news that Langley would indeed be charged with murder.

In the end, no such boycott took place and feelings have gradually become moderated by the passage of time. Hugh is concerned that when Thomas Langley's trial begins, it will stoke up these angry divisions once again. Hugh grew up in this part of the world. Despite devoting a few years to studying and living in Scotland, he has spent the majority of his life here. His parents, Kathleen and Gerry, live just up the road in Maldon itself. The Croft family still have many friends in the area. It concerns him deeply that his own community should be embroiled in such an unpleasant turn of events.

Hugh waits until the bracing and bright Saturday morning after the book launch to broach the subject with his wife. They have enjoyed a leisurely walk along the promenade in Maldon, passing the multitude of dog-walkers who take this picturesque route along the banks of the river Blackwater every weekend. The couple sit down on a bench looking out across the water, slowly sipping cappuccinos from cardboard cups held in their gloved hands. This is the moment Hugh chooses to tell her about his decision.

Imogen takes a few moments to absorb the information before she responds. 'That's a big responsibility, Hugh. It's a very high profile case. This is more than you've ever taken on before and it will be in addition to your normal teaching, remember.'

'Yes,' he replies, 'but I think the university will be keen for me to do it. It will be good for the department's reputation. They might even lighten my teaching load a little. How do you think Ian will feel about it?'

Imogen and Hugh's teenage son had become quite friendly with Nikki and Will Carlow over the summer holidays. They all attend the same sailing club in Maylandsea. Ian still absolutely loves spending his free time out on the water. Nikki and Will are cousins of the boy who was killed by Thomas Langley, although Imogen has always sensed the two branches of the family were not particularly close.

'I'm genuinely not sure. I get the distinct impression that Nikki and Will's parents prefer to keep their distance from Rick's brother and his wife. They are both such lovely kids. You couldn't imagine in a million years either of those two being involved in an aggravated burglary.'

'Quite so. Within some extended families, cousins can be absolutely hand-in-glove, especially if they are close in age. They can often appear to be more like siblings. With the Carlows, I don't think that's the way it is. Although, poor Rick had to shoulder some of the fall-out from Danny's misadventures - it was *his* shops the local farmers were threatening to boycott.'

Imogen sighs, 'it wouldn't have been very fair if they had. But in a way, I can understand their strength of feeling.'

Hugh's wife had herself grown up on an isolated farm on the Scottish island of Garansay, so she had certainly understood the strong reaction by local landowners to Langley's treatment at the hands of the authorities.

'Mum was living on her own at Lower Kilduggan for all those years. It was always my greatest fear someone might break in while she was there all by herself. The Carlow boy had taken a crow-bar to old Langley and it looks fairly likely he was about to do it again when Thomas let off the shot-gun. I cannot see how it constitutes cold-blooded murder. To *me*, it sounds much more like self-defence.'

Hugh is surprised to hear his usually liberal-minded wife adopting this view.

'I'd certainly like to find out from Langley himself what happened during those few moments before the gun was fired. My understanding is that Darren Beck's testimony was taken less seriously than Nash's because he had a criminal record. Joshua Nash had never been in trouble with the police before. It does interest me how Beck appeared to be defending *Langley* rather than Danny Carlow. It makes his testimony seem the more convincing of the two.' Hugh looks across the river, watching a barge make its way out of the quay and slowly glide towards open water.

'Let me speak to Ian about it. I'll try to explain that you aren't actually going to be taking sides with Thomas Langley, but simply providing your impartial opinion,' Imogen says this thoughtfully, tipping her head to one side and letting her ebony black hair fall across her shoulder.

Hugh turns back to his wife with a look of concern on his face. 'I don't want to cause any problems for us as a family by doing this. Or for Mum and Dad. I just feel it might be possible for me to throw some new light on the case - does that make any sense?'

Imogen leans in and places a tender kiss on her husband's lips. 'I know exactly what you mean, darling.

Somehow, I get the impression justice is not being properly served for Thomas Langley. Whatever you need to do, I will support you.'

Emboldened by Imogen's response, Hugh contacts Penny Mills first thing on Monday morning. He wants to find out what is going to be expected of him. Again, Penny sounds relieved to hear back from the psychologist, as if she hadn't quite believed he was genuine when he had agreed to provide his services at the party. Indeed, she has to take a few moments in which to locate the Langley file before she can fill him in on some of the details.

'What I will do for starters,' the lawyer says briskly, 'is to e-mail you Langley's army record and a bit of background information about the family. I can also send over the notes his counsellor has made so far. I will have to wait to get those from her, so it might be a few days from now until you receive them. It is Langley's solicitor, Clifford Maynard, who is liaising with the client. I'll get him to send me everything he's got and then I can work with you directly, okay?'

'That's fine. I'd like to take some time to examine his army career. If I could look at his medical file too it would be a great help, Penny. After that, I will be ready to see him. It's important I build up a relationship with Langley in order to produce my assessment, so the sooner we get a meeting arranged the better,' Hugh concludes decisively.

'Okay,' Penny says and Hugh can tell she is smiling on the other end of the line. 'You're beginning to sound more enthusiastic about the case than I am! I'll ring Clifford and see what I can get fixed up. Thomas has been given bail, as you know, although we didn't think it was wise for him to return to the farm - for his own safety. He is staying somewhere outside the area. I'll have to organise clearance for you to be given the address, which will take a little while, I'm afraid.'

Hugh finds to his surprise he spends the rest of the working day with one eye on the e-mail inbox, waiting for Penny's promised information to arrive. He is keen to begin the background work which will be necessary to produce a psychological profile good enough to be submitted to a court of law. It needs to be sufficiently convincing for him to be rigorously cross-examined upon. But it is not only this. Hugh has become intrigued by the case and he is eager to meet the old man who appears to be at the centre of it all.

Chapter Three

Imogen Croft is an attractive brunette in her early forties. She had her first child when she was relatively young and he has now left home for university. Imogen was, at one time, an English teacher. Since having her three children, she divides her time between tending to their many needs and providing a little home-based tutoring; mostly for the offspring of her local friends.

In recent months, she has acquired an interest in research. It developed out of the investigation she found herself entangled in following the death of her mother a few years back. Imogen has since discovered she is quite adept at solving tricky puzzles, particularly of the kind which involve people. Imogen likes to feel she has a good instinct for the idiosyncrasies of human nature and that her insights might be of some value to Hugh in his new role.

In the meantime, she has been given the unenviable task of discussing the Langley case with her seventeen year old son, Ian. Imogen waits until Bridie is engrossed in her homework before she approaches him with her news.

Ian Croft possesses a tall and ungainly frame. His dark colouring and olive complexion indicate that once he has filled out a little, he will become a good looking young man. Hugh and Imogen's middle child has always been a source of worry for his parents. When Ian was only two years old he was diagnosed with type 1 diabetes. This has meant a daily injection and the close supervision of his diet throughout childhood and adolescence.

As he gets older, Imogen is trying to delicately steer a path between allowing him the space to manage his own condition and making sure he remains in good health. It is a balancing act which hasn't always proved successful. She is very much aware Ian may be leaving home for college in a couple of years and he needs to learn how to fend for himself in the wider world. As far as Imogen and Hugh are concerned, his interest in sailing has always been very beneficial. It has kept him active and outdoors. He loves it so much that it has stopped him from brooding on his predicament and letting it get him down.

This new found friendship between her son and the Carlow twins immediately struck Imogen as a very good thing, being founded as it is on a shared love of messing about on the water. She does not wish to jeopardise the relationship in any way. They are great kids and seem to have brought Ian out of his shell. He is obviously very relaxed in their company.

Imogen decides to approach the topic by asking her son's general opinion about the Langley case. Ian is lying on top of his Manchester United bedspread when his mother enters the room. Several magazines are discarded haphazardly about him on the bright red duvet. He has begrudgingly shifted a large set of headphones down to rest on his shoulders. Ian has stubbornly left the mp3 player running. The distant hum of the music provides a faint background noise. It is designed to send his mother a clear message that as far as he is concerned, this conversation will not be lasting long.

The teenager shrugs his shoulders. 'I dunno, Mum. Everyone was pretty shocked about it when we got back to school. Some of the older kids knew Langley from the Young Cadets and they didn't like him very much. 'Said he was really strict and mean, so there was a lot of talk against him - some of the boys were even saying he enjoyed shooting at children - that kind of stuff.'

'I see. Did you ever talk about it with Will and Nikki? They must have been very upset when the whole thing happened. Didn't they miss a week at the club?' Imogen presses.

'Yeah, but we didn't really mention it when they came back. I got the feeling they were a bit embarrassed to be honest, so I never brought it up. Look, Mum, you know what Danny Carlow was like. He was pretty much the most out of control kid we ever had in our school.' Ian places both of his hands on the headphones, indicating to his mother this is all he has to say on the matter.

'Ian, how would you feel if Dad were to produce a psychological profile for Thomas Langley's defence lawyers? It doesn't mean he is going to go out of his way to help the man - he will just be providing his honest opinion - good or bad.'

The boy shrugs his shoulders again. 'I don't mind if he does, but hasn't Dad got a bias - because of the way Danny used to pick on Ewan when they were both still at school? Won't that mean he can't be involved with the case?'

Imogen is silenced for a moment or two as she had not even considered this. It seems as if Ian is not going to be the problem after all. Imogen had completely forgotten that Danny Carlow was the boy who had caused Ewan so many problems back when he had been in his final year of GCSEs. Considering the number of meetings she had attended about it and how upset they had all been with what Carlow seemed to be allowed to get away with during school hours, Imogen is amazed it could ever have slipped her mind. But Ewan is so happy and settled now in Manchester. The whole thing feels as if it happened a lifetime ago.

Imogen decides to let her son off the hook and leaves him to his music. Instead, she goes to stand and gaze out of the large windows that run the full length of the elevated sitting room and give fabulous views out over Cooper's Creek. The sun is just beginning to set and the water is steadily darkening. Imogen does not switch on the lights but remains perfectly still, lingering at the glass in order to savour the early evening glow that remains.

She sees the headlights of Hugh's car slowly approaching down the bumpy track. Imogen is absolutely confident the difficult time Ewan had with Danny Carlow won't affect her husband's impartiality as an expert witness in any way. In fact, Hugh was never very closely involved with their eldest son's problems back then. He had been very busy at the university during that period and Imogen had shouldered most of the burden of it by herself, with some help from Hugh's parents, of course.

The car is pulling up onto the driveway. Imogen decides she'd better switch on a lamp or two otherwise Hugh will think it peculiar to find her standing here in the dark. Before she does, Imogen looks briefly towards the shadowy trees and marshland below. Now Ian has reminded her, all sorts of memories from that time are flooding back. What strikes Imogen more than anything else, is the clear recollection that whatever Carlow did or said back then in his schooldays, the boy always seemed to follow it up with the threat of violence.

The following day, Hugh's dad is due to come over to the house and do some tidying up in the garden. This is part of a regular arrangement. On this occasion, Imogen has decided to ask her mother-in-law to have coffee with her whilst Gerry is hard at work. She wants to get another opinion on the Langley case.

Kathleen brings a homemade fruitcake with her, sealed inside a festively patterned circular tin. Imogen cuts a couple of large slices for them to eat with their coffees. She knows from long experience it will be some considerable time before Gerry comes back into the house for refreshments. If she makes the mistake of plating his up now, the cake will have dried out and the drink will become stone cold before he finally gets around to them. The ladies sit themselves at the breakfast bar and after a brief chat about how the children are coping at school and college, Imogen introduces the topic of Langley's assessment.

'So, Hugh has been asked to be an expert witness, has he?' Kath says with more than a hint of pride in her tone. 'It's such a high profile case. Not that *we* would ever buy the rag, but it's been on the front page of 'The Daily Informer' most days for the last couple of months.'

'I know,' Imogen adds with a heavy sigh. 'We don't want to upset any of our local friends by getting involved. People have certainly got themselves very heated up about the whole incident.'

Kath takes a dainty sip from the coffee cup, placing it carefully back into its saucer. 'Yes, they have and Gerry and I have our own opinions about it too. Hugh is a professional and he must do what he believes to be the right thing - without being swayed by what others may think.'

'If you don't mind me asking, Kath, what do you and Gerry make of the whole thing? Did you remember Danny Carlow was the boy who gave Ewan such a hard time when he was in Year 11?'

'Oh yes, Imogen, I certainly remembered the boy, although I had to remind Gerry about it. Of course, it's tragic a young man is dead - I can see that. However, I can also recall how upset the Carlow boy had made Ewan all those years back. He was not a pleasant character at all. Gerry and I were very close to suggesting you take the children out of that school and move them to Hugh's old place. We were prepared to help pay the fees. I couldn't have borne another second knowing that vicious thug was preying on our grandson.' Kath takes another sip of her drink. Imogen can see her hand is visibly shaking.

She is genuinely surprised her mother-in-law is still so angry about the bullying, even after all this time has passed. 'Then the situation suddenly got better. That very pleasant P.E teacher got involved and he seemed to find a way of sorting the problem out, thank God. Carlow probably moved onto someone else afterwards, but at least it wasn't Ewan anymore,' Imogen supplies.

'Once these incidents are cleared up, they are quickly forgotten by the children involved. Ewan seems not to have experienced any lasting damage. We weren't quite so resilient. Gerry and I were very upset about it for a long time. We wouldn't go into the hardware shop any more. We had to start driving miles out of our way to the B&Q in Chelmsford - it was quite an inconvenience really.'

'But the store is owned by *Rick* Carlow - Will and Nikki's dad. They don't have very much to do with Danny's family.'

'Oh, it wasn't about him. It was because Wendy Carlow works in there. Not every day, just part-time, but it was enough for us. I couldn't bear to be served by the mother of that terrible boy. So we took our business elsewhere,' Kath says decisively.

Imogen hadn't known Danny Carlow's mother worked in the store. It certainly helped to explain why the local farmers had been planning a boycott of the shop. At this moment, Gerry comes in from the cold. While he is removing his mud-laden boots, Imogen pours out his drink and cuts a fresh slice of fruit loaf.

The conversation quickly turns into a discussion about autumn jobs for the garden. It is not until after Hugh's parents have gone that Imogen suddenly realises Kath had not told her what their opinion on the Langley case had actually been.

Chapter Four

As far as Hugh Croft is concerned, his new book is a self-help manual of a very specific type. There are a number of army barracks situated near to the university campus in Colchester where he works. Over the past twenty years, his department have been at the forefront of research into the psychological disorders which have plagued many of the local servicemen and women who have seen action during that time.

Hugh wanted to convert his findings into a form returning personnel could refer to in their everyday lives. To help them deal with the bewildering array of symptoms traumatic stress can lead to. He has been accused, by some of his more pompous colleagues, of attempting to 'dumb down' their painstaking research. However, Hugh feels the whole point of his work is to help soldiers overcome their difficulties, not simply to gain the accolades of his fellow academics.

He is not expecting big sales from the new book, mainly because Hugh does not believe there are more than a few hundred people in the entire country who actually suffer from PTSD itself. Although, he makes it clear on the dust jacket 'blurb' that his techniques can help anyone to overcome all forms of nervous disorder.

Despite it having played such a fundamental part in his working life, Hugh is healthily sceptical about the use of such a broad brush term as 'Post Traumatic Stress Disorder,' anyway. Originating in the U.S. about a quarter of a century ago, the label has been used to encompass a wide range of psychological problems.

PTSD is sometimes used as a mitigating factor in criminal cases. As an expert witness, Hugh must apply certain behavioural criteria to a person who has been accused of a crime. This is so that he, and later a jury, can decide if PTSD, or a similar condition, had affected the defendant's judgement in any way. In the case of Thomas Langley, Hugh will not be making any decisions about his mental state until he meets the elderly man face-to-face. Before then, he will purely be looking at his background and finding out some more about the kind of military career Langley had served.

Hugh received Penny's e-mail a couple of days ago. Since that time, he has been browsing through Thomas Langley's files. The Professor has a spare hour or so between lectures so he pours himself a strong coffee from the filter machine he has jammed into a small space on one of the tall bookshelves that line the walls of his tiny office. He settles back and pulls over the pile of papers.

Langley was born in 1934 and his parents lived on the outskirts of Birmingham. His father fought in the Second World War and returned home to his clerical job towards the end of 1945. Thomas's education appeared to have been severely disrupted by the war. He left school by the age of 14 with few qualifications. He joined the army at 16 years old and his first experience of action was during the Korean War of the early fifties.

Hugh reads how Langley was part of the Gloucestershire Regiment whilst serving out in Asia. The name of this Regiment rings a bell for him. He makes a note and decides to ask his father about it. Gerry didn't fight in the Korean War himself but he is very keen on military history and will probably be able to fill in the gaps.

Langley doesn't appear to have seen much action after that. Not until he was sent over to Northern Ireland in the late sixties. He returned to this posting on and off until the mid-seventies when he ended up in West

Germany for the remainder of his army career. Langley retired from active service in 1980. That was when he and his wife bought the farm in Essex. It seems Thomas's wife, Rose Langley, (née Palmer) was from the Maldon area herself and wanted to take her sons back there.

It appears to Hugh like a fairly straightforward military record. Keeping the peace in Northern Ireland during the height of the troubles would have been very tough, but Langley had avoided serving in the Falklands War. Hugh is used to the impact of conflicts like those in Iraq and Afghanistan through his work. This experience has made him feel, rightly or wrongly, that these modern theatres of war are far more brutal and life-shattering than anything which came before.

The Langleys had two sons; Rob and Andy, who joined the army just like their father. In his interviews, Thomas described how his boys served in the Falklands War and latterly in Northern Ireland. Hugh doesn't have access to their individual records so he doesn't know where else they might have seen action. Both men now live outside the area. It could prove tricky for Hugh to get an interview with them, although he would certainly like to. Rose Langley died in 2010 at the age of 72. There is no real mention in the counsellor's notes of how Thomas had reacted to his wife's death.

Hugh glances at the old classroom clock on the wall and begins to prepare for his next lecture. He allows himself a few moments to call his parents. He asks if his father would like to meet him for a quick pint after work. Hugh does this very rarely, but when he does, it is always a pleasant experience. His mother complains heartily that Gerry is stiff and tired after the morning he spent working hard in Hugh's garden. His father chips in loudly from the background, saying he would be very pleased to meet his son at the usual place and time, so Kath is compelled to relent.

The Queen's Head pub is situated on the Hythe Quay. In summer, it provides a lovely place to sit and watch the boats coming and going on the River Blackwater. This evening it is almost dark as Hugh enters the red brick building and locates his father perched up at the bar. The Queen in question is Anne Boleyn. Her portrait adorns the hanging sign outside. The second wife of Henry VIII could perhaps more accurately be described as the *mother* of a great queen, but she remains the pub's figurehead, nonetheless.

There is an interesting Tudor connection with the town of Maldon. Mary Tudor, as a princess, had very nearly escaped the strict protestant rule of her younger brother, Edward, when a fleet of Imperial ships anchored just off the coast here in 1550. The ships were sent by the Holy Roman Emperor, Charles V, and were ready to take her to the sanctity of Catholic Europe. In the end, Mary developed cold feet and the plan was abandoned. But the notorious Queen is still closely associated with the town.

It was Gerry who had originally entertained Hugh with this historical titbit and he is hoping his father's extensive knowledge will not fail him now. With pints of Suffolk ale in their hands, Hugh enquires if his drinking companion knows anything about the role the Gloucestershire Regiment had played in the Korean War.

'I'm not supposed to discuss the case, Dad, so I'm afraid I can't go into any more detail than that. It's just when I saw the name of the Regiment, there was something familiar to me about it, but I wasn't sure why.'

'Well you *should* know, Hugh. They were actually involved in quite a famous incident. Maybe you would have been better taking that History A-Level after all.' the older man smiles to himself before continuing. 'There was a battle during the spring of 1951, in which the Chinese forces were aiming to recapture Seoul from the Americans. To achieve this, they had to cross the Imjin River, which was defended by U.N forces made up predominantly of British and Belgium troops. From what I recall, the 'Glorious Glosters' were pushed back by the Chinese until they were isolated on a hill, cut off from the other regiments and from any supply lines. The Glosters held out against the enemy for three days and nights until a small number of them managed to escape.' Gerry takes another sip from his pint glass.

'How many of the Gloucester Regiment would have survived, do you know?'

'From what I can recollect, only a handful escaped. About fifty or so were killed in the battle and the majority of the rest became prisoners of war. There are all sorts of memorials at the site of the stand-off. Veterans go out to Korea every year to commemorate their dead comrades. If Langley served with the regiment and he was involved in the incident then I would guess he most likely ended up as a POW. A number of the soldiers died in captivity, so conditions must have been pretty awful for those who were interned.' Gerry drains his glass and places it on the bar. He asks Hugh if he would like another.

'No thanks, I'd better be getting back. Look, I suppose it's fairly obvious I'm referring to Langley's war record, but I'm not really allowed to pass this information on, so just keep it to yourself, okay Dad?'

'Of course, Hugh. What I will tell you is that it would have been terribly traumatic for any young man to have been involved in the Battle of Imjin River. The fact they held out for all those days and nights against constant bombardments is incredible. It would have pushed those men to the brink.'

'I don't know where you store all of this information, Dad. Thank you. I will look into it further. It seems there was a long gap between Langley serving in Korea and him taking part in any other kind of active service - if he had been a POW that would certainly explain the delay. I'm sure he wouldn't have been fit to fight for a long time after his release. If Langley really was experiencing post-traumatic stress, this could very well prove to be the incident which had first triggered it.'

Chapter Five

About once or twice a year, the Maylandsea Sailing Club host a big fund-raising dinner. Imogen Croft is on the organising committee. She is gratified to note that the event, which takes place this evening, has finally sold out of tickets. The venue for tonight's festivities is the clubhouse itself, which has a large and modern dining room facing the placid waters of Lawling Creek.

The Crofts have been involved with the club ever since they moved to the area just over ten years ago. They get on with some of the sailing families better than others. Tonight, Imogen has arranged for them to be seated with Will and Nikki Carlow and their parents. She hopes this will provide company for Bridie and Ian during the meal. Imogen has always found Caroline and Rick to be very amiable people. As Hugh and Imogen get dressed for the evening, it provides them with an opportunity to compare notes on the Langley case.

'Had you remembered, Hugh, that Danny Carlow was the boy who bullied Ewan a few years ago?' Imogen asks, as she slips into her black cocktail dress. She turns round, holding her voluminously dark curls in a twist on top of her head; an unspoken gesture which indicates that her husband should zip up the back.

'No, I had not,' he replies quietly. While Imogen moves silently across the thick bedroom carpet to the dressing table he states, 'Is it going to prove too difficult for me to get involved with Thomas Langley do you think? I feel a little awkward about sitting with the Carlows tonight. It is going to feel as if I'm doing something shifty behind their backs.'

'I know what you mean, darling. But I don't think you should be put off. Your Mum said yesterday that you must follow your professional instincts and not be swayed by what others might do or say. She is quite right. No one will be better at producing this profile than you, so of course you must do it and to hell with everyone else.'

Hugh steps towards his wife and scoops her up into an embrace. 'Sometimes you are full of surprises, Mrs Croft,' he whispers softly in her ear.

'Did you expect me to disapprove?' she suddenly asks, withdrawing from him a fraction.

'If I'm honest, yes I did. I thought you would be worried about the impact on the family of my getting involved in a case which is so contentious. I certainly wouldn't have blamed you for it.'

Imogen considers this point for a second before replying, 'my reaction was quite the opposite.' She lays her head onto Hugh's shoulder. 'I believe this case is so important to our local area, that unless it is resolved fairly and with justice having been done, I think it could tear the community apart. With you involved, we might just have an opportunity of making sure we actually find out the truth about what happened.'

*

After the dinner, an unmemorable speech is made by the Chairman of the Club and a fundraising auction held. At the first opportunity, Hugh and Rick Carlow escape to the bar area. The teens disappear off to the dancefloor, joining the other young guests who have congregated there. Imogen and Caroline remain seated at the table, unhurriedly finishing their coffees.

Caroline Carlow is rather tall, with a willowy figure and fine, light brown hair which she wears in a short, layered style that suits her almond shaped face. She is pretty and athletic but in no way 'showy' about her looks. Imogen has always got on well with Caroline, who possesses a sharp wit and is as happy to chat about politics as she is the latest club gossip. She is intelligent and well-read. Imogen finds her good company. Her husband is equally pleasant, but he is fundamentally a practical man. Rick has built up his hardware stores from nothing and must have significant business acumen. However, he likes to talk only about boats and his work. As long as you can stick to those subjects, it is possible to get on very well with Rick Carlow.

'Has Ian mentioned anything to you about 'The Blackwater Boys' yet?' Caroline asks her friend, placing the empty cup carefully into its saucer.

'No,' Imogen replies, caught off-guard by the question. 'I've never heard of them.'

'It's this outward bound club Mark Gilbert runs. Well, the boys are supposed to organise it themselves but with Mark supervising. The lads go off on treks and stuff on their own. Mark has the job of inviting new members and that kind of thing,' Caroline explains.

'Where have I heard his name before?'

'He's one of the P.E teachers at the school. He's a very nice guy and really good with the lads, very encouraging. Anyway, Mark has asked Will and Ian if they would like to join,' Caroline concludes.

Imogen pushes aside her coffee and reaches instead for the open bottle of white wine on the table, pouring herself a fresh glass. She is a little embarrassed Caroline knows all about this invitation. But then Imogen has a pretty good idea why Ian hasn't mentioned it to her yet. 'Okay. Are you going to allow Will to get involved? What sort of activities do they get up to?'

'I was waiting to discuss it with you before making a decision,' Caroline chuckles, 'a bit feeble of me, I know. It seems fairly harmless; they sail together, go on treks and occasionally they might have a camping weekend. It sounds like great fun - Will is very keen.'

Imogen sighs before responding, 'I'd love to be able to immediately say yes to Ian joining, but there's the complication of his diabetes. I don't feel happy with the idea there isn't always an adult with them. Hugh would never allow it.'

A startled look passes across Caroline's face. Imogen can tell her friend is surprised by how much she and Hugh limit Ian's actions. It makes her feel deeply uncomfortable. 'Well, Rick and I are probably going to let Will join - although we would be far happier if Ian was there too. Have a think about it Im, they don't go very far afield. You could always have a chat with Mark - he would set your mind at rest, I'm sure.'

Imogen nods and smiles whilst quickly changing the topic of their conversation. She has no intention of being railroaded into anything this evening, certainly not before she has discussed the whole thing with Hugh. After a couple of dances the Crofts are ready to call it a night. They gather outside the sailing club in the crisp, cold air and say their goodbyes to the Carlows.

As both families climb into their cars, Caroline calls over, 'let me know what you decide about 'The Blackwater Boys' - I can always organise for us to have a coffee with Mark sometime to find out the details.'

Imogen waves back but says nothing. Ian immediately pulls his headphones down over his ears and stares out of the window at the black and motionless creek beyond.

'What was that all about?' Hugh asks his wife as they begin the drive home.

'There's a kind of outward bound group Will and Ian have been asked to join. It's run by one of the teachers at their school. It is meant to allow the boys to become more independent, so they take part in expeditions on their own. They have a sort of hierarchy - you know, like the brownies or the scouts. They earn commissions and each member has to follow the orders of their superior in rank. I remember a little about it now I've had time to think, although I'm sure it used to be called something different. Ewan never wanted to get involved with them, I seem to recall.'

'Only because Danny Carlow was in it,' Bridie chips in from the back. 'Ewan said there was no way he was going to take orders from that thug.'

'It sounds like a nightmare to me,' Hugh adds stonily.

'I think Ian is going to be really keen to join - especially if Will Carlow does,' Imogen says tentatively.

Ian is still keeping his eyes steadily fixed on the moving darkness outside. His mum isn't entirely sure just how much of their conversation he can hear.

'He needs supervision in order to take his injections, Imogen. There might be a possibility Ian can become involved in some way or another with this gang, but he wouldn't be able to take part in all of their activities,' Hugh concedes, without any enthusiasm.

'I'll talk to him about it.' Imogen sighs, suddenly feeling tired.

'Why aren't girls allowed to join?' Bridie pipes up from the rear.

'That would be my question exactly, sweetheart,' Hugh calls back to his daughter. 'I've never trusted any organisation that deliberately excludes certain people. It automatically makes me believe they must have something to hide.'

*

Chapter Six

Imogen has observed that you inevitably become more c̲ community. Even if your offspring do ... myriad of clubs and societies that flourish within ev̲e̲r̲y̲ town and village, the mere fact they attend a nearby school or college means you are automatically entwined in the affairs of your neighbourhood.

A working couple, residing in their own house, might find it fairly easy to live out their lives without ever coming into meaningful contact with their neighbours at all. Especially those people who commute to a distant city every week day and return only under the cover of darkness. Imogen has often felt it must be sad to exist in such a way; with one's home providing nothing more than a base for a night's rest, before heading off to lead a life which takes place somewhere else entirely. There are times, however, when becoming entangled in the concerns of your community can be oppressive or even dangerous. Imogen had never really experienced this side of the coin, until now.

No attempt had been made to keep Hugh's involvement in the Langley Farm case secret. Ian must have told his friends about it, because while Imogen is ambling along the High Street in Maldon, on a foggy November morning, she has an unpleasant encounter with Wendy Carlow.

Imogen has just stepped out of the bakers and is concentrating hard on arranging the flour-dusted paper bags inside her shopping basket, when she literally bumps headlong into Danny Carlow's mother.

brashly blond woman barring Imogen's way
ly exclaims, 'I hear your husband is helping to
murderer off the hook.'

'I beg your pardon?'

'You heard me. My Matt told us your husband is helping Langley's defence team. Talk about betraying your friends and neighbours - and you with a son the same age as my Danny was. There's no explaining some people is there?' Wendy spits the words out from between thin, blood-red lips.

Imogen is tempted to reply that Danny Carlow had been no friend of theirs but she does not. 'Hugh has been asked to produce a psychological profile. It will be completely objective. He is not allowed to take sides.'

'He didn't have to agree to it though, did he? They could have found someone else. It's not like he hasn't already got a job. The man who killed my son is going to get off by using some kind of loop-hole isn't he? With clever-types like your husband helping him to do it,' Wendy's words taper off as she tries desperately to fight back a sob.

Imogen sighs, 'Wendy, I'm genuinely sorry for your loss, it's an absolute tragedy. I promise that Hugh simply wants to find out the truth about what happened to your son, he has no other motive for getting involved than that.'

Wendy looks up then, her attractive face is smeared with loosened mascara but her mouth remains fixed in a grim line. 'It doesn't make a difference what *he* wants though does it? It is how those people are going to *use* his words that matters. They can twist whatever he says to suit their argument and if there's any doubt in the minds of the jury, Thomas Langley goes scot free - that's what my solicitor says - 'I must prepare myself for disappointment'.' she lets out a humourless laugh, 'story of my life that is.'

Realising there is not much more to be said, Imogen mutters something which could be interpreted as an apology and then walks away. During the drive home she takes some time to consider Wendy's words. Imogen has to concede there might well be some truth in the woman's fears. Although Hugh will do his very best to produce an unbiased report, it would be naïve to think Langley's solicitors aren't going to use it to their advantage. Perhaps even to the extent that if Hugh decides the old man is completely free of psychological disorders, they may decide to disregard his testimony entirely.

Imogen doesn't get the chance to consider this unsettling prospect any further. While she is putting away the shopping in their narrow kitchen which looks out across the creek, the phone in the hallway starts to ring. It turns out to be a call from Abigail, her brother's girlfriend, and she sounds very upset.

'Abigail, just explain that to me again, nice and slowly, would you? Has Allan been taken ill?'

'Yes, but it's nothing physical,' she manages to get out between sobs. 'He's checked himself into a private clinic. The doctors have given him an assessment and they told me he is suffering from 'severe nervous exhaustion'.'

Imogen allows herself a few moments to absorb this information. Good for him, she thinks. Imogen is always vaguely aware of the niggling concerns she has for her middle brother's well-being. Allan's drinking is a perennial worry for her. The news that he has recognised he has a problem himself, she views as something of a breakthrough. 'Which clinic is he staying at?'

'It's called 'The Sanctuary' and it is just behind Hampstead High Street - near to the Heath,' Abigail explains, sounding calmer now she has shared her revelation with someone else.

'Can he receive visitors at all?' Imogen asks in a matter-of-fact way.

'Yes, you can come along with me this evening if you'd like. Allan is checking out on Friday and he will continue his treatment at home. The Doctor has signed him off work for a few weeks.'

'Yes I will, if you don't mind, and Abigail, please try not to worry. He just needs rest and relaxation for a while. A break from the Bank will do him the world of good. None of us can possibly claim we haven't seen this one coming.'

*

Abigail and Allan own an attractive first floor flat in Highgate. It is part of a 1930s building which is full of wood panelling and spacious, airy rooms. Imogen parks outside on the street and waits for Abigail to come down and join her. The sky is already darkening. When her brother's girlfriend emerges from the front door of the property, Imogen notices how blotched and red-faced she appears, as if she has been crying almost non-stop since their phone conversation several hours ago.

'It's a bit of a way, but we can walk to the clinic from here - unless you want to get the bus?' Abigail gushes, as she embraces her visitor warmly.

'Let's walk, it's very mild.'

The trek from Highgate village to the fringes of Hampstead Heath provides Imogen with an opportunity to find out exactly what has been going on with Allan over recent months.

'His mood has been up and down for weeks,' Abigail explains, 'he's had to work long hours on this merger deal the Bank is involved in and then there's his drinking, of course.'

'Was there a particular event which finally prompted Allan to seek help? I'm very glad he did.'

'Well, in the last few days he suddenly got worse. He said he was too frightened to travel on the tube and he wasn't eating at all. He said he couldn't even have a brandy to calm his nerves - because it tasted disgusting to him. Allan decided then he needed professional help.'

'It sounds like a breakdown to me. His poor nerves have just taken too much strain,' Imogen replies kindly, although she thinks how typical it was that Allan was only prompted to seek medical assistance when he could no longer enjoy a drink.

Abigail turns towards her walking companion and says plaintively, 'does this mean he's unhappy in his relationship with me? I know he can be a pain, but I do love him, Imogen. I try my best, though I just can't seem to make him happy.' The young woman crumples into sobs once again and Imogen places a supportive arm around her shoulders.

'Don't take this the wrong way, Abigail, but it has absolutely nothing to do with you. Allan has things on his mind and they are causing him unbearable stress. I'm pretty certain none of those concerns relates to your relationship. I know how hard it is for you. However, the very best thing you can do is to remain calm. Just let him know you are here for him. If Allan senses you are upset it will only worry him more and prolong his recovery.'

Abigail nods and makes an effort to compose herself, taking deep breaths and dabbing at her eyes with a handkerchief.

The Sanctuary Clinic is a modern, single storey building set in landscaped gardens which blend seamlessly into their wooded environment. Everything about the institution is deliberately discreet. Even the immaculately uniformed receptionist addresses the two visitors in hushed tones.

Allan's room is very comfortable and although the curtains have been drawn, it faces out towards the Heath and no doubt provides a pleasant view. Allan himself is quite groggy and passes in and out of wakefulness whilst the ladies are with him. The nurse informs Imogen this is a result of his medication. The doctor wants him to be fully rested before he is sent home. Allan's weakened state makes his sister concerned about how the couple can possibly manage when he returns to their flat in a couple of days from now.

Obviously thinking the very same thing, Abigail suddenly implores, 'I should really take some time off work, but I just can't. Although it's only the beginning of November, my head office classes this as the 'Christmas period' and I'm not allowed any leave.' Abigail is the manageress of a large clothing store in the west-end of the city.

Worried she may burst into tears again, Imogen quickly supplies, 'I can drive back on Friday morning and take Allan home with me for a while. Ewan's room is free and I am around in the daytime to keep an eye on him. It's very peaceful in our little hamlet. We can take some walks along the estuary together, once he is feeling better. I promise Hugh and I will look after him for you.'

Abigail smiles with obvious relief and immediately takes hold of the older woman's hand. Imogen realises in this moment that Allan's long-suffering girlfriend is very probably in need of a break from him herself.

Chapter Seven

The Croft household is unusually peaceful. As Hugh sits at the desk in his study, in the pale blue light of early morning, he can hear nothing except the sound of a freshening wind along the channel. The reason for this quietness is that it is not yet six a.m. Long gone are the days when the Croft's children would be up and about at such an ungodly hour.

Hugh is taking advantage of the stillness to read through his notes on the Langley case. Penny called late last night to say her client is free to speak with him today. She wanted to know if it was possible for Hugh to make the meeting at such short notice. He was a little hesitant at first, but with some last minute shifting around of his teaching schedule, it was just about achievable. Hugh wants to be sure he is absolutely ready for the interview. He was awake before dawn, so it seemed a good opportunity to start the planning.

Hugh doesn't like to prepare specific questions before a session. He prefers to allow the conversation to evolve naturally. He does, however, make sure he is fully briefed on the client's medical and psychological history before he begins any meeting.

The first interaction between psychologist and patient is always crucially important, as it sets the tone for all future exchanges. For the first time since his very early career as a young practitioner, Hugh is feeling apprehensive about this encounter. Perhaps because the case is so close to home and the consequences for Langley are so serious.

Penny has supplied him with Langley's temporary address. The old man is staying in a flat in Buckhurst Hill, which, although still in Essex, is right on the border of the East London suburbs. Hugh hasn't been out that way for years but he used to know the area quite well. A good friend of his had attended a boarding school situated just on the edge of Epping Forest. He had visited him there on a number of occasions when they were both teenagers.

Sounds of movement and activity are finally beginning to fill the house. Hugh can tell his wife has entered the kitchen to make a start on breakfast. Feeling he is as prepared for the interview as he will ever be, Hugh goes out to join her. Imogen is shuffling around in her dressing gown, busily placing clean coffee cups on the worktop, with her thick, shiny dark hair lying loose about her shoulders.

'How's the patient this morning?' Hugh asks in a hushed voice.

'Still asleep. Those sedatives are certainly doing their job.'

'He's reducing the dose now though, isn't he?'

'Yes, but he still seems pretty knocked out. Should I try and encourage him to do something today?' Imogen enquires.

'See how he feels when he wakes up, darling. Take it slowly - he needs lots of rest and no pressure. When he is a little more robust I can begin to teach him some techniques for dealing with stress and anxiety. I might even try and get to the bottom of what's really bothering him.'

'Hmm, I've got a few theories on that myself,' Imogen adds, putting her arms around Hugh's neck and resting her cheek against his. 'I just want to see Allan back to his old self again, however annoying he can be.'

'We'll have to give it time. His nerves need to repair themselves properly and there aren't any hard and fast rules about how long it might take. He will get better, I promise.'

*

Buckhurst Hill is punctuated by smart Victorian villas and a traditional High Street full of boutiques and independent shops gives it a village-like feel. In fact, since the coming of the railway here in the mid-19th Century, Buckhurst Hill has been a busy suburb of London. It marks something of a boundary between the hinterland of the city and the more rural nature of the Essex towns which lie beyond it to the east.

Hugh parks up outside a reasonably modern, large and well-tended residential building, just off Palmerston Road. The man who answers the door of the second floor flat is not as Hugh had expected.

Thomas Langley is tall, with a muscular build. Despite his advancing age, there is nothing in the slightest bit frail about the gentleman who greets Hugh with a firm shake of the hand.

'Please come in Professor Croft,' Langley says, leading his visitor into a neatly presented, spacious living room.

'Call me Hugh.'

'Okay, Hugh, would you like a coffee?' He responds in a friendly and unguarded manner.

'I'd love one, thank you.'

Whilst Langley retreats to the kitchen area to prepare the drinks, Hugh takes in his surroundings. This flat is meant only to provide temporary accommodation for its current occupant but Langley has kept the place very orderly and tidy nonetheless. Hugh can see a number of photographs displayed on the mantelpiece above an old-fashioned gas fire. Two of them are of young men in army uniforms who he assumes must be Langley's sons. The boys are as sturdily built as their father.

'Are these your sons, Thomas?' Hugh enquires, pointing at the pictures as Langley returns with a tray.

'Rob and Andy- they're a bit older than that these days, mind you. Andy left the army about five years ago, but Rob's a Major now. He's still out in Afghanistan. He'll be coming back within the next few months.'

Langley sits down on the sofa and gestures towards the armchair opposite. Hugh selects a steaming mug and settles into the comfortable seat. Now he has had time to look at Thomas properly, he can see the man's age etched out in the lines on his face. Hugh notices the purplish stain left by the wound on his forehead. It is in the final stages of its healing process, but will no doubt leave behind a permanent scar. He looks tired and a little drawn, although there is an element of peacefulness to his demeanour which Hugh had not expected.

'I'd like to make a start with my questions, if you wouldn't mind, Thomas,' Hugh states, kindly.

'Of course,' the old man replies, with a hint of weary resignation in his voice.

The psychologist discreetly switches on the Dictaphone he keeps in his trouser pocket and begins. 'Could you tell me, in your own time, exactly what happened on the night of the burglary?'

Hugh knows Langley will have given his account of the event many times and there will be a rehearsed element to it by now. He still wants to start from this point and move backwards, it is simply the way he always likes to work.

'It was a normal evening for me. I locked up the cottage and went to bed at about 11pm. I was tired because I'd come back from visiting my brother-in-law that day and it's a long drive. I went to sleep quite quickly. Something woke me up. I glanced at the clock and it was half past twelve. I heard a noise, outside in the yard. I got up and put on my dressing gown, went downstairs and pulled on my boots. Then,' he coughs a little before continuing, 'I unlocked the cabinet and took out the shotgun. I carried it outside with me. I could see straightaway the doors to the big barn had been forced open. I went up to the entrance and shouted inside. The gun wasn't cocked. I had it slung across my arms. It was pitch black in the shed and my eyes hadn't had time to adjust properly to the dark before I was violently shoved over. I fell to the ground. When I looked up, I saw there was a tall figure standing over me. This person paused for a fraction of a second and then brought down something hard and metal on my head.' Langley absent-mindedly moves his fingers up to feel the inflamed, jagged line across his temple.

'Did you lose consciousness?' Hugh enquires.

'Only very briefly, I was more stunned than anything else. I knew the wound was bleeding but I had a sudden compulsion to chase the thieves. I was fully aware they must have taken the lead flashing from the barn - there wasn't much else of any value in there. I needed it, you see. I'd painstakingly removed all the lead sheeting from the roof of my old cottage. I was going to sell the metal to pay for the upkeep of the place. I'm not able to look after the farm buildings and land any more without outside help. So I got myself up and then ran in the direction of the fields - the ones that take you towards the wooded copse. I could actually see the men a few yards ahead of me because the moon was so bright. There were three of them and they each had backpacks on - full of my property. I knew I couldn't possibly catch the blokes, so I released a shot up into the air - just to frighten them, you know? I wanted to stop them from getting away. That's when they all dropped to the ground. Then I couldn't see where they were at all.' Langley pauses to take a sip of his coffee.

'How far away were the men when you fired the first shot?' Hugh asks.

'Only about a hundred yards. I've got a licence for my gun. It's all perfectly legal. When I knew they weren't going anywhere I shouted that they must give me back my property and then I would allow them to leave. One of the lads raised his head above the undergrowth and asked me if he would be free to go if he gave me his rucksack. I nodded to him and he threw it over. Following that, he scarpered towards the trees.

After the first lad had taken off, there was complete silence. I knew the other two must be nearby somewhere but I had absolutely no idea of where. I shouted out again that all I wanted was the flashing. I heard nothing for several minutes. Then I sensed a movement by my feet. It all happened in a split second. My legs were pulled out from under me and a tall figure jumped up and raised his weapon over my head, temporarily blotting out the light from the moon. Suddenly, there was another person behind him. This man grabbed the tall fella's arm and shouted something, although I'm not sure what he said. You have to understand these events all occurred pretty much simultaneously. When the lad raised the crow-bar I let off the shotgun - but I hadn't had time to aim it or anything. I was never conscious of actually firing it. I was acting purely instinctively, in the heat of the attack.'

'What happened after that?' Hugh presses, knowing from the witness statements it was not Langley himself who had called the emergency services and curious to understand why not.

'I believe it must have been the adrenaline that had kept me going up to this point, what with my head wound and everything, because after the gun was fired I sort of collapsed. It went very quiet. I was vaguely aware of the sound of moans and whimpers - sobbing maybe. Then I blacked out. The next thing I knew the medics were lifting me into the ambulance and there were police milling all around the farm.'

Hugh asks a few more questions about how Langley has been coping since the incident. He then invites Thomas to list some of the emotions he experienced in the aftermath of the boy's death. Langley is cooperative in all of these tasks and appears to be answering honestly.

'You're probably wondering how on earth I can afford to have such a top flight defence team,' the old man suddenly says. 'It's my son who's paying for it. Rob's not married and he hasn't any children so he insisted on covering the legal bills. I want to help as much as I can to clear my name - for my sons' sakes more than anything else. My reputation doesn't matter much to me anymore but I wouldn't like my boys to carry any stigma. I may never be able to go back to the farm - whatever happens at the trial, I know that. I don't much care, Hugh. It was Rose who wanted to return there. She longed to bring the boys back to where she grew up. The area really means little or nothing to me.' Langley places the empty cups back onto the tray.

Hugh would love to take Thomas's lead and probe more deeply into the past of the Langley family, but he knows he must leave this for another day. He has plenty of evidence to work through for the time-being and he doesn't wish to tire the old man out. The psychologist thanks Thomas Langley for his hospitality and then takes his leave, eager to return to the Essex coast before he gets caught up in the busy rush-hour traffic.

Chapter Eight

'Langley wasn't at all as I had expected,' Hugh comments, as he pours himself a coffee from the freshly filled *cafetiére* on the breakfast bar.

'In what respect?' Imogen replies, in an absent-minded way, as she moves efficiently around the narrow kitchen, carefully filling a line of lunch boxes, placed open on the counter-top.

'Well, I thought he was going to be *elderly* - you know, in the full sense of the word. I had obviously been far too influenced by the newspaper and television reports, where he is constantly portrayed as a frail old man.'

'The British media seem to think anyone over the age of 55 is decrepit. Look at your dad - he's fitter than we are and he is only a few months younger than Langley.' Imogen pauses from her activities for a second and takes a sip from her mug of tea. 'It might affect the opinion of the jury, perhaps. When they discover Thomas isn't the weak and aged figure they're expecting to see.'

'You can tell he's in his seventies, don't get me wrong. It's just that Langley is rather tall - at least six foot I'd say and even though he was wearing a thick shirt I could still make out the muscles on his arms and torso.'

'He *is* ex-army and he's been running a farm for the last thirty years. It's a job that keeps you fairly fit,' Imogen observes. 'From what you told me last night about Langley's testimony, it seems increasingly clear to me he was acting in self-defence. I'm mystified as to why he is still facing a murder charge.'

'He *chased* those boys across the field, Imogen. He fired a shotgun and pretty much held them hostage until they returned his property. Whether Thomas wants to admit it or not, the implication was that he would have shot them if they hadn't done what he said. It could be argued it was *Danny Carlow* who was acting in self-defence, not Langley.'

'All those two lads needed to do, was return what they'd stolen - just like Joshua Nash had done. Then they could have run off home and no one would have got hurt. It was *greed* which made Carlow go for old Langley. He wanted to keep his loot. Danny took a gamble and it went terribly wrong for him - it's as simple as that,' Imogen replies, turning round to place each lunch pack into the correct bag.

Hugh leans over and gives his wife a brief peck on the cheek. 'Have a good day, darling,' he adds, grabbing his tatty leather briefcase and making his way out to the car.

Hugh can certainly understand Imogen's point of view. Since meeting the old man, however, he can't shake his growing suspicion that whatever happened at the Langley Farm on that summer's night was *anything* but simple.

*

When Allan awakes in his nephew's bedroom, he is feeling more alert than at any point since arriving at the Croft household. As he gingerly raises himself up, Imogen brings in a cup of tea and a brioche; thickly smothered in butter and marmalade. She places the tray on a table by the window.

'How are you doing?' she asks quietly, sitting herself down on the edge of the bed.

'I'm a bit disorientated to be honest. But I do feel hungry, which must be a good sign.'

Imogen takes the hint and lifts the tray over, placing it squarely on her brother's lap. He begins to take small sips of the hot, sweet liquid.

'Do you want to talk about it?' she enquires in a light tone.

'There's not much to say, really. I've overdone it at work and been relying on the booze to calm my nerves. Things just got a little out of hand, that's all. Do you know what's peculiar, Im? Since I've been here, away from my flat and my London life, I feel incredibly peaceful - as if a ton weight has been lifted off my shoulders.' Allan adds between healthy mouthfuls of buttery brioche, 'I've been having these vivid dreams too. They're mostly about our childhood back on Garansay and in some I'm still married to Suz. The overall mood of them is happiness and tranquillity.'

'That's the drugs, I'm afraid. They do induce a kind of euphoria in the short-term. The lifting of your mood also comes from having removed yourself from the source of your stress. It was at the flat you experienced your breakdown and removing yourself from that environment will make you feel immediately better. Once your nerves have recovered enough, you will be able to return to your old life, without all those unpleasant associations. It's just going to take some time.'

'At this precise moment, it feels as if I couldn't ever go back. I can almost visualise a physical wall between me and my life with Abigail. It is like a huge barrier I am completely powerless to pass through.' Allan reaches suddenly for his sister's hand.

'That's your nerves playing tricks on you, Allan. Nothing has really changed except your perception of things. Simply take each day as it comes. Hugh will be able to help you through this much better than me. For the time being, I want you to relax and do whatever you like. Our home is entirely at your disposal.' Imogen sweeps her hand in a circular motion to indicate the walls of her elder son's room, where posters of sinister looking rock bands cover every free surface. To her great relief, Allan starts to chuckle and she feels confident enough to leave him to finish his breakfast in peace.

It is a clear and cloudless day. The sky over the creek is a beautiful cornflower blue and the low lying afternoon sun is piercingly bright. It feels remarkably mild for early November. Imogen is rummaging about in the double garage underneath the house in her thin woollen sweater and no coat. She is trying to locate a bin bag full of guest bed-linen which she recalled storing in here a few years ago. Imogen has just concluded she must have been mistaken, when the mobile phone in her trouser pocket starts to buzz.

'Hello,' she snaps, unable to keep the frustration of half an hour's fruitless efforts out of her tone.

'Oh, hello, is this Mrs Croft?' enquires a hesitant male voice.

'Yes, this is Imogen Croft.' She carries on manoeuvring herself free of the untidy garage, clambering out into the relative warmth of the sun-lit driveway.

'My name is Mark Gilbert and I'm calling from The Beeleigh School. It's absolutely nothing to be concerned about. Caroline Carlow asked if I would give you a ring, she said you wanted some information about 'The Blackwater Cadets',' he explains.

It takes a few moments for Imogen to make the connection. 'Okay, I see. Well, yes, I would like to know more, certainly. Caroline told me you had invited Ian and Will to join the club?'

'That's right. They have both excelled themselves in my classes this year. I felt your son would benefit from taking part in some exciting new activities. There are nine lads who are currently members of our group and they range in age from 16 to 20 years old. Most attend the school, although a couple have now left full-time education. Caroline might have told you already how we operate a military-style system of ranks within the cadets. Depending on length of service and the number of tasks the lads have undertaken during their membership, they can earn certain commissions. The boys seem to find these rewards very motivating and it gives them a great sense of achievement.'

'You mentioned they perform certain tasks, could you give me an example, Mr Gilbert?' Imogen asks.

'Call me Mark, please. Well, we tend to organise one big expedition per term - which might be a sailing day or just a long hike. Each of the lads is given a responsibility; which can vary from skippering the boat to cooking us all up lunch on the gas stove. The boys learn to do new things and the rest of the group depend on them to get it right. They pick up very useful life-skills as a result, Mrs Croft. I've seen some pretty tough young men, who don't usually respond well at school, happily work their way through a pile of washing up when asked.'

'If you don't mind me saying, you've just highlighted one of my concerns. I always got the impression 'The Blackwater Cadets' were set up to help the more 'challenging' students at the school find activities where they can learn a few practical skills. Ian and Will really don't fall into that category.'

Mark Gilbert takes a couple of seconds to respond and when he does he sounds irritated. 'I'm deeply saddened we have gained that reputation, Mrs Croft. It's not what we are about at all. You are probably referring to the fact Matt Carlow is one of our senior members. I can assure you he is a very mature and sensitive young man. The rest of my cadets are a mixed bunch - some are 'A' grade students, while others are less academically minded. We don't tend to pay much attention to those types of labels. We have a 'live and let live' policy within our group.'

Imogen can tell she has offended the teacher with her remark. She silently notes to herself how this 'live and let live' policy does not appear to extend to allowing girls to join. 'I will certainly have a word with Ian and my husband about the possibility of him getting involved. May I ask about something else, Mr Gilbert?'

'Of course,' he answers curtly, not objecting this time to Imogen's formal term of address.

'Caroline suggested there might be times when the boys take part in expeditions by themselves - without you or another teacher present. I wondered if this were the case and, if it is, who is then in charge of them?'

Gilbert responds swiftly to this, his tone softening once again, 'Oh, Caroline must have got herself a little muddled up there. Sometimes the lads might have a planning meeting without me - if I'm away refereeing a football fixture or something. But I'm always with them for the expeditions, Mrs Croft, please rest assured on that score.'

'I'm very glad to hear it, thank you very much. Just one more thing, Mr Gilbert, before you go - what exactly does the club call itself? Caroline referred to you as 'The Blackwater Boys'. That's not your proper name though, is it?'

'No, not at all,' Gilbert chuckles good-naturedly. 'It's a kind of nickname that the boys themselves started to use a few years ago and I'm afraid it has begun to stick. I'd prefer it if we went back to our official title, to be honest, otherwise it gives the wrong impression about us, I think.'

'So girls *can* join the organisation then, if they want to?' Imogen can't stop herself from asking.

'Of course,' he immediately responds, a little too quickly perhaps. 'We'd love to have more female members. Unfortunately, girls just never seem particularly keen to get involved. It's not for want of trying, I can promise you, Mrs Croft.'

'Well, you've certainly set my mind at rest, Mr Gilbert,' Imogen says politely as they end the call, when in fact she is thinking the exact opposite.

Imogen did not know that Danny Carlow's younger brother was a member of these 'cadets' and finding this out only makes her more nervous than ever about the whole set-up. All she can do now is to hope her middle son, by some miracle, has gone off the idea altogether.

Chapter Nine

The weather along the Blackwater estuary has turned decidedly colder, but Allan Nichols is becoming brighter and more positive with each passing day.

It is a fine, sunny morning and Imogen has persuaded her brother to accompany her up the coast to St Lawrence Bay from where they can take a boat trip to St Peter's Island. St Peter's is the smallest of the three land masses which arise out of the River Blackwater. It lies to the east of its counterparts and has provided a first line of defence against the many invaders who have threatened this part of the coastline over the centuries.

Being such a tiny, exposed and generally featureless strip of land it has never actually attracted any long-term residents; although these very characteristics have created an irresistible pull for those on the pilgrimage trail for many hundreds of years.

Imogen relays some of the history of the island to Allan, as they enjoy the pretty drive through the villages of Latchingdon and Mayland, en route to their final destination.

'The island was settled first by the Celts, who felt its remoteness had a spiritual importance. They built a small church there. Then, when the Christians arrived, they used the place as a kind of religious retreat and they named it after the ancient chapel at Bradwell. I think there was a connection with the Beeleigh Abbey in Maldon too at one time - the monks had obviously recognised the bleak and peaceful beauty of the place.'

Allan nods his head politely, but says very little during the journey. They arrive at the riverside settlement of St Lawrence in time to join the small group of people who are lined up at the harbour. They are waiting to climb aboard the gaily painted pleasure cruiser which will ferry them across the turbulent, grey waters.

In summer, these cruisers are packed full of eager visitors. In the middle of November, it is noticeably less popular. Imogen and Allan are wrapped up warm in thick coats and woolly hats. Imogen suddenly hopes she has not been too ambitious with this expedition. She gives her brother a hand ascending the narrow walkway and then assists him as they clamber down into the deep hull of the vessel, where wooden benches are fixed around the gunwales.

'Are you okay?' She asks, as they take a seat near the stern and wait to pay their fare.

'I'm fine,' Allan replies, placing an arm around his sister's shoulders. 'This is far preferable to me than being sealed inside a packed carriage and whisked at high speed through an underground tunnel.'

'Well, when you put it like that, the cruiser does seem like a pretty civilised way to travel. Despite the fact I'm bloody freezing!' Imogen smiles at her companion, leaning comfortably into his bulky form.

Although bitterly cold, the boat ride is exhilarating and takes them around Osea Island before stopping at a small jetty on the north side of St Peter's. They have just half an hour here before the cruiser will take them back to the mainland again. Imogen feels this will certainly give them enough time, as there is precious little to see.

They proceed first in the direction of the tiny church on the eastern tip of the island which is almost in ruins, but still very pretty, in a bleak kind of way. All that remains of it is a crumbled stone structure which would once have possessed a tall wooden tower, now long since rotted away. There stands an ugly, concrete pill box a short distance along the shingle beach from the little church. Imogen and Allan make their way towards it, instinctively bowing their heads into the strong, north - easterly gale.

The pill box provides the only obvious evidence of 'modern' life on St Peter's Island. It was constructed during World War Two as a defence against a possible German invasion. Imogen peers into the small, uneven entrance-way and, although it would provide them both with a temporary respite from the weather, she decides not to venture down the small flight of steps. It is pitch black inside and smells of stale urine and dampness. Something about the place makes Imogen shiver and place her arms tightly across her chest.

Walking around to the more sheltered side of the man-made structure, they sit themselves down on a low stone wall which protrudes from the grassy hillock opposite.

'When did you say this boat was coming back?' Allan asks dryly.

Imogen laughs, 'We've got quarter of an hour left. Sorry Al, I didn't think it was going to be as cold as this. I'd forgotten we'd be totally exposed to the elements out here. I sort of thought this might be a peaceful and spiritual experience for us.'

'I did wonder what your rationale was, my dear. Well, you've certainly succeeded in getting me out into the fresh air.'

'Can I ask you something?'

'Sure, we've got some time to kill.'

'Did you ever tell Abigail about your affair with Alison Dickson?' Imogen isn't quite sure where this question has sprung from. She would never have dared to ask it if they were back at home, in their everyday life.

Allan says absolutely nothing for several minutes. Imogen senses he has been taken completely by surprise. He is clearly battling with himself over how to respond.   'No, I have not.'

'It's none of my business, I realise that. But when you've been married to a psychologist for over twenty years, you do pick up a few things. You see, one of the main causes of nervous breakdown - along with bereavement, of course, is carrying a burden of guilt. It can start to eat you up inside after a while.'

In the moments which follow, Imogen watches her breath condense into tiny water particles in the icily cold air.

'That might well be the case, but it's no good reason to destroy another person's happiness,' Allan replies flatly.

'Oh, I quite agree. I'm not suggesting you should confess to Abigail - the poor woman doesn't deserve that. What I am saying is how you must try to forgive *yourself.*' She takes hold of his gloved hands, 'Abigail would eventually forgive you if she knew - the girl loves you to bits. You've got to let it go now Allan - you made a mistake - hell, it's not as if you murdered somebody.'

'Here's the boat coming,' he calmly observes, helping his sister up from their stony seat.

The return journey to Cooper's End is not as awkward as Imogen had feared it might be. Allan actually seems a little more animated in the car than he had been on the way, particularly after the heaters have warmed them up. Imogen takes the opportunity to tell him about her conversation with Ian's teacher and her reservations about the organisation her son is so eager to join.

'I'm tempted to say you must allow Ian to do what he wants, otherwise he will only resent you both for holding him back,' Allan advises. 'But I don't like the sound of this Gilbert fellow. It seems as if he's saying one thing to you and something else to Caroline Carlow. Ian and Bridie are already involved in the local sailing club - I don't see why they need anything else. It was certainly enough for my two.'

'I'm really uncomfortable about Ian being in a position where he is thrown together with Matt Carlow. I know he's not as wayward as his brother was, but in the current circumstances - what with Hugh becoming so tied up in the murder case, I sense it would not be wise.' Imogen keeps her eyes steadily fixed on the road ahead.

'Best to keep your heads down for a few weeks, you mean? I quite agree. Ian's a sensitive lad, really. I've often thought he's a lot like my Robin - takes stuff to heart, you know? I could try having a word with him if you'd like?'

Imogen is momentarily stunned. She had never thought Allan ever paid that much attention to her children - certainly not to the extent of forming such an in-depth judgement about one of them. 'You are free to have a go, by all means, but don't expect much of a response.'

As they pull up the drive, it is nearly dark. Bridie and Ian both have after-school clubs this evening. Hugh will be fetching them on his way home from work and the house seems conspicuously empty. The security light above the garage comes on as Imogen begins to climb the steep steps leading to the front door. Something makes her glance back over her shoulder, towards the wooded area that lies just on the other side of the track. For a fraction of a second she imagines there is a flickering movement out there in the darkness, between two of the larger trees. As she stands for a moment, peering more closely into the gloom, she sees nothing.

Imogen makes a start on dinner. They have never attempted to put blinds up at the vast window which runs the entire length of the second floor of the house; largely as it would prove too difficult, but also because they are not at all overlooked. Beyond the marshy coppice to the north of them lies Cooper's Creek and then the wide, lazy river itself. As a result, privacy has never seemed much of an issue to the Crofts.

Allan has been sitting quietly in one of the armchairs which are angled to get the best view from the impressive picture window. Abruptly, he stands up, making his way purposefully towards the Crofts' drinks cabinet, which is placed along the dividing wall between the sitting room and the narrow, galley-style kitchen.

'Could you pour me a gin and tonic please?' Imogen calls from the other room, when she hears her brother's movements. For once, she is actually reassured that Allan is feeling recovered enough to fancy an *aperitif.*

Before he has a chance to respond, there is a sudden, ear-piercing sound - like a loud crack. It is followed by a weighty, reverberating thud and a second later the huge pane of glass which extends along the full length of the sitting room splits into several large pieces. Within moments, these shards simultaneously crash down onto the wooden floor below.

Chapter Ten

The immediate after-effect of the brick hurtling through the Crofts' sitting room window was oddly devastating. Luckily, the glass in the kitchen held firm and Imogen was completely unhurt.

The thunderous noise brought her running into the lounge, where the scene was almost apocalyptic. Allan was crouched down on his haunches next to the drinks cabinet with his hands clasped over his head, whimpering and sobbing quietly. The brick itself was lying innocently in the centre of the room, where it had etched a deep score into one of the polished floorboards.

What was really peculiar to Imogen was the huge, open expanse of freezing blackness which had replaced the glass. The window itself had been shatter-proof, so there were several large and jagged pieces lying directly where they had fallen. One such shard had dropped like a guillotine onto a soft armchair - viciously slicing the upholstery straight down the middle.

Imogen was forced to quickly decide upon a sensible plan of action. Firstly, she called the police and then she gently led her brother out of the front door and down the steps to the car. Once he was comfortably secured into the passenger seat, she accelerated out of the driveway and along the single lane track as fast as was humanly possible.

*

'What if Ian and Bridie had been at home?' Imogen declares in shocked disbelief. 'If it was any normal evening then they certainly would have been. It's bad enough that poor Allan's been reduced to a nervous wreck. What on earth I am going to tell Abigail? He was supposed to be coming here for some peace and quiet!'

Kath brings over a large glass of brandy but says nothing. She simply places an arm around her daughter-in-law's shoulders.

Imogen arrived at Hugh's parents' substantial Victorian villa in Maldon about an hour ago. She immediately called her husband to instruct him to bring the kids straight there. Gerry drove back over to Cooper's End to meet with the police at the house. Hugh has just this moment left in order to join him. Imogen and Kath are left alone in the beautiful, high-ceilinged living room.

'Allan will be fine. I've given him one of my sleeping tablets. He's just had a shock, that's all. It won't set him back, he only needs to rest. You will simply have to be thankful Ian and Bridie weren't there. For some reason, fate has intervened, thank goodness. They are currently holed up in the snug watching movies and eating dinner, blissfully none the wiser.'

Imogen slumps back into the armchair, taking a long sip from her glass and feeling her mouth go numb. 'I suppose we should have seen it coming. Have we been fools, Kath? Was it obvious something like this would happen if Hugh took on the case?'

'No, it wasn't.' the older lady makes herself comfortable on the dark green velvet sofa opposite. 'Are you absolutely positive it has anything to do with the Langley trial? Has something happened over the last few days which might possibly have prompted such an attack?'

Imogen closes her eyes and thinks carefully. 'Well, Hugh had his first interview with Langley a couple of days ago - but I can't see how anyone else would know about that. It was arranged purely between Hugh and the lawyers; even Langley's whereabouts are strictly hush-hush. The only other thing was the run-in I had in the High Street with Wendy Carlow.'

'Oh, yes,' Kath says, with a steely edge to her voice.

'She was upset about Hugh agreeing to be an expert witness for Thomas Langley. Wendy said he had 'betrayed his friends and neighbours' or something like that. She said her son, Matt, had told her about it.'

'That's it then,' Kath adds decisively. 'It must have been the Carlows trying to warn you off. Young Matt might even have known that Ian had an after school club and would be out of the house. He probably wanted to send you and Hugh a message. He gets on quite well with Ian, doesn't he? So, perhaps Matt Carlow made sure his friend wouldn't be there at the time he struck.'

Imogen has to admit Kath's theory is quite convincing, although, she isn't totally happy about her mother-in-law grouping all of the Carlows together into one criminal unit. Imogen hopes the police investigation comes up with some answers quickly so they can discover if Kath is right.

Gerry and Hugh stay overnight to guard the house, trying their best to erect some makeshift boards in order to temporarily secure the property. Hugh manages to return to his parents' place by mid-morning the following day, eager to fill the ladies in on the latest developments. Imogen leads her husband straight into the large, open-plan kitchen where Kathleen pours him a cup of strong, black coffee.

'What did the police have to say?' Imogen asks warily.

'There were no prints on the brick and obviously, whoever had thrown it was long gone. The police were convinced they must have come to the house on foot. Apparently, they can tell if there have been any fresh, unfamiliar vehicle markings and there was no sign of any. There *was* evidence of recent human activity in the woods opposite, though. Branches and twigs were disturbed and at some point a camp fire had been lit. The police asked if it could have been Bridie and Ian playing over there but I said no - they never do - that is right, isn't it?' Hugh looks towards his wife as he sips the hot drink.

'Yes, it's a bit too marshy for that. Look, I've just remembered something. I saw a movement amongst the trees yesterday evening - just as Allan and I had returned home. It was more of a *sense* of a movement really, because when I turned around, there was no one out there.'

'We'd better let the police know. It will confirm what they already suspect. That someone was watching and waiting in the woods.' Hugh appears very down-mouthed. 'I'm sorry Imogen, Mum, if I knew this was going to happen I would never have agreed to help Penny with her case.'

Imogen goes over and lays a hand on his arm. 'We don't actually know yet if the attack on the house was connected to your decision to profile Langley.'

'I can't begin to imagine what else it could be about. We've lived perfectly safely in our home for the last decade, but as soon as I interview Thomas Langley we find ourselves subjected to some kind of guerrilla warfare,' Hugh retorts.

'A brick thrown through a window is a cowardly act,' Kath interjects. 'The results were so terribly damaging because of the size of that particular window. The person throwing it may not have expected to make such a shocking impact. It's got the look of a childish prank gone wrong to me.'

Almost as if his mother has not spoken, Hugh suddenly states, 'I'll phone Penny now and let her know I'm not taking the profile any further. I refuse to put my family at any risk.'

'Please just hear me out for a minute, before you make a decision, Hugh,' Kath says. 'Our friends, John and Barbara, invited us to go away with them for a couple of weeks to the Peak District. We were in two minds about it, but I think now that we will go. Then you can all stay here for a while - only until the trial is over, of course. The Police Station is at the end of the road, so no one would *dare* try to do anything to you while you're here. Once the window is fixed and the Langley case is resolved, you can go back home.' Kath vigorously wipes a cloth across the solid wood worktop before adding, in a very level voice, 'we aren't really going to let the Carlows get away with bullying this family for a second time, are we?'

Chapter Eleven

Hugh's parents grew up during the hardships brought by the Second World War and are of that generation who feel they must never give in to intimidation of any kind. It is a quality Imogen deeply admires but isn't sure she can always successfully live up to.

After a sleepless night and much fraught deliberation, the Crofts finally decided to accept the offer to stay at Kath and Gerry's place for a short while. Whether or not Hugh should continue to act as an expert witness for Langley's defence team, proved to be a harder issue for them both to resolve.

In the end, Imogen pointed out the damage had already been done. She added that even if Hugh were to give up his role, short of taking out an advert in the local paper, very few people would get to know about it. Whereas, if he carried on meeting with Langley and produced his report for the lawyers without making a big song and dance about it, the whole thing would eventually blow over.

Hugh has taken a couple of days off work. He and Allan have been moving the most essential and valuable items out of the house in Cooper's End. The new glazing is on order but could take several weeks to arrive. In the meantime, the insurance company have thoroughly secured the gaping hole at the front of the property with wooden boards. Imogen has tried to keep the youngsters away from their home for the time being, as it looks terribly depressing. It is almost as if the eyes of the building have been plucked out and then haphazardly covered over, as if to hide something gruesome underneath.

Ian and Bridie are extremely pleased to be staying at their Gran and Grandad's house. They can now walk to school and even meet their friends in the High Street for a coffee after classes have ended. It is obvious to Imogen just how much her children are relishing this new found freedom. It makes her realise what they have previously missed out on by having to be ferried to and from school every day and not having any of their close friends living nearby.

Kath and Gerry left for the Peak District yesterday morning and instructed their son and daughter-in-law to contact them immediately if there was any more trouble. There was something in the retired couple's contented expressions as they cheerily waved goodbye from the front seats of their little hatchback, which indicated they were perfectly confident there would not be.

What the Victorian townhouse in Maldon lacks in terms of isolation and views it makes up for in beautiful period features and easy accessibility to all of the local amenities. To be there almost makes Imogen feel as if they are on holiday. Last night, Allan stayed in to mind the kids whilst his sister and her husband took a leisurely stroll along the waterfront to the Jolly Sailor for a quick drink.

Imogen can't remember the last time they were able to act with such freedom and spontaneity. They had asked Allan when they returned if he felt ready to go back to his London flat. Hugh and Imogen both noticed the shadow which passed fleetingly across his face as they mentioned it. Allan replied that he still needed more time. His sister insisted, quite genuinely, he was welcome to stay for as long as he liked.

'In fact, I could do with your company during the daytime, to be honest. The kids are acting as if they've been awarded the 'keys to the city' and I've hardly seen anything of them.' Is what she had said.

Allan appears to be slowly recovering. His appetite is improving daily and every so often, one can clearly discern the briefest glimmer of his previous self. Imogen has certainly seen a glimpse of the old Allan in the way in which her brother is telling anyone who will listen how he was saved from being cut in half by a sheet of falling glass because of his sudden desire for a whisky and soda. Imogen chats to Abigail on the phone most days and she senses the girl is keen to come and visit for a weekend. Allan must be putting her off, as no concrete plans have yet been made.

Imogen is busy familiarising herself with the layout of Kath's kitchen when her mobile phone starts to buzz.

'Hello?' she answers, whilst simultaneously peering into drawers and cupboards.

'Hi, Imogen? It's Caroline here. I'm so sorry about what happened at your house - how are you all doing?'

'Hi, Caroline. We're a bit shell-shocked, but no one was hurt and the glass can easily be replaced. The most horrible part was the realisation someone out there might want to do such a terrible thing to us. It leaves you with a pretty nasty feeling,' Imogen replies.

'Look, would you like to come and meet me for a coffee? How about Lucio's - I'll treat you to a Latte?'

'What a great idea. We're staying at Hugh's parents' place so I can be there in five minutes,' Imogen gushes.

'Even better. Bag us a table by the window, will you? I'll join you as soon as I can.'

Lucio's is a trendy Italian café and restaurant on the High Street. Its interior is an impressive ensemble of dark woods and burgundy upholstery. It could potentially be gloomy inside if it wasn't for the two large bay windows which make up the frontage of the building. It is on a comfortable sofa at one of these windows that Imogen settles herself down to await the arrival of her friend. As she removes her woollen scarf and coat she feels a little thrill at the fact she was able to stroll out of the house and straight into the hustle and bustle of the town.

Glancing at her wrist watch, Imogen notes that it is now a quarter of an hour since her conversation with Caroline. She gazes idly along the High Road to see if she is approaching. Imogen quickly spots her. Caroline is standing in the semi-circular entranceway to Clarkewells Department Store. She is talking animatedly to somebody who Imogen doesn't recognise. Caroline's companion has his back turned towards the café but Imogen can see he is wearing a long, dark coat and is tall and wirily built. The man has on a deer-stalker style hat; of the type which has recently come back into fashion. His face and head are largely obscured from view.

For some reason, Imogen feels inclined to sit forward in her seat and observe the pair more closely. As the conversation continues, the expression on Caroline's face begins to change. Imogen's friend is clearly becoming agitated and then appears to be remonstrating with the man. He remains still and impassive throughout the exchange. All of a sudden, Caroline says something to him with exaggerated emphasis and walks quickly away. Disappointingly for Imogen, the man does not turn around to watch Caroline go, but instead lingers to browse in the shop window for a few moments before disappearing inside.

Imogen swiftly turns her attention to the menu on the table in front of her. When Caroline enters the café, she is slightly flushed, but in no other way does she seem to be ruffled by her recent encounter.

'Oh fab, you managed to get the window seat. Sorry I'm late, Im. I had to get some P.E socks from Clarkewells and the assistant took *forever*. Haven't you ordered yet? Don't worry darling, I'll go and get you that Latte I promised.'

When Caroline returns from the counter with their long glasses of milky coffee, she is completely composed. She removes her camel coloured coat and gives Imogen a kiss on the cheek. 'How are you? I felt just awful when Will told me about what happened - have you any idea yet who could have done such a thing?'

'The police don't know. The brick was thrown by someone who had run up to the driveway of the house. They think whoever it was had been hiding out in the woods opposite. The general consensus is that it was kids, but we're no further on than that.'

'And nobody was hurt? Will said Ian and Bridie were out of the house when it happened - thank God. So what was the point of it all? They didn't try to break in or anything?' Caroline looks genuinely eager to get to the bottom of the whole incident.

'No, someone simply hurled the brick and ran. Hugh's mum believes whoever it was didn't know it was such a large pane of glass and hadn't realised how dangerous it was. I'm not sure if I agree with her or not,' Imogen pauses for a second, wondering if she can afford to take Caroline into her confidence. 'I did think for a while it might have had something to do with Hugh helping out the Langley defence team.'

Caroline sits back in her seat. 'I won't lie to you, Imogen. Steve and Wendy were pretty furious when they found out Hugh was going to help Langley to mount his defence. I had to put up with her complaining to me on the phone a number of times. But they've not mentioned it recently and, to be honest, I'm fairly sure it was all just bluster.' She lowers her voice a little. 'Deep down, both of them knew what Danny was like. Wendy was at her wits end in the months leading up to his death. He'd been kicked off his apprenticeship at the garage for stealing some of the tools. She's very angry and upset at the moment and although she'd never admit it - she's actually angry with Danny - for being stupid enough to get himself killed. So I just can't see them being responsible for this, I really can't.'

'What about Matt?' Imogen ventures.

'He's a good lad. Matt is determined not to go down the same road as his brother. He's seen first-hand what it has done to his parents. I think you're barking up the wrong tree here, Imogen. It's not his style at all.'

Imogen says nothing and changes the subject. She is oddly surprised at how vehemently Caroline had defended Rick's family. Before now, her friend had barely said a good word about them. But Imogen is fully aware that in times of crisis families pull together, it is only natural. Although she does note to herself how this usually happens when there is an individual within that family who has something they wish to hide.

Chapter Twelve

The wind is blowing a gale as Hugh climbs out of his car at Thomas Langley's apartment building. He makes a desperate attempt to prevent his precious notes from taking flight down the street by stuffing them rapidly into his battered old briefcase.

The psychologist is flustered and windswept by the time his client lets him into the warm and comfortable flat. Thomas Langley takes Hugh's coat and strides off to begin his coffee-making ritual. This is the third time the two men have met. Their second encounter was at Penny's Chambers in Lincoln's Inn, where Hugh was invited to attend a strategy meeting. What had struck him on that occasion was how chaotic the proceedings were. None of the briefs, including Penny herself, seemed to be well versed on the details of the case. Hugh didn't get the sense they were pursuing any clear line of defence. He wondered at the time what Langley must have made of it all, as it had certainly not filled Hugh with much confidence.

When Thomas returns from the kitchen, they fall into what is now becoming a regular pattern. The older man sits, tall and upright on the sofa, whilst Hugh gently asks his questions.

'Could we talk a little about your childhood today, Thomas?'

'Of course,' he replies politely.

'Your father fought in the Second World War, is that correct? So you didn't see much of him during those years?'

'That's right. I was just me and my Mam for the first few months of the fighting. We lived in a small terraced house in the suburbs of Birmingham. I was evacuated, did you know? Towards the end of 1940 - I was sent down to Devon and stayed there for the next five years, give or take. It was quite an elderly couple who took me on and they left me to my own devices mostly. Lovely cottage they had; so pretty it was.' Langley's face lights up at the memory. 'I've often thought since, how my Mam and Dad would have had more children if it wasn't for the war. It had separated them just at the wrong time in their marriage. Because when Dad came back we didn't really know him anymore and he certainly didn't know *me*.'

Hugh nods with understanding. This was a situation which had played out in many families after the Second World War was over, his own father's included. 'It must have changed things for a lot of couples. What kind of education did you get during those years?'

'All of us evacuees went to the village school, where we joined the local children. I had already missed several months of formal teaching and never really caught up. We covered all of the basics of course, but I didn't have much interest in going beyond that when I was a boy. Everything I've learnt since has been from books. I came to it all a bit later than most.'

'Your father returned home in September 1945 and went to work for his old firm,' Hugh prompts, glancing at his notes.

'Aye, a few years after Dad came back I left school and got a job in the city. I was a luggage collector at the station. It wasn't a bad gig at all. There was plenty of life to be seen there and I was still living at home, so I could save up my money too. Then, as soon as I turned 16, I joined the army.'

'Was that the career you had always wanted?'

'I suppose so. Having grown up in the war, the military sort of gets imprinted on your brain - you think about your father and what he might be doing out on the battlefield the whole time and it becomes a part of your life. That was how it was for me, anyway. Plus, I knew an office job would never have suited my character. So the army it was.' Thomas smiles a little. Hugh recognises how hard the man is trying to be thorough and cooperative, most likely because his son is footing the bill for all this.

'Your first exposure to overseas action was in Korea, is that right?'

A shadow passes across Langley's face and for the first time he looks uncomfortable.

'I've never talked about those years, Hugh. Not even to my wife and sons. I'm happy and willing to help, but I won't talk about that.' Langley clasps his hands together in his lap and his face looks determined.

Hugh is surprised by the sudden change in him. Then he realises that Langley was being so forthcoming about his civilian life, because he was compensating for the fact he was not prepared to divulge anything at all about his experiences in the army.

'I can totally understand. However, if I am to produce a full psychological profile, we will need to explore your military experiences, I'm afraid. It will not be an easy process, but it may well be our only real chance to help you at the trial.' Hugh immediately recalls the shambolic strategy meeting with Langley's lawyers.

'Let me tell you about my family first, *please* Hugh. My early army days were certainly my worst. I'd like to tackle those memories in my own time, okay?'

Hugh knows he has been fobbed off, but decides to let Langley lead the conversation for the moment. He is beginning to feel frustrated. Hugh is putting his own family in a difficult position in order to help this old man. If Thomas refuses to cooperate fully then it will all have been for nothing.

'I came back from Korea in '53. I'd been a prisoner of war and wasn't very well. I spent a few months in an army hospital and then went home to my mother. She wasn't in the best of health herself and found it a burden to have me there, although she never would have said so. My father had passed away by then and Mam was all alone. I wasn't fit for active service for a long time, but when I was well enough, the army sent me to Suffolk. It was a desk job and I hated it. It did have its advantages, though. One of the Major's secretaries was a young woman called Rose Palmer. I took her out for a drink on a few occasions and we became an item. Rose and I got hitched in 1957. We spent our early married life living on the base. Rob was born in 1961 and Andy in '63.' Langley pauses and asks Hugh if he would like a fresh cup of coffee. The psychologist shakes his head, becoming increasingly exasperated that the man isn't telling him anything which is not already of public record.

'I wasn't a good husband at first, Hugh. I was dissatisfied with my administrative job and wanted to return to the field. I'd also seen some things out in Korea that no young lad should have witnessed. It made me get angry sometimes and difficult to live with - but I never raised my hand to Rose or the boys - I wouldn't have done that.' Hugh sits forward a little, as Langley's testimony becomes more interesting to him. 'I was restless with my lot and in '64 we took a boat out to New Zealand to begin a new life.'

'I wasn't aware of that. It didn't get mentioned in your record,' interrupts Hugh, who begins to flick briskly through his file, just to check he hadn't somehow missed it.

'Well, we were only in New Zealand for a few years. I asked the army for some time out and they agreed, as long as I did a bit of liaison work while I was there. We arrived in Christchurch during the Christmas of 1964 but we returned to England in '68. I did a number of different jobs during that time, mostly for the New Zealand government. The boys really enjoyed the climate and the outdoor lifestyle which went with it. I liked it too. Rose, however, was terribly homesick. She missed her parents and her brother and his family. We kept waiting for her to settle in and feel better about the place but she just never did. I couldn't allow my Rose to be unhappy so finally, we packed up and shipped ourselves back home. Our time out in New Zealand had done my health the world of good. When we got back to the UK, I was assessed as being fit for active service once again. We moved around between military bases for a good few years. I was posted to Northern Ireland for a while, but overall it was our happiest period together as a family. We made good friends and Rose was able to visit her folks whenever she wished.'

Hugh glances at his watch. He should really start to wrap things up for the day. 'Did you ever regret not having stayed on in New Zealand?'

'There was a time, later on, when we regretted it bitterly. Life wasn't easy for us in the seventies. At certain moments, things had seemed very bleak. We tried not to torture ourselves with 'what ifs' because there's no point in it, is there Hugh? Rose just wasn't content in New Zealand, so we could never have stayed. Nevertheless, she did beat herself up about it. The fact it was *her* who made us all come back to the UK with its strikes and power cuts and rubbish in the streets. I always told her not to brood on it - what is done is done. God most likely had a plan for us, is what I always used to say, isn't that right, Hugh?'

Hugh nods politely and decides to end it there. As he says goodbye to Langley in the doorway of his pleasant little flat, he thinks how the old man's fatalistic attitude is probably what has got him through the darkest episodes of his long and eventful life. It is a mind-set which has certainly left him with a noticeable aura of inner strength and calm. Hugh is surprised to discover that he is almost envious of it.

Chapter Thirteen

Having mastered the appliances in Kath's kitchen, Imogen is beginning to feel quite at home. She particularly likes the fact that the youngsters can sit around the large dining table whilst Imogen fixes breakfast or dinner. It seems to make the whole process a more sociable experience. This afternoon, it is Allan who is in there with her, sharing out a *cafetiére* of coffee, whilst his sister prepares the evening meal.

'So, Caroline's got herself a mysterious gentleman friend, you say?' He comments innocently, taking a sip of the strong, dark liquid.

'No, I said she was arguing with a man outside Clarkewells but she deliberately didn't tell me about it afterwards,' Imogen patiently clarifies.

'Well, if this other person wasn't Rick, he must have been her fancy-man. There aren't really any alternative explanations for it. Caroline's 'a bit of alright' from what I can remember and her husband's a crashing bore, so it's not terribly surprising.'

Imogen can't prevent herself from smiling. 'I think you may be jumping to conclusions. I didn't sense there was anything romantic about this encounter. In a funny way, it had a look of pure business about it.'

'Ah, blackmail then? Or a dastardly plan to swindle the sailing club out of its petty cash?' Allan smiles too and gets up to rummage in the cupboard for biscuits.

'There *is* more to life than sex and money, you know. Don't eat too many snacks, Allan, dinner will be ready in 20 minutes.'

'Tell me *your* theory then, sis. No doubt you've got one.' Allan helps himself to a couple of chocolate digestives, completely ignoring Imogen's advice.

'I was too far away to work out what was going on. All I'm saying is there may have been a number of different explanations. It could have had something to do with Rick's shop, for example. The man might have been a creditor who hadn't paid his bills. Or, it's possible it was related to the children. He could perhaps have been the father of a kid at school who is bullying Will or Nikki. What I did notice, is that this chap was very keen not to be recognised by anyone. His hat was almost completely obscuring his face and he rushed off into the shop as soon as Caroline had walked away.'

'So he didn't know you had seen him arguing with her?' Allan asks.

'No, he never turned in my direction at all. I don't think Caroline knew I'd seen them either. There's another thing - I don't believe their meeting was planned, otherwise Caroline wouldn't have suggested I take the seat by the window. She would have been too worried I'd spot them.' Imogen turns down the light on the stove and comes over to sit with her brother.

'Let's hope this fellow wasn't responsible for throwing the brick through your sitting room window. They might very well have been rendezvousing to plan something else - or perhaps Caroline was angry with him because the brick caused more damage than they had originally planned. On the other hand, it could have been quite the opposite. Maybe she was infuriated because they hadn't succeeded in running you out of town.' Allan's expression looks serious now.

'I don't think so, Al. Caroline's a really good friend of ours. It's a little far-fetched,' Imogen automatically retorts, although Allan's theory has placed a tiny seed of doubt in her mind.

He throws his hands up in a gesture of surrender. 'Hey, I was only following your lead by considering all the possible scenarios. How good a friend is she? Would she tell you if she were having an affair?'

Imogen goes quiet for a moment. 'I'm not sure, probably not if I'm honest. We've never spoken about that kind of stuff. You know, like problems in our marriages or our past relationships. I would only ever discuss something of that nature with a really old friend or with you or Michael.'

They both sit in comfortable silence for a minute or two and then Imogen glances up at the antique clock above Kath's stove. 'The kids are late home. Dinner's going to be ready soon. Maybe I'll give Ian a call.' She digs out her mobile and finds his number. It rings for a while, but no one answers.

'Where were they going after school?' Allan asks.

'They were both meeting a group of friends at Café Crème for a hot chocolate. They must have lost track of the time.'

'I'll go over and fetch them if you'd like?' Allan suggests, standing up and making his way into the hall.

'Wait a second, I'll come with you,' Imogen adds, turning off the hob and firmly placing a lid on the pot's bubbling contents.

The cold air hits her as soon as they step out of the front door. Imogen looks upwards and sees that the dark sky is cloudless and dotted with the pattern of distant stars. They walk without conversation along the leafy street. It is empty except for a large grey cat, sitting on one of the stone walls which mark out the neighbour's front garden, warily eyeing them as they pass.

They turn down a narrow passageway which leads straight onto the High Road. Immediately, Imogen can tell something has happened. A group of people are standing around in a circle on the other side of the street. They seem to be gathered in the layby, where the local taxi cabs park up and wait for passing fares. As they get closer, Imogen can see something that looks like a bundle of coats lying on the ground. Then, she notices the hair. It is a deep, honey-brown colour and is splayed out across the damp road.

Imogen grabs at Allan's coat. Speaking in no more than a whisper, she gasps, 'Bridie?'

'Let me find out what's going on,' he says flatly.

But Imogen is already running. Straight towards the congregation of onlookers, not waiting to check if the road is clear, pushing one of the inert spectators out of her way. Now she is nearer, Imogen can see there is frantic activity taking place down on the ground. A young man with dark, closely cropped hair is leaning over the bundle, taking charge and applying first aid to the girl. Imogen's mouth is open although no sound is coming out. She feels a hand gripping her arm and distant voices shouting.

'Mum? It's Nikki Carlow. She was hit by a car. We didn't see it happen. She must have stepped out into the road. She left the café before any of us, because she said she was late for her tea. Mum, can you go and get her dad? He will be working in the shop - Mum?' Ian shakes her gently until she finally turns towards him and registers his presence.

Beside her son stands Bridie, looking cold and shocked, but otherwise perfectly alive and well. Before responding, Imogen reaches out and pulls her daughter into an embrace. 'Oh, Thank God,' she mutters. Then she wills herself into action. 'Has someone called an ambulance?'

'Matt's already done it, we're just waiting for them to arrive. He's also got Nikki into the crash position and made her more comfortable. He says we shouldn't risk moving her any more than that.'

'I'll go and get Rick. Bridie: you come with me.' Imogen takes her daughter by the hand. They run down the street to the Carlows' hardware store.

Rick Carlow is serving a customer, but when he catches sight of Imogen's expression he stops what he is doing and says, 'what's the matter?'

'It's Nikki, please come quickly.'

By the time the three of them get back to the layby, the ambulance has arrived. A medic is busily assessing the girl's injuries. After a few minutes she is lifted carefully and efficiently onto a stretcher. Her father doesn't utter another word but follows his daughter into the back of the ambulance, looking like a condemned man about to mount the gallows, with his son trailing along close behind.

The crowd begins to disperse, leaving just Imogen and Allan, standing side by side with Bridie, Ian and Matt Carlow. Imogen turns towards the assembled teenagers and demands; 'tell me exactly what happened.'

'A group of us were in Café Crème, Mrs Croft,' says Matt Carlow, taking the lead. 'We'd been in there since the end of school, just hanging out and having a hot drink. Will was with us but Nikki came along later. She'd been shopping first, I think. We were there for another hour or so and Nikki suddenly said she and Will had to get home, or her mum would be cross with them. But Will didn't want to leave just yet so she went ahead without him. Then, about five minutes later, we heard this terrible commotion on the street. We all ran out to see what was going on. Somehow, we knew it had something to do with Nikki.'

'There were all these old ladies kneeling down, who were trying to lift Nikki up, but Matt took charge. He told them he was a first-aider and that she shouldn't be moved - she might have a neck injury. Those ladies did tell us the car had just driven off, without even stopping. Matt checked her breathing and made her comfortable and called the ambulance. We wouldn't have had a clue what to do without him,' Ian explains.

'It's no biggie. It's just what I learned doing my first aid qualification through 'The Blackwater Boys'. Mr Gilbert suggested I do it because I want to become a medic, when I finish college.'

Allan leans over and shakes the young man's hand. 'Well done. It was very lucky you were on the scene. Would you like someone to drive you home?'

'No thanks, I've already called my dad. He's going to pick me up. We'll drive to the hospital together and see how she's doing. I'd like to be with my parents while they are there. They've had some pretty awful experiences of those places in the last few months. I wouldn't want them to have to face it alone.'

Chapter Fourteen

The Croft children are finally settled and asleep by midnight. It was a fraught evening of telephone calls and anxious waiting. No one felt much like eating the meal Imogen had prepared. It remained untouched in the saucepan until someone eventually scraped it into a container and shoved it in the freezer.

'Any more news?' Hugh asks, as he walks back into the sitting room after checking on Ian and Bridie.

'Caroline says the doctors have described her as 'stable' and 'out of danger'. Nikki has a broken collar-bone and she took a nasty knock to the head. They've given her a scan and are awaiting the results. She has been awake and lucid so they are fairly confident of a good recovery,' Imogen explains.

Hugh drops heavily onto his parents' velvet sofa. 'It's very sobering. In just a matter of seconds, your whole life can come crashing down around you. The bastard simply drove off, did he?'

'It looks that way,' Allan adds. 'Matt Carlow and I waited for the police to arrive. When they finally did, one of the customers in the café came out to give a statement. He said the car was a dark blue, medium-sized hatchback; a Golf, maybe or an Astra. He said it was revving its engine hard, which is why he looked up from reading his paper. He saw Nikki standing in the layby, between two stationary cars. She took a step out into the road and this blue car just kind of clipped her. Nikki fell to the ground and the car carried on going.'

'Might the driver not have realised he'd hit someone?' Hugh ventures.

'The impact must have made quite a thump. I don't think it's very likely - and the driver could have been a woman, Hugh.' Imogen leans forward to take another sip of her brandy.

'I suppose so, but in my experience, women don't tend to loudly rev their engines.'

'They might do if they aren't particularly familiar with the car,' Imogen suggests.

'I know this observation isn't very P.C., but can you *really* imagine a woman leaving a young school girl, lying injured and possibly dead by the roadside?' Allan inquires.

'I think that's probably an old fashioned sentiment, Allan. Although, I believe you are correct in as much as 'hit and run' crimes are predominantly committed by young men.'

'He could even be somebody local,' Imogen muses. 'At that sort of time in the evening he was most likely returning home from work. The street was so busy with people, I'm sure the police will be able to identify him.'

'I was rather impressed by young Matt Carlow. He kept his cool and showed a great deal of resourcefulness and presence of mind,' Allan states.

'It often happens in families where one of the children has died. The sibling left behind finds themselves having to support grieving parents and, occasionally, being required to take on the running of the household for a while. This situation forces them to grow up more quickly than they otherwise would. A significant number of those who end up in positions of high office suffered the loss of a close relative during their childhood. It's a well-known phenomenon,' Hugh explains.

'It's a case of 'what doesn't kill you will only make you stronger' I suppose. Although, I think Matt was always a nicer lad than his brother. They broke the mould after Danny Carlow was born, thank goodness,' Imogen mutters, almost to herself.

'Well, there's nothing more we can do for Nikki right now, except to get a good night's sleep,' Hugh declares, raising himself up from the seat. Imogen nods in silent agreement and they begin the ritual of making sure the house is securely locked up.

*

Imogen feels a little uncomfortable as she walks from her car to the entrance of the Intensive Care Unit at Stourfield Hospital, on the outskirts of Chelmsford. She has a gift for Nikki and is keen to give Caroline and Rick her full support. However, she is nervous about the possibility of bumping into Wendy and Steve Carlow. Imogen has no idea what kind of reception she will get from Danny's parents.

The unit where Nikki is being treated is eerily quiet. The rooms which run down the right-hand side have been built with large windows facing out towards the corridor, presumably so that the critically ill patients can be observed at all times by staff. About halfway along the passage, she sees Caroline, sitting on a seat outside one of these rooms, with Wendy beside her. Imogen takes a deep breath and approaches them.

Caroline jumps up to greet her friend. 'Imogen, thank you so much for coming, we've had such an awful night.'

'I know,' she soothes, 'how is Nikki doing?'

'She's asleep most of the time, but the doctors say it's quite normal after a bad blow to the head. They've given her pain killers for the collar-bone too. The scan came back okay, so we're just waiting now for her to get better.'

Caroline looks tired and worn down. Wendy, however, appears brighter than when Imogen had last encountered her. She seems healthier and less troubled. 'Hello Imogen,' Wendy says. 'I'm glad you came.'

Their brief exchange is interrupted by the arrival of the men. Steve and Rick stride towards the ladies with brimming cardboard cups in their hands. They are immediately recognisable as brothers. Steve is the older and taller of the two and, although beginning to grey, his hair is still thick and wavy. Rick, on the other hand, is thinning on top and his skin is sallow. He is physically smaller than his sibling, who holds himself deliberately upright, as if to accentuate this difference between them. Their facial features are very alike. Small-eyed and determined, it suddenly occurs to Imogen how they resemble a pair of terriers; or some similar breed of tenacious hunting dog.

'Would you like a drink, Imogen?' Rick asks without much enthusiasm.

'No, thank you. I won't stay long. I just wanted to see how Nikki was getting on.'

"Stable', is the best anyone can tell us.' Rick looks defeated - as if all the fight has been knocked out of him.

'You were at the scene of the 'hit and run' weren't you?' Steve asks bluntly, 'did you see what happened?'

'I'm afraid my brother and I arrived shortly after the car had driven away. We only heard what the witnesses told the police,' Imogen replies.

'That it was a blue hatchback, revving its engines,' Caroline supplies.

'There might be CCTV footage.' Steve glances at his brother. 'You've got a camera outside the shop, haven't you?'

'Yes, but I've no idea if there is one anywhere near the spot where Nik was knocked down. The police haven't told us a damn thing yet.'

Steve grimaces at the mention of the police. 'They're a bunch of useless sods. I wouldn't expect much from the coppers if I were you. The law ain't on the side of the victim any longer and the sooner you realise that, the sooner you'll spare yourself from bitter disappointment.'

Not wishing to stick around for Steve's tirade, Imogen announces she had better be getting back home. Caroline quickly volunteers to walk with her friend to the hospital's entrance.

Once they have left the ICU, Caroline says, 'I know it's ungrateful, but I do wish Wendy and Steve would go home. Being here is obviously bringing back unpleasant memories for them and I'd rather just sit with Rick and wait for her to wake up. I'm sure it will change, but at this present time I don't much care who is responsible. I only want my little girl to get better.'

They embrace, and Imogen promises to call her friend first thing the following morning. On the long drive back to Maldon along the A414, where she is caught in the inevitable queue of traffic waiting for the lights to change at the crossroads in the pretty village of Danbury, Imogen thinks carefully about the events of the last 48 hours.

It strikes her as a tragic coincidence that two dreadful misfortunes should befall the Carlow family within such a short space of time. Also knowing this kind of bad luck is not unheard of. Firstly, she considers if it is a coincidence at all or if the incidents are in some way connected. Imogen quickly dismisses this idea as there is no evidence to support it.

As the traffic finally begins to move more freely, a truly horrifying thought pops unbidden into her head.

She recalls how last evening, in the semi-darkness, seeing a glimpse of Nikki Carlow's honey-brown hair had made her immediately fear that it was *Bridie* who was lying there on the ground. Imogen now wonders if the driver of the dark blue car, seeing a young girl in a Beeleigh School uniform, with shoulder length chestnut coloured hair, standing at the side of the road, had, momentarily, thought that it was Bridie too.

Chapter Fifteen

'That's crazy,' Hugh states flatly, as he sits down at the kitchen table opposite his wife. He loosens his tie and picks up the mug of steaming coffee she has placed in front of him.

'I know it's far-fetched. It's just the 'hit and run' happened so soon after we had a brick thrown through our front window. I can't help but feel a little paranoid.'

'Our theory was that the attack on the house had something to do with me helping Langley. So, it would have to have been carried out by one of the Carlows or their sympathisers. If that's the case, and they then decided to target Bridie; they aren't going to knock down a member of their own family in the process, are they? Or even mistake Nikki for Bridie - it doesn't make any sense.'

'No, you're right. Also, Steve Carlow was really keen to find out who knocked Nikki down and I'm sure his desire was genuine. All the local support for the Carlows in the aftermath of Danny's shooting has come from people who are shocked and disgusted at the tragic death of a young man. I can't see any of those people, including the Carlows themselves, harming *another* youngster in order to make their point.'

'If Mum were here,' Hugh adds, 'she would say that the throwing of a brick through a window and the deliberate knocking down of a child, are two very different crimes. She would suggest they were not committed by the same person. There is a theory that criminals will gradually 'escalate' their use of violence with each illegal act. But I believe it's too much of a leap in too short a space of time in this instance.'

'Plus, we don't even know if Nikki's accident *was* deliberate. So, are we decided this 'hit and run' was not connected to us in any way?' Imogen looks pensively at her husband for reassurance.

'Darling, I truly don't think it was. It's simply a tragic thing to have happened. If you are worried, make sure the kids head straight home after school for the next week or so. We're quite safe here.'

Imogen takes a few minutes to consider this. 'I don't believe that is the answer. Ian and Bridie usually get driven to and from school every day. Only when they are at the sailing club do they have any real freedom. At their age I had considerably more independence than they have. I believe the real danger here is that I will become so worried about the threats which may or may not be lurking out there, that I will prevent my children from developing the skills which will actually *help* them to survive in the outside world. The fact is, if Nikki Carlow hadn't stepped out into the road from between two parked cars, she would never have been run down. And, if Matt Carlow hadn't been well trained in first aid, then the end result could have been far, far worse.'

'What are you saying?' Hugh senses his wife is building up to something.

'I've decided we should let Ian join 'The Blackwater Boys'. He's seventeen years old now, Hugh. If we try to hold him back he will never forgive us. I had judged Matt Carlow before I'd even met the lad. It turns out he's a good kid. We are safer if we allow Ian to become a proper part of the community; with friends to support him, rather than trying to keep ourselves out on the edge.' Imogen turns to fill the dishwasher, unsure of how Hugh will react.

'Okay. I agree. But we think very carefully before he sets out on any expeditions, alright?'

Genuinely surprised by his response, Imogen rushes over and places her arms around her husband's neck. 'I think it's the right thing to do, darling. I'm just going to have to learn to overcome my fears about letting the children go forth into the big bad world.'

*

Hugh glances around the busy restaurant. Penny Mills is seated at a table which is tucked into an intimate corner of the room. She raises her hand to catch his attention. Hugh smiles and slowly weaves his way over to join her.

Penny requested they have a lunch meeting in order to discuss the Langley case. She is due back in court later in the afternoon so she suggested this Italian restaurant on Fleet Street. Hugh notes how the place is full of lawyers. However, it is not grandiose in any way and he opts for a simple pasta dish with tomato sauce and clams.

Penny is looking very business-like in a dark, close-fitting suit, with her blond hair pinned back severely from her face. 'Thank you for coming all this way, Hugh. I really appreciate it.' She lays her hand briefly on top of his. Before the gesture has time to become awkward, Penny withdraws it again.

'I needed to spend a couple of hours in the British Library, so it really wasn't a problem.'

'Let me fill you in on where we are with the Langley Farm case,' Penny begins. 'To be honest, we aren't feeling confident. My Head of Chambers thinks it's on a knife edge. We've got the recent changes in the law to help us, of course. The 2011 Act means home-owners are no longer required to 'retreat' from an intruder. It also states that one can act 'instinctively' to protect one's property. These tweaks to the wording will help me to build my case.' Penny takes a sip of Soave.

'What are our greatest obstacles?' Hugh enquires.

'Have you ever witnessed the effect on the human body of a shotgun fired at close range?' Penny rests her green eyes steadily upon her companion.

Hugh shakes his head.

'The impact is similar to that of shrapnel wounds from a small bomb. Darren Beck was hit in the shoulder by some of the stray pellets. But the side of Danny Carlow's head was horribly injured. The fact that the boy lived on for a few hours makes the whole thing even worse. The prosecution have post-mortem photos which the judge has agreed the jury can see.'

Hugh lets his mind drift to the old man living in the neat little flat in Buckhurst Hill.

'The boys were running away, posing no immediate threat. We think it's going to come down to the jurors' opinion of Langley himself. At this point in time, Hugh, I'm not convinced the jurors are going to take to him. He's not the doddering old geriatric they're no doubt expecting. And, between you and me, he's too cool. Not enough remorse is evident for my liking.' Penny sits back and allows the waitress to set down her main course.

'What do you feel personally about the events of that night, Penny? Don't you have any sympathy for Langley at all?'

'It doesn't really matter too much what I think, Hugh. Since you ask, it strikes me as odd that Langley chased them down. It's an aspect of the case I don't like; it just doesn't sit very well with me.'

'I can understand. You've read my interview notes haven't you? Langley knew the boys had taken his lead. It was all he had to keep the farm going. I believe it comes under the category of 'instinctive' that he would pursue the men in order to get his property back. Langley is an army man. He isn't used to showing his emotions; it's been conditioned out of him. By the way, did you know the Langleys lived in New Zealand for a while in the mid-sixties? They would have stayed out there for good, but Rose Langley was homesick.' Hugh tucks into his pasta, which he discovers is delicious.

'Our researcher must have missed it. Does it assist us in any way, Hugh? Are you finding any evidence of PTSD? We need every bit of help we can get to win over that Jury.'

'It takes time, Penny. He's telling me about his family first. Then we'll move onto the military stuff. It does sound to me as if he was suffering from the symptoms of severe anxiety after he returned from Korea in the early fifties. So there is a history of it. I'm afraid at the present time I agree with you. He seems too calm to be a PTSD sufferer. However, if he was placed in a position where he was in mortal danger, it might very well be an entirely different matter.'

Penny nods her head and takes another sip of wine. They finish their lunch in amiable discussion but Hugh senses he has failed to provide the lawyer with the news that she had really wanted to hear.

Chapter Sixteen

The rain is pounding onto the windscreen of Hugh's Volvo estate. The wipers are working furiously to combat the onslaught, squeaking pitifully in the process.

The cold and clear spell has given way to days and days of wet. Low-lying fields are flooded and the ground across the Dengie Peninsula is boggy and sodden. This afternoon, Hugh is heading west along the A120 from Colchester to the eastern fringes of London. He is meeting Thomas Langley again and hopes to reach a judgement today about the man's state of mind on the day of the shooting.

The trial is just a matter of weeks away and Hugh knows that Penny is becoming jittery. The legal team received some bad news. Darren Beck is threatening to withdraw as a defence witness. His testimony is crucial as it supports Langley's claim that Carlow was about to strike him with the crow-bar when he let off the shotgun. Penny still has Beck's sworn statement to the police - he has not withdrawn that. However, she was hoping to call him to take the stand. Now he is refusing to cooperate. Hugh had always felt this was a long shot anyway. He is not surprised to hear the boy has developed cold feet. Penny said that as soon as the lad had completed his community service sentence he became a lot less helpful.

Hugh suddenly spots the turning which leads to his and Penny's old school. He can't make out much today, but when it's clear, you can see the imposing Victorian building from the road. The school had not been admitting girls for very long when Hugh joined the

Senior Prep. Penny was one of only a handful in his academic year. She had needed to be tough to get herself noticed back then by the old-fashioned school masters. Hugh had certainly noticed her. Penny was feisty, clever and extremely pretty.

Penny Mills had been his first serious girlfriend. They had gone out for the best part of two years. Hugh recalls that her parents had lived somewhere nearby - Coggeshall, he thinks. When Penny got her place at Oxford and Hugh decided to go and study up in Edinburgh, they had split by mutual consent. They barely saw anything of one another over the following few years. Then, one Christmas break, at the end of the term in which Hugh had met Imogen, they bumped into each other in a pub in Colchester. He has never told his wife about it.

He and Penny got pretty drunk that evening. She told Hugh how she still loved him and suggested they should get back together. This admission had come at just the wrong time for Hugh. His relationship with Imogen was very new. She was a couple of years younger than him and hadn't yet fully understood his background and what made him tick like Penny did. Or that was how it had felt, for a short while, on that drunken and nostalgic night in the pub.

What makes Hugh feel guilty now, is that he had taken several days to consider it. He had two years of shared history with Penny but only a few months of a blossoming relationship with Imogen. Thankfully, Hugh's good sense had eventually kicked in. He had known there was something special about Imogen Nichols, right from the very beginning. Hugh wasn't so naïve as to be blind to the fact Penny was the kind of girl who desired what she could not have and once she had obtained it, would quickly lose interest. He suspected this was still the case now and probably the reason why

Penny hadn't managed to settle down with anyone for the long-term.

The rain is easing off when he arrives at Langley's flat. As he walks into the warm hallway Hugh can see Thomas has been out. A sopping wet umbrella is propped up in the corner and a pair of old walking boots, plastered with mud, are sitting on the mat.

'There's a park across the main road from here where I like to go and walk. I'm starting to miss the open-space of the farm. Though I didn't think I would,' Langley says, as if he could tell what Hugh had been thinking.

When they are settled into their customary positions, Hugh switches on his recorder and states, 'I never like to rush my patients, Thomas. But I am aware time may be running out for us. If I may, I would like to speak now about the death of your wife and what life had been like at the farm for you after she passed away.'

Langley appears rattled. After a few quiet moments he starts to talk. 'Rose was diagnosed with breast cancer in 2004. We fought it for a good number of years but eventually lost the battle. At first, I considered selling up and moving on. In fact, I was pretty much decided upon it. I'd offered the place to Andy, because it was around the time he retired from the army. He didn't want to take it on. I put the place on the market. It was back in 2010 when the credit crunch was probably at its worst. Barely anyone came to look at the farm and the one's that did kept muttering about how much it needed spending on it.'

'You must have had some developers interested though?' Hugh chips in.

'Aye, a couple - but new houses weren't selling back then either; no one could get a mortgage for love nor money. You've got to remember, my farm is out in the middle of nowhere. Someone'd need to build a proper access road and everything. I decided to take it off the market and stay put - only until the economic situation got better.' He laughs bitterly. 'Strangely enough, it never has.'

'In a sense, you found yourself trapped at the farm.'

'Not just in a sense, Hugh.' He chuckles, but in better humour this time. 'Do you remember the winter of 2010? It was bitterly cold and there were snow drifts of ten or eleven feet on some days. I was completely cut off from the local village that Christmas; the first on my own in 53 years.'

'It was a difficult time for you, then. Did your sons come to visit much?'

'Rob was overseas and Andy had decided to move down to the south of France. He's still there now. He runs a guest house with his partner. I'm pleased for Andy; he says the climate there is good for his injuries. They have a decent life. I certainly wouldn't have wanted him to be stuck here like me, but I had to give him the choice.' Langley gazes out of the window and Hugh is aware the old man's composure is slipping.

He waits for a moment and then asks, 'how were you feeling about living at the farm when the break-in occurred? Were you still keen to sell it?'

'I'd pretty much resigned myself to being there. Taking down the lead to sell on was hopefully going to keep me going at the farm for a few more years. Now I wish I'd just accepted any old price for the place and got the hell out of there. Then that poor boy would still be alive.'

Hugh is surprised. This is the first time he has heard the man display any kind of remorse for Danny Carlow's death. 'Do you now think you shouldn't have tried to get the lead sheeting back - that you shouldn't have chased those boys?'

'No, Hugh. Nothing on that night could have happened any differently than it did. What I'm saying is that I should never have been the one still living there. If I'd sold up, it would have been some other wretched bugger who encountered those boys. Then I wouldn't be in this awful mess.'

On the drive back home, the clouds have lifted and the sky is finally revealing some patches of blue. It provides such a contrast to the weather earlier in the day that Hugh cannot stop himself from staring out at the scene. The wispy clouds have been tinted a bright orange by the setting sun and the horizon looks as if it has been painted using a small child's choice of colours; with broad strokes of turquoise and purple; the end result appearing almost gaudy to his tired eyes.

Hugh had seen a different side to Thomas Langley on this visit. He was reflective and self-pitying. The calmness he had observed during their previous sessions was less evident. Hugh doesn't think this is a bad thing. Langley actually came across as more human. He *did* care about what had happened to Danny Carlow, after all. But something is puzzling him. Langley had said that nothing could have changed what occurred on the night of the burglary, yet he had also seemed to suggest that if *someone else* had been living at the farm at the time of the shooting, Danny might not now be dead.

Hugh isn't sure what the old man meant by this. He could have been referring to his decision to take the shot-gun outside with him to confront the intruders. He might even have been making a comment on his own state of mind. Perhaps he meant that someone else would not have been so quick to pull the trigger when under stress. Hugh doesn't know yet, but he is certainly feeling that they are finally starting to get somewhere.

104

Chapter Seventeen

'I would like us all to extend a very warm welcome to our newest recruit; Ian Croft.'

A gentle ripple of applause echoes around the half empty classroom. Mark Gilbert vigorously shakes Ian by the hand and then indicates he may return to his seat.

'It's great news that Will and Ian have accepted our invitation to join The Blackwater Cadets. With more troops, we can try out new things and push ourselves even further as a group. I sense we have some exciting challenges ahead of us. I'm very much looking forward to what the future has in store.'

An older lad with shoulder-length, shaggy blond hair who is sitting, perched on the edge of one of the desks at the back of the room, raises his hand.

'Yes, Darren.'

'What rank will Ian and Will start at?'

Gilbert considers this question for a moment. Then he turns to look at his two new recruits. 'Lads, as you are brand new to this whole system I think we'd better introduce you slowly. If you both take on the rank of private for the time being, I will find some suitable tasks for you and we might just be able to fast-track the process a little as we go on.' The teacher smiles to himself, obviously proud of the meritocratic structure he has adopted.

Matt Carlow gets up and moves forward. He stands next to Gilbert at the front of the classroom, suddenly announcing; 'Will and Ian. It might take a while for you to pick up on the way we like to do things here. It's going to be a bit different from what you are used to. There are only a couple of things you really need to remember. What we value most in 'The Blackwater Boys' is loyalty and service. I've been a member now for, what, six years?' the young man glances at his mentor who nods and beams indulgently. 'I've learnt many skills and led many expeditions, yet I've only just managed to gain my Officer Cadet rank. Now I am in the Officer class, Mark and I can work together on devising new and ever more demanding activities for us to try. If you have any suggestions of stuff you'd like to have a go at, then write it down and pop it into the box that we will pass around at the end.'

'We don't have limitless funds, but we do endeavour to try something different each term - within reason, of course!' Gilbert quickly adds. 'I'll give you each a few minutes to chat about your ideas. Please use the paper and pens on the desks to record the best and most sensible suggestions. Ian, why don't you go and work with Darren's group and Will; you can stay here with Matt.'

Gilbert wanders about the room whilst the boys launch into an eager and positive discussion. He is a good-looking man in his late thirties. Although tall and obviously physically fit, he has a lean build which is better suited to an athletic track than a rugby pitch. He glances at his watch. 'Okay, guys, your lifts will be arriving soon. Choose your favourite proposals and chuck them in Matt's blue box. Next week, I'll let you know if any of them are contenders. Ed, I hope you've not canvassed for that alpine ski trip again - though it's always worth living in hope, I suppose!' Gilbert gives a boy with dark greasy hair and pitted skin a playful slap on the back. The youngster chuckles shyly in response. Several scraps of paper get folded up and dropped into a tatty old cardboard box.

'Same time next week!' Mark Gilbert calls out cheerfully to the backs of his departing students.

'How did it go?' Imogen asks, as soon as her son climbs into the back seat of the car.

'Yeah, it was okay. We've got to choose what the new expedition's going to be; we'll find out at the next meeting.'

'Who decides what you do?'

'All of us. We've had a discussion and written down our ideas. Then Mr Gilbert will take a look through them and work out what's within our budget.' Ian places his hand expectantly on the headphones lying next to him on the seat.

'What was *your* suggestion, then?' Bridie enquires, in a tone of voice which Imogen does not feel is entirely supportive.

'I'd like to sail out to one of the islands - when the weather improves a bit.'

'Sounds like a great plan, sweetheart. Let's hope the others go for it too,' his mum replies, turning her attention back to manoeuvring the car out of its cramped parking space. As she reverses towards the side of the school building she sees Caroline, sitting impassively in the front seat of her people carrier, obviously still waiting for Will to come out. Imogen stays where she is for a moment, watching as the boy finally emerges through the swinging doors. He is exiting the building with another lad, who looks to be a few years older than him.

'Who's that young man with Will?' She asks, without taking her eyes off the pair.

'It's Darren Beck,' Bridie replies. 'He left school years ago. I don't know why he's still involved with this club; he needs to get a life.'

Imogen twists around, ready to reprimand her daughter for denigrating Ian's new found interest. She discovers that her son is thoroughly absorbed in his music and hasn't heard a word. So instead, she says, 'was Darren in Ewan's year group? I don't think I remember him.'

'No, he was a couple of years younger, I think. He was in the Science Society when I joined it in Year 7 and he was still in the sixth form then. Darren's quite clever really.'

'I wonder why he didn't go off to college or university then.'

'I dunno. His parents don't have much money - so maybe they couldn't afford to send him. They live in one of those big caravans, like the one Gran and Grandad have got at Mersey. They don't just use it for holidays; they live in it *all the time*.'

Imogen knows where Bridie means. There is a large static caravan park out towards Great Totham. Darren Beck must have got plenty of stick for that when he was at school, she imagines. Then Caroline spots them and waves. Imogen waves back and makes a gesture which indicates that she will call her.

'When's Nikki coming back to school, Mum?'

'Not for a few weeks yet, sweetie. She's still in the hospital. It takes a long time for our bodies to get better after an accident.'

Bridie simply nods her head and turns back to the book on her lap. Imogen accelerates out of the school grounds and heads for home.

Chapter Eighteen

'Of course I still love you, darling.'

It is Saturday morning and Hugh and Imogen are trying their best to carry on as normal around the heated phone conversation taking place out in the hallway. Abigail called about ten minutes earlier, asking to speak with Allan as a matter of some urgency.

'Well, Im has got stuff planned for us over the weekend. Hugh and I need to go and check on the house for starters. Make sure everything's ship shape up there, you know?'

Imogen fills up the filter coffee maker.

'Yeah, okay. I hear you, Abigail. I'm getting there but it takes time. A complete break is what the doctor said. I'm only following his orders. Yes, *of course* I'll see you at Christmas, that's weeks away. Just hang in there for me darling, will you? I love you too, see you soon; take care, goodbye... bye.'

Allan strides back into the kitchen, picking up a warm brioche roll from the basket on the counter and intently seeking out the marmalade.

'Would you like a coffee, Al?' Imogen asks, hovering with the glass jug poised over a set of cups.

'Great, thanks.'

'Look, Abigail is welcome to come here anytime, you know. Just because we're in Hugh's parents' place doesn't mean she wouldn't be welcome. There's plenty of room,' Imogen states.

'I know that guys and I appreciate it. But I really do need this break. I feel like a different person being away from London. I'm worried that when I see Abigail again things will go back to the way they were.' A dark shadow seems to pass across Allan's face.

'They might well do - for a little while at least. You're on the road to recovery now. You have to see Abigail at some point and as soon as you begin to build good memories and experiences with her again, the sooner you can get back to being a normal, happy couple. It's tough for her as well, you know. She feels shut out.' Hugh lays a supportive hand on his brother-in-law's shoulder.

'But it seems to be Abigail who triggers my 'bad feelings' - if I can call them that. When I see her innocent and trusting little face, all I feel is a guilt so heavy I think it's going to crush me.' Allan takes a sip of his coffee.

'Then you need to consider if she really is the one for you,' Imogen surprises herself by saying. She quickly glances around to make sure the kids are not within earshot. 'If you don't intend to confess to your affair with Alison, then perhaps you are always going to feel this way. In which case, you need to set her free to find someone else - because you will never be truly happy with Abigail again.'

Hugh finds himself smiling, but not unkindly. 'I wish I could be so blunt with my patients, sadly I'm not allowed. I think Immy's right. You need to be able to move on from your guilt over the affair; *or* you must leave everything associated with it in the past. I *can* help you Allan, whichever route you choose.'

Allan delays his response for a moment by generously buttering the French roll, taking his time to open the weighty jar of marmalade and then sculpting the orange jelly into a thick swirl on the top. 'I know you're both talking sense. I simply don't want to make that decision just yet. I've no intention of torturing the poor girl, but I need to be ready. I need to be seeing clearly through the fog first, because I really don't want to make the wrong move on this. Heaven knows I've made enough of those in my time and if I cock this up, it could be the biggest mistake of my life.'

*

Imogen stands on the coastal path, watching Hugh help Allan and the youngsters to push their little boat out into Lawling Creek. There is a sharp easterly breeze today but Imogen's brother is an experienced yachtsman. She is confident he will control the boat with ease. The tide is high and when they have manoeuvred the tiny vessel out of the secluded bay, she knows they will have a wonderful sail.

Once the Skipper is on the water, Hugh strides back up the shingle beach to join her. 'Poor guy. I hope a morning's sea air will help him to clear his head.'

'I hope so too,' Imogen replies. 'You know, Hugh. I've been thinking a lot about Alison Dickson in the last few weeks.'

Hugh gives his wife an enquiring look.

'I've been considering just how skilfully she used Allan to her advantage. She was twenty years old when she started sleeping with him. Allan was just seventeen - the age Ian is now. And he was a *young* seventeen at that. Alison didn't fancy Allan back then - it was Michael who she was interested in romantically. Alison simply realised she could *use* him - that if she had sex with him, she would gain a power over Allan that would make him do all kinds of things for her.'

'Like helping her to steal your mother's bag, for instance.'

'Yes. They shared a secret, you see - about their illicit relationship. Alison fuelled Allan's fear that Mum would find out. The whole thing was unequal from the very beginning. I believe the situation between them was similar to the dynamic which exists between the abuser and the abused.'

'Hey,' Hugh nudges his wife gently. 'I'm supposed to be the psychologist around here.' He goes quiet for a minute. 'I think you're right. The hold that Alison had over Allan was very strong. So when he saw her again, years later - when they bumped into one another in Glasgow, it was very difficult for him to resist it.'

'It was a problematic time in his life too. He had only just divorced from Suz and his relationship with Abigail was very new and fragile.'

'So what did Alison want from him that second time, I wonder?' Hugh muses.

'Perhaps it had something to do with her extorting money from Mum. She certainly enjoyed playing with people. It might have given her a real kick to know she was sleeping with Allan whilst at the same time blackmailing his mother.'

'Maybe. Allan was also a grown man by then and had filled out into those Nichols good looks you're always telling me about.'

Imogen laughs and playfully pretends to shove Hugh towards the steep bank. She suddenly stops and her expression becomes more serious. 'Yes, that's right. Allan was looking more like me and Michael by that age. What was it Allan had said to me back on Garansay? Something about him always being the 'poor substitute for the real thing'. Do you think she could have been planning to somehow get close to Michael again? Her affair with Allan had started up not long after Miriam died. Is it possible she knew about Miriam's cancer and saw it as some kind of opportunity?' Imogen shudders at the thought.

'There's no point in trying to second guess the woman's motives now - she's long gone. What *is* important is that Allan shouldn't really be blamed for falling into her trap for a second time. He was programmed from a young and highly suggestible age to obey Alison Dickson. It would have been almost impossible for him to refuse it. We can't excuse his actions entirely, but I think it would be very cruel to make him pay for the mistake forever.'

Chapter Nineteen

The ground under foot is sodden and slippery with thick, wet mud. Hugh is fighting hard to maintain his footing through this difficult section of the run. His feet are pounding the sludge to a regular rhythm and each step sends a filthy spray up the back of his legs.

'Keep the pace up, old thing,' Allan shouts back encouragingly. 'It won't be quite so hard going when we get to the woodland path.'

Hugh doesn't answer. He is using all the puff he has simply to keep moving. Luckily, Allan doesn't seem to require a response. Imogen's brother comfortably leads them both to the edge of this vast farmer's field. He finally stops for a breather by the gate that marks the entrance to Limbourne Woods.

When Hugh catches him up he stops and bends over, planting his hands on his knees; panting furiously. 'I can't believe you've been running this route every morning,' he exclaims, once he has regained some level of composure. 'How do you have the energy to do anything else for the rest of the day?'

Allan laughs. 'It does get easier, you know. Otherwise people wouldn't do it. I run around the Heath most weekends when I'm back in London. You pass through a kind of pain barrier and then you actually start to enjoy it.'

Hugh cannot imagine ever having the stamina to progress beyond this miserable stage. Although, he thinks that perhaps at his age he should really try.

He and Imogen have walked this route many times. You follow the public footpath past the old Anglo-Saxon church at Mundon and then across several farmers' fields until joining up with the path again at Limbourne Woods. Eventually, you will reach the village of Cold Norton. You could even carry on into North Fambridge if the fancy takes you. It's a very pleasant stroll over some lovely, unspoilt countryside.

'Are you ready to carry on?' Allan asks, not looking hopeful.

'I might just walk for a bit. Could I meet you on the other side of Limbourne Woods?'

'Sure, I'll do a circuit of the forest and then we can head back if you'd like? It looks as if the rain's about to come on anyway. Okay, catch you later.' Allan strides off smartly along the twisting path.

Although it is only mid-morning, the clouds have suddenly thickened and under the dense canopy created by the trees, it becomes really quite gloomy. Hugh walks briskly along the well-tended footpath. He has brought the kids for bike rides through here on a number of occasions, so he knows that after a short distance the path will split into two. If you take the left hand turn it leads to a little visitors' centre providing children's activities and housing a few nature displays. When Hugh reaches the crossroads, he veers to the right, deciding instead to explore where this alternative track comes out.

Hugh had often played in these woods as a young boy. Climbing the gnarled branches of the old oak trees and getting dirty following the course of one of the tiny tributaries of the Mundon Wash. Now, the woodland activities laid on for kids are far more organised. These days, Hugh reflects, he and Imogen would look askance at anyone who let their child spend a day roaming around a lonely place like this all by themselves. It wouldn't even cross his mind to let Bridie do such a thing.

As he gazes about him, Hugh can see the evidence of a recently constructed bonfire. The sticks and kindling have been packed tightly together to form a kind of solid wigwam. It looks as if someone may be planning to come back to it at a later stage. It isn't big enough to be part of the forest management programme. Hugh immediately wonders who would choose to set up camp in the middle of the woods in late November.

In front of him, Hugh can see a distant tunnel of brighter daylight; indicating this track has led him straight through the woods to the other side. When he reaches the stile which marks the western edge of the forest, Hugh scans the horizon beyond. He recalls that Thomas Langley's farm isn't far from here. Hugh decides to go and take a look before Allan returns.

Finding a burst of energy from somewhere, he jogs across the empty field and then pauses briefly when he reaches a small copse of trees. He weaves his way around the wide trunks of the imposing oaks which seem to predominate in this tiny wood. In a matter of minutes, he comes out into the wide, open countryside again. Staring ahead of him, Hugh can see the collection of run-down barns, the little white-washed cottage and the clapped-out pieces of machinery which constitute the Langleys' Farm.

Hugh takes a look in the largest of the barns first. He can see immediately where Carlow had forced the padlock open. The wooden panels have almost split in half lengthways with the force that was used. The barn itself is simply full of worthless clutter. Hugh wonders what happened to the lead flashing.

He takes a look at the cottage next. It's a neat building with a rendered exterior and a pretty gabled entrance porch which at one time clearly supported some kind of climbing plant. Hugh feels as if this house once had a heyday; but that it was a long, long time ago.

He tries the wooden front door but finds it locked. Hugh peers through the grubby window of the sitting room. Everything appears much as Thomas must have left it. There is an old-fashioned television in the corner and magazines and papers lie strewn across the coffee table. He sees photographs on the mantelpiece. A wedding shot perhaps and a portrait featuring two boys; one of them sitting on the other's lap.

Hugh doesn't like the feel of this place. He is not a sentimental or a superstitious person, but he still senses the residual trace of an overwhelming sadness. He recalls how Langley was stuck out here during the harsh winter following his wife's death. It must have felt like being under siege. He wonders if it triggered the memory of when, as a much younger man, he was surrounded by Chinese snipers on that hill in Korea; trapped, and with no supplies for three days and nights.

Hugh walks around the cottage and then stops to face in the direction of the trees. He tries to picture that night in his mind's eye. He walks from the kitchen door of the house to the barn. Then he proceeds across the disordered yard to the field. Hugh tries to imagine where Langley would have stood as he let off the first shot. The boys were about half-way to the cover of the trees when they heard it. He weighs up how much time it would have taken Carlow to back himself along the ground and been in a position to launch a surprise attack on Langley.

It strikes him then that Carlow, Beck and Nash must have spent quite some time planning the burglary. They knew where the lead flashing was kept. Beck and Nash claimed it was Carlow who had told them the metal would be found in the largest barn; the one nearest to the woods. So how did Carlow know about it? There's no reference to it in the police report.

Langley has always claimed he didn't know any of the boys who invaded his farm that night. Beck and Nash corroborated this. But Carlow had possessed at least a rudimentary knowledge of the place. Hugh wonders how. Did Carlow hang about in these woods as a youngster, just like he had done? Had he stood over there, under the cover of the trees, watching the farm and carefully working out this robbery in his head?

Hugh is jerked away from these thoughts by the chiming of his mobile phone.

'Hi? Hugh? Where are you?' Allan's voice demands.

'I'll be with you in five minutes.'

'Thank goodness. I thought you'd either abandoned me out here or were lying in a ditch somewhere having a heart attack. I didn't much fancy explaining the last scenario to Imogen and that's a fact.'

Chapter Twenty

'If you were having an affair with someone, where would you go in order to meet up with them?' Imogen suddenly enquires, as they sit around the table after dinner. 'Oh - sorry, Allan, that wasn't a very tactful thing to say.'

'On the contrary, Imogen. I always enjoy answering your hypothetical questions.'

'What on earth makes you ask that?' Hugh exclaims, laughing heartily at the same time.

'I was just thinking about Caroline and the man she was talking to on the High Street the other day. I don't actually believe there was anything romantic going on between them; nevertheless, a thought has struck me. If Caroline *were* to carry on an affair with somebody, I simply can't imagine where they could have the, err... liaisons. Wherever they went, she would be bound to bump into a person she knew. And Caroline couldn't go too far afield, because then her family would start to notice the absences.'

'For some people,' Hugh says, 'it's the risk of getting caught which makes the affair more exciting.'

'It certainly wasn't that way for me. I only met up with Alison when I was in Scotland on business. Even then, I was constantly terrified a friend of Mum's would spot us together.'

'If someone is regularly away on business trips, I can imagine how an affair would be fairly easy to pull off. If you're a housewife or you work locally, I don't see how it could work. Hotels are another option, I suppose. But you might still get seen. Also, it's expensive and it shows up on your bank statements.' Imogen pours them each a glass of port.

Allan sits forward in his seat, leaning towards his sister and brother-in-law in a conspiratorial kind of way. 'Okay. Cast your minds back to when you were teenagers. Imagine you are in the sixth form and you've got a girlfriend or boyfriend. The two of you are at a stage where you want to start fooling around a bit. Take it to the next level, as it were. So, where do you go?'

'Well, if one of you has a car, then you could drive it to somewhere secluded and do it there, in the backseat,' Hugh responds.

'It's a little sordid, isn't it?' Imogen immediately comments.

Allan laughs, 'says she who began this entire debate!'

'Fine, I get the point. The only problem with the car thing is that you've still got to park it up somewhere. The police might discover you or, if they don't, you're going to have to choose a very quiet and isolated place to be sure not to be seen by anyone.'

'There are always holidays and camping trips,' Hugh adds, 'if your parents happen to be foolhardy enough to let you go away with your mates.'

'But they are only very few and far between,' Allan responds.

'I suppose if you're a sixth-former and you have free periods, then you could go home and meet your lover during the daytime. If you knew the house was going to be empty, of course,' Imogen supplies.

'Which would also work for a housewife; like Caroline,' Allan says.

'Meeting at home would be very risky,' Hugh counters. 'You've got the neighbours to consider and a chance that the husband or children might pop home unexpectedly.'

'There *is* an angle we've not taken into account.' Allan sips his port with a devilish glint in his eye. 'It's a tactic as old as the hills and yet always amazingly effective.'

'Go on then.' Imogen is beginning to wish she had never started this discussion at all.

'When Alison and I began our secret liaisons, back when we were teenagers, we had a number of clandestine meeting places. Most of which were outside. For example, down by the sand dunes on the beach was a good one. Or, in a remote part of the hillside or woods; it works better in summer than in winter time, obviously. Best of all were the seldom-used empty buildings, like old sheds and barns.'

'Wow,' Imogen interrupts, opening her eyes wide, 'this is like an adultery master-class.'

They both giggle stupidly and Imogen measures out the thick, sweet liquid evenly between their three glasses once again. Hugh is sitting quietly, not joining in with the joke. He looks as if he is thinking carefully about something.

'You mentioned meeting in the woods.'

'Oh yes, that was always a great place for a rendezvous. Most people have an aversion to hanging around wooded areas at night; they seem to find it frightening for some reason. So, you hardly ever see another living soul. The trees provide you with a certain amount of protection from the weather. There are also lots of dips and ditches for hiding yourselves away in. I suppose if you were adept at outdoorsy stuff you could set up an encampment; light a fire and make it really quite cosy. I'm afraid as a teenager I never showed a girl quite as good a time as that; it was strictly coats and a flashlight for me.'

'It isn't something you are likely to do as an adult though, is it?' Imogen states. 'For some reason, teenagers don't seem to feel the cold. But for anyone over the age of twenty five, I can't see them wanting to have hanky-panky outdoors. For someone of *our* age, I mean, forget it.'

'It might depend upon how desperately you wanted to be with the other person.' Hugh is looking really quite serious now. 'If you loved them or even simply lusted after them; with a kind of obsessive longing. You would want to meet with them under any circumstances, wouldn't you?'

'But you feel it more strongly when you are a teenager. The excitement and desire you experience during those initial acts of intimacy. It creates a stronger sensation for being the first time it has happened, don't you think?' Imogen drains her second glass, feeling a little queasy at the thought of the sweet, sticky alcohol lining the inside of her mouth.

'Not necessarily. For some people that kind of feeling comes only later in life. When it does, the strength of it can be almost overwhelming.' Hugh stands up to clear the table.

'Point taken.' Allan has a serious expression on his face now, too. 'What prompted all of this again?'

'I wanted to know how Caroline would have managed to have an affair, under the noses of her husband and kids. It was just a piece of idle and childish speculation, really; sparked by having seen her arguing with the mysterious man.'

Hugh moves back over to the table. 'If two people feel strongly enough, they will always find a way to see one another. They'll rationalise the risks involved. In the course of providing relationship counselling, I noticed how women rarely entered into an affair with the expectation of simply walking away again. They quickly became emotionally attached to the object of their desire. They then imagined running away with them and starting a new life. For the man who indulged in his attraction for a married woman; he tended to do so mainly because he knew he would be able to extract himself fairly easily from the liaison. There are always exceptions to the pattern, of course. Generally speaking, that is what I found to be the case.'

'What emotions are left when the affair ends? I mean, if the man suddenly decides he doesn't want to carry on with it any longer and breaks it off?' Imogen asks.

'Well, heartbreak and upset at first. This is very rapidly replaced by anger and resentment. Then they both simply switch their attention back to their previous lives.'

Imogen lets her mind return to the heated exchange she witnessed outside the department store in Maldon. She had not picked up on any kind of romantic sentiment between those two people. Perhaps she had been mistaken. Maybe she was observing a relationship which had entered an entirely new and altogether different phase; the one which evolves between two people after all of the love and sexual desire have finally been extinguished.

Chapter Twenty One

Hugh is running late. Grabbing a piece of buttered toast he picks up his briefcase and rushes out to the car. It looks as if it will be another clear and sunny day. Ian is watching him through the bay window of Kath and Gerry's living room. Hugh gives him a quick wave before driving off.

He is going to see Thomas Langley for a couple of hours this morning. Then he has a meeting in the afternoon with his publishers, who want to discuss the possibility of him writing a book about his work on the Langley Farm case, after the trial is over. Hugh is a little reluctant to appear to be 'cashing in' on his role in the investigation, but he promised his agent he would at least discuss the proposal. Martin has set up a conference at the publishers' offices in Farringdon Road at 2pm.

Driving a little faster than he might usually have done, he reaches Langley's flat at just after nine. Hugh finds it trickier to get a parking space today, as there seem to be more cars about than usual. He circles around for a bit and ends up having to pull onto the curb a little further along Palmerston Road, hoping he won't lose his wing mirror as a result. Hugh walks the short distance to Langley's building, glancing briefly over his shoulder as a man walking his dog turns abruptly out of the park and falls into step behind him.

Thomas Langley is in a different mood from Hugh's last visit. The routine is just the same, but the old man's calmness has once again returned. Today, the psychologist is prepared to let his patient take the lead and the topic Langley chooses to discuss surprises him.

'You wanted to hear about my time in Korea, Hugh. If you're still interested, then I'd like to tell you about it.'

'Of course.'

'I was one of the youngest in my platoon. A new recruit, and completely unprepared for what I was going to see. The 'Glosters' were a wonderful group of men. Many of them were a good few years older and they fathered me a bit. They were the gentlemen of a previous generation. Those chaps were incredibly brave and loyal. When we were holding out, up there on Hill 235, we simply got lost in the immediacy of it. I certainly didn't have the time to take it all in. It was later on, after I and so many others had been picked up by the Chinese and taken to a prison camp. That was when the events of those terrible few days started to roll back over me, like I was facing those endless lines of troops all over again. There were human waves of Chinese soldiers coming for us. Their leaders didn't appear to care how many men they lost in the process of taking those vantage points and getting to Seoul. We just couldn't compete with that.

Our battalion was almost entirely wiped out. I'd been shot in the leg but I received very little medical treatment in the camp. Luckily, it was a fairly clean wound and it eventually healed. Most of us were in the POW camp for two years. It was tough, as you can imagine. When I was finally released and shipped back home I was very ill. Under-nourished and malarial, it took several months for me to even begin to think about working again. I had to sleep with the light on for years. It used to drive Rose mad, especially when the boys were tiny.

The slightest little thing would make me angry. If Rob or Andy dropped a toy, or suddenly shouted something loudly, I would nearly jump out of my skin. Then I would get so cross with them my vision would actually get blurry. You know the expression 'seeing red'? Well, that was exactly what it was like. It is strange what your mind can do to you, isn't it? Those extreme emotions gradually faded, over years rather than months, mind you. Going to New Zealand probably banished the worst of it. I felt as if I'd escaped something there.'

Hugh nods his head. 'Were you ever given medication?'

'No. I never saw a counsellor or a psychiatrist either. I thought it was just a normal, unpleasant side-effect of being in the army. It certainly never put me off; I was desperate to get back out into the field again. When I went over to Northern Ireland I was pretty much recovered. My nerves were fine under pressure. What still haunted me - and still does now, was the napalm. It was one of the first things I witnessed when I arrived in Korea. The Americans were dropping napalm onto the Chinese troops in battle and I couldn't forget the men's screams. And the terrible smell - of young men being burnt alive, Hugh. That remains the single, most wicked thing I've ever seen on this earth. How could I ever forget it?'

'But you've learnt to live with the memory.'

'If 'living' is the appropriate word, then yes, I have.'

'Did you ever relapse and experience those nervous symptoms again, Thomas?'

'There was a time in the late seventies and early eighties when money was very tight and things at home became difficult. Some of the symptoms returned then.'

'What form did they take?'

'Insomnia. Being short-tempered. Oh yes, and I developed a recurrent feeling of claustrophobia back then too - came right out of nowhere that one did.'

'They're all perfectly recognisable manifestations of nervous illness. How long did the symptoms last?'

'A couple of years perhaps, but it was a milder case than when I'd got back from Korea in the fifties, it was maybe more like depression the second time around. You develop a way of dealing with it over time.'

'Thomas. You said you'd never had any previous contact with the three men who broke into your farm. But Danny Carlow seemed to know very quickly where he would find the lead. He knew all about the little copse of trees and how it would provide them with cover as they approached the place. Are you absolutely certain you had never seen the lad before? He might have been staking out the farm from the woods for weeks or even months beforehand. Did anyone of his age ever come and perform any work for you? He was training to be a mechanic, like his father. Perhaps he had fixed your car or some of your machinery at some point.'

Langley takes a moment to consider this. 'I have a man who does all my odd-jobs. I've never used anyone else. I've always taken the cars over to a garage in Colchester - they know me there. The only thing I can think of is how at one time I used to help out with The Young Cadets. It was a club which was connected to the school. Rob got me into it, he thought I might enjoy passing on my skills to the youngsters. He was right, I did enjoy it. Sometimes the Cadets came over to the farm and we performed drills and stuff - out on the field. I was like their Sergeant Major. The kids seemed to appreciate it; there were girls as well as boys if I remember rightly, but they all appeared much the same to me. I couldn't pick one now out of a bunch. I was never on my own with them, mind. It was Mr Pickering who ran it and he was always there with us. He had to do a 'risk assessment' on the farm before he brought the students. He was the Head of Games, I think, and I stopped when he retired. I got the feeling his replacement thought I was an old-fashioned oddity. My services weren't called upon again. I had a nice little send off. The Headmaster gave me a bottle of whisky and shook my hand. Bill Pickering and I still exchange a Christmas card every year. Although I don't know if he'll be doing that now, not after what's happened.'

'Did you tell the police this, Thomas?'

'No one's ever asked me about it before you did. I'd not made any kind of connection between those boys and The Young Cadets. They were all kitted out in military gear on the night of the burglary, but I still don't think any of them would have been Pickering's lot. The Cadets were a good bunch. Those kids wouldn't have used their uniforms to do something bad - do you know what I mean? They had pride in the organisation. Those three boys who broke into my farm were just *playing* at being soldiers. They had all the correct get up, for sure, but it was part of a nasty game - one with no bravery and no honour. If those boys had ever had a taste of real army life, they wouldn't have lasted five minutes.'

Chapter Twenty Two

Glancing up at the carriage clock, Hugh realises he is going to be late for his afternoon meeting. He apologises to Langley and hastily grabs his old briefcase.

When he reaches the car, Hugh decides to give Martin a call to let him know he's been delayed. Reaching inside his jacket pocket he discovers the phone's not there. He must have left it behind in Langley's flat, he thinks irritably. Locking the car again, he rushes back towards the building. Seeing a different set of entrance doors, facing out onto the main street, he quickly pushes through them and dashes up the stairwell.

'I'm really sorry Thomas, but I think I've left my mobile here somewhere,' Hugh says breathlessly, as Langley invites him inside for a second time.

'I found it just after you'd left. I was waving at you from my lounge window, but you didn't seem to see me.' Langley hands the phone to the psychologist with a friendly smile. 'I hope you aren't going to be late for your next appointment.'

'I hope so too. My agent gets pretty cross with me when I am. Look, I know it's a bit cheeky, but I couldn't just use your bathroom before I go? If I get stuck in the London traffic, I might be on the road for some time.'

'Of course.' Langley chuckles to himself and gestures towards a closed door, leading off the central hallway.

As Hugh is busily washing his hands at the basin, he hears a dull thud outside in the corridor. Wondering what Langley is up to, he finishes quickly and steps into the hall. When Hugh opens the bathroom door he smells the paraffin. Before he has a chance to shout out a warning of any kind, he sees a lighted splint being dropped through the letter box. As soon as the flames touch the pungent liquid, which is soaking through a thick bundle of papers, the fire immediate ignites, with a low, rushing roar.

'Thomas!'

Frozen with fear, Hugh stands absolutely still in the middle of the hallway. Feeling the intense heat from the flames, he watches as they lap up at the base of the front door; slowly melting the plastic guard which runs along the bottom.

When Langley reaches the entrance to the sitting room, he stops dead in his tracks. 'Dear God! I'll call 999.'

'Is there a fire escape?' Hugh cries out desperately.

'No. We're supposed to exit down the main stairs in an emergency. Come into the living room, Hugh. We can break one of the windows in here and climb out onto the roof.'

Hugh edges his way down the narrow corridor, holding his arm up to cover his face, constantly aware the fire is raging just a few feet away from him. Once he is safely inside the lounge, Langley immediately slams the door shut behind him.

They can hear the sound of the building's main fire alarm, trilling remorselessly somewhere in the distance. Hugh imagines that the smoke must have spread out from underneath the front door. It must by now be filling the communal corridor; which at least means the fire brigade should soon be on their way.

Langley places cushions along the base of the living room door and then he turns his attention to the windows. The flats were constructed in the sixties and the whole of one side of the room consists of a large double glazed unit which is divided into two halves by thin wooden frames.

Hugh rushes up to the window and peers down. 'I can't see how we can get to the roof from here; it just looks like a sheer drop to me.'

Langley has begun coughing violently. He brings out a handkerchief, which he holds up to his mouth. 'Perhaps we are too far along. Let's get the window broken and then we'll have to jump for it. That flimsy door will only hold off the flames for a few more minutes.'

Hugh feels his eyes becoming sore and weepy due to the acrid fumes seeping through the cracks in the door. He knows they haven't got long. The smoke inhalation will do for them before the fire does.

Hugh picks up a sturdy side table and swings it at the lowest pane of glass. The window holds firm for several blows and then finally collapses outwards. Hugh takes off his jacket and wraps it around his arm so he can clear away the worst of the jagged glass fragments from around the now empty frame. The rush of cold wind on his face feels wonderful and he greedily drinks in the fresh, clean air.

'Thomas, come closer to the window,' he calls, but the old man doesn't look good. His breathing is heavily laboured. Hugh drags him towards the open space left by the broken pane of glass. Langley is shaking and cowering in his arms.

'Thomas, we haven't got long, we're just going to have to lower ourselves out, one after the other, and jump. I don't think we can wait for the emergency services to get here. The air coming into this room is only going to stoke the flames and make the fire worse.'

The old man is struggling for breath. 'You go first, Hugh. I'll follow.'

In that moment, Hugh realises Langley has absolutely no intention of jumping out of the window. Whether he is frightened of the fall or simply resigned to his fate, Hugh isn't sure. He is faced with a difficult decision. He glances towards the lounge door, which now has yellow flames encircling it; like a monstrous pair of hands reaching into the room, desperate to find any living soul it can get a grip on.

Hugh sits with his feet dangling out over the twenty foot drop. Tiny shards of glass are piercing through his trousers and digging into his buttocks and thighs. He glances back at Langley, sitting slumped next to him, breathing thinly through the smoke stained linen of his handkerchief.

'Make sure you follow me, okay?' Hugh shouts, before he shifts painfully forwards and then allows himself to fall, silently and with a certain bitter resignation, onto the wet grass below.

Chapter Twenty Three

'Your husband has broken his pelvis and his left wrist. He is also suffering in a minor way from the effects of smoke inhalation. Other than that, he's absolutely fine.' Hugh's doctor beams positively at Imogen, whilst intermittently flicking through a complicated looking medical chart.

'What is the prognosis?' Imogen enquires of the attractive Indian lady opposite her.

'Well, for the moment, your husband's pelvic fracture is stable. It is what we would refer to as a type A. We will keep him here for a few days longer and make sure there is no abdominal bleeding we have missed. He fell from quite a height, so we want to observe him for a little while longer. His wrist has only a very slight break. It is still painful for him. It will need to be elevated for a couple of weeks. Full recovery will take at least six weeks, I'm afraid. But he should be up and about before then - as long as there are no further complications.'

'Thank you. Is it alright for me to speak with him now, doctor?'

'Sure. He's a bit drowsy because of the pain relief, but the police have already been in to interview him and I gave it the okay.'

When they are alone, Imogen moves forward and places her hand tenderly on Hugh's arm. 'Are you awake, darling? How are you feeling?'

'Im? I feel a bit sick. The doctor said it's the effect of the smoke.'

'Do you want the bowl?'

'No, I'm fine. Come closer.'

Imogen perches on the edge of the bed and lightly rests an arm across her husband's chest, leaning in towards his face. 'What is it?'

'It's all my fault.'

'Don't say that!'

'Nobody was supposed to know where he was staying. Someone must have followed me to the flat.'

'We don't know that's the case, Hugh. They could have found out another way. They might have got the information from his lawyers' office.'

'I sensed something was wrong that morning. I felt as if I'd been watched coming out of the car and walking into the building. I was so flustered about running late that I didn't act upon it. I've been such an idiot, Im. What's the latest on Thomas?'

'He's not any worse. The medics gave him oxygen at the scene but he's suffering very badly from the smoke. He's on a ventilator at the moment. I spoke to one of the firemen, just after I got here; he said it was better that Thomas hadn't jumped. He didn't think the old man would have survived the fall.'

'Whoever did this wanted Langley dead. There wasn't any other route out of that flat.'

'If you hadn't been there to break the window he probably would be.'

'But I *shouldn't* have been there. I only came back to pick up my phone, which I'd left at Langley's place by mistake. First, I exited by the doors which led out into the car park. Then, once I'd realised I needed to go back, I re-entered by the doors at the front of the building, facing the main road. So if someone had been watching the flat from the car park, they would have thought I had left for good. They would have believed Langley was the only one in the flat.' Hugh's face creases with concern.

'What does that mean?'

'Well, it could simply imply that whoever did this had no intention of murdering anyone but Langley. Or, it might possibly suggest that the people who set fire to the flat are in some way known to us and they didn't want me to get hurt in the process.'

'The Carlows?' Imogen mutters.

'It's a pretty rough form of justice if one of the Carlows did this - 'an eye for an eye' and all that. Are Steve, Matt or Rick *really* capable of carrying out arson?' Hugh lays his head back against the pillows and stares blankly up at the ceiling. 'Thomas didn't turn out to be as resilient as I had thought he was. When we were trapped in the living room, with the fire raging out in the hall, he just crumpled.'

'One of the medics told me Thomas had been wheezing very badly in the ambulance. He said he thought Langley probably had a history of asthma.'

'He never mentioned it before. It can't have been too severe, otherwise he wouldn't have been considered fit to join the army.'

'I'll leave you to get some rest, darling.' Imogen leans over and gives him a brief kiss.

'Oh, Im. Please let Mum and Dad know they don't need to come back from the Peak District. Tell them I'm absolutely fine.'

Imogen smiles as she straightens out his sheets. 'I think it might be a little late for that Hugh. I suspect they are already on their way.'

*

Allan offers to make the teas and coffees. Imogen has hastily purchased some iced cakes from the bakers which she places on pretty china plates arranged around the kitchen table. It would appear to an observer as if they are about to host a celebration of some kind.

The sombre looks on the faces of the newly arrived guests give a clue as to the real reason for this impromptu family gathering.

'Right,' Kath declares, dumping her case heavily on the chequered floor of the hallway. 'What's been happening?'

Gerry slowly follows her in, carrying the rest of their bags.

Allan silently pulls out a couple of chairs for them to sit on whilst Bridie unexpectedly launches into an explanation. 'Dad went to interview Mr Langley again and someone must have followed him, because when he went back into the flat; they put a petrol bomb through the letter box. Dad had to jump out of the window, but he's actually okay.'

Imogen steps forward to pour out their tea. 'It was paraffin and a lighted splint,' she clarifies.

'It amounts to the same effect,' Gerry says pointedly.

'Didn't the police have anyone watching the place? Isn't Langley under any kind of protection?' Kathleen asks, refusing Bridie's offer of a slice of Madeira cake.

'I don't think they've got the resources for that kind of operation. Besides, his lawyers had organised a safe house, so he shouldn't really have been found.'

'Hugh is certain they followed him, is he?' Gerry enquires. 'Did they tail him all the way from Maldon?'

'He isn't sure, no. The only time he became suspicious was as he was walking up to the apartment building.' Imogen sits down at the table to join them.

'This is so much more serious than throwing a brick through a window. It amounts to attempted murder,' Kath says in a puzzled tone.

'The fire could easily have spread and killed someone else in one of the other flats. It's very worrying.' Gerry leans back in his seat and everyone is silent for a few minutes.

Striding into the kitchen, Ian impatiently proclaims, 'when can we go and see Dad?'

Imogen glances at her watch. 'We'll set off in about half an hour, sweetheart. Please don't worry about him, he's fine. Just a few broken bones, that's all.'

'And how is old Langley bearing up?' Gerry says.

'He's still on the ventilator. He's a sturdy chap and I'm sure he will pull through.'

'When can we go home?' Bridie announces. 'To *our* house, I mean. Thanks Gran and Grandad; for letting us stay here and everything. But I'm ready to go back, I miss all my stuff.'

'The new windows are in place,' Allan pipes up. 'It looks really terrific. Listen, Imogen. Langley's in hospital now and Hugh isn't going to be doing any more interviews with him. You said yourself that whoever attacked the old fella didn't intend to hurt Hugh in the process. I think it would be fine for you to go back home. You can't hide over here forever.'

Ian steps forward and says, 'Uncle Allan is right. Those people were after Langley, not Dad. We can go home now.' Then, as an afterthought, he adds rather oddly, 'I'll make sure nothing happens to us. I promise that from this moment on, we'll all be perfectly safe.'

Chapter Twenty Four

Penny Mills stands by Hugh's bedside, carefully arranging the bunch of Asters she brought with her; placing them one by one into a tall vase. As he begins to shift about and open his eyes, Penny rests on the edge of the bed and takes Hugh's hand in hers.

'How's the patient today?'

'Sore and uncomfortable, but still alive.'

'Well, that's okay then.' She leans forward and places a gentle kiss on his cheek. Hugh picks up on a hint of jasmine. The lingering scent sparks a sudden feeling of nostalgia within him.

'Did you bring the photographs?' He enquires.

'You're very keen.' Penny smiles and goes to fetch her bag. Removing a small bundle of mug-shots, she brings them over and places the package on Hugh's lap.

'Have you ever read any of Josephine Tey's novels?'

Penny shakes her head.

'Tey's detective; Inspector Alan Grant, thought he could tell an enormous amount about a person just by looking at their face. He believed criminals tended to be of a specific type. Tey suggests that all the best policemen can judge a person simply by the placement of their features. It's a technique which would be frowned upon nowadays - and quite rightly so.'

'I've seen a lot of people who've been accused of crimes over the years and I have to admit I tend to make a judgment about their innocence or guilt fairly quickly. Perhaps we all use this method to a certain extent - in conjunction with the evidence, of course.'

'But you would never allow someone's appearance, or a feeling you might have about them, to *override* the evidence.'

'No, absolutely not.'

Penny begins to carefully divide out the photographs, each of them clearly having been taken in a police station somewhere. She points at each in turn. 'This one is Danny Carlow, taken a few years back when he was arrested for stealing tools from a Garage. This is Darren Beck, taken after the shooting in August. Lastly, this is Joshua Nash, again, just after the incident this summer.'

Hugh can immediately see the flaws in Inspector Grant's theory. Just by dint of these photos being mug-shots, the three young men immediately appear shifty. If he were gazing at a set of informal family snap-shots, he would most likely form an entirely different opinion of them. Context is crucially important.

'Why were you so eager to see the pictures?' Penny asks.

'As I was walking in the direction of Langley's flat, I saw a man with a dog. As soon as I had passed him, he stepped off the path leading towards the park and fell into step behind me. It might be absolutely nothing. I didn't have a particularly good view of his face, but I just wanted to take a closer look at the boys who broke into the farm.'

'Well, it wasn't Danny Carlow.'

'No. But it could have been a member of his family. I already know what Steve and Rick Carlow are like.' Hugh carefully examines the first of the three photographs. Danny had closely cropped fair hair and the same small, determined eyes of his father. Rick looks much the same facially, but Hugh recalls how Will and Nikki's dad possesses a much smaller frame than his brother and two nephews.

'Steve Carlow is the same age as us, did you know that?' Penny suddenly adds. 'I knew him for a while, when we were both very young.'

Hugh places the photo back down again. 'Did you? How?'

'I went to primary school in Maldon, before my parents moved me to Stane Hall. Steve was in my class, along with thirty or so others.'

'What was he like?' Hugh shifts himself up a little, feeling a pain immediately shoot through his abdomen.

'Naughty.' Penny chuckles. 'I quite liked him. It was all fairly innocent stuff he used to get up to. He was actually a charming little boy.'

'Yes, I've heard he can be a bit of a lady's man.'

'He wouldn't recognise me now, I expect. We're talking about nearly forty years ago. God, that makes me feel old.'

'Well, you haven't changed much and I suspect that neither has he.'

Hugh picks up the other two photos. Darren Beck looks younger than Carlow and has a mane of shaggy blond locks. His face appears quite pleasant. Mainly because he has rather large, greenish, puppy dog eyes. Nash, on the other hand, simply looks terrified. He seems very young and has closely cut dark brown, very nearly black hair. 'It might have been Beck that I saw, although I could never be certain. I'm pretty sure it wasn't Nash. The guy who followed me definitely wasn't Afro-Caribbean or of mixed race.'

'I'll pass on your observations to the police. Do you think the man with the dog could have been Steve, Rick or Matt?'

'I have a feeling he had fair skin and a pale complexion, which means it wasn't Matt. He was also quite tall, so that puts Rick out of contention too. Let's face it - it could have been anyone.' Hugh hands the pile back to the pretty lawyer.

'What progress is Thomas making?' Hugh then asks.

'Still on the ventilator, unfortunately. We're currently making an application to the Judge suggesting he will be unfit to put on trial.' Penny's face crinkles up with concern.

'What will that mean?'

'The Judge will probably just delay for a few months. We'd still like your final psychological report, Hugh. I want to be able to clear Langley's name if at all possible.'

'I'll work on it whilst I'm stuck in here. Have Thomas's sons come to visit him yet?'

'Rob is still in Afghanistan but he emailed his solicitor this morning to say he's got compassionate leave and should be flying back within the next few days. We haven't heard anything from Andy at all.' Penny gathers together her stuff and slots the papers neatly into her briefcase. She keeps her eyes facing downwards as she says, 'I'm sorry I dragged you into all of this. I know you could have been killed. I've behaved very selfishly, Hugh. I was struggling with the case and clutching at straws with the whole PTSD defence. Also, I wanted an excuse to see you again.'

Hugh remains silent for a while. 'I make my own decisions, Penny. I went into this with my eyes wide open. I've enjoyed seeing you again too, but you know I've got Imogen and the kids now, don't you? Sometimes, if things were meant to be then they would already have happened. We choose the paths that we do for good reasons, Pen.'

'But occasionally, people come back into your life at a different time and in a different place and you look at them in a totally new way. It makes absolutely anything seem possible.' Penny lifts up her bag, gives Hugh's hand a quick squeeze and then is gone, leaving the professor to his own thoughts.

Hugh quietly considers what Penny has just said to him. He agrees that in some circumstances two individuals can find one another again at a later stage of their lives, when previously insurmountable complications appear to have fallen away. They are often able to happily spend the rest of their days together.

Hugh is not free in this way, nor does he wish to be. Though for some reason, when Penny was making her parting statement, he got the distinct impression that it was not the two of them she was referring to, but someone else entirely.

The tops of the tallest trees in the wood are bending with the strength of the freshening breeze. Far below, a tiny tent sits incongruously at the base of a small hollow; almost buried within a deep layer of fallen leaves. The flimsy structure is largely protected against the worst of the elements. Which is just as well, as the wind is now blowing sheets of freezing cold sleet remorselessly across the bleak landscape.

The thin drizzle of cold rain which has managed to filter through the dense foliage helps to extinguish the dying embers of the camp fire. A woman wrapped up in waterproof clothing carefully dampens down the last of the flames and then crawls inside the tent, sliding the zip down resolutely behind her.

'It's bloody freezing out there,' she mutters under her breath.

'Well, come over here then,' a male voice replies.

'I'm too old for this. My back's in absolute agony from crawling in and out of this bloody thing.'

'But we don't have to worry about anyone else being around, do we?'

'There's always some crazy dog-walker or runner who ventures out in all weathers.' The woman removes her boots and jacket, then manoeuvres herself onto the opened out sleeping bag lining the bottom of the tent.

'Not at this hour. Now, I said come here.'

The woman smiles and folds herself into his embrace. They kiss with a keen sense of urgency, quickly undressing one another with the restless hunger of a desire not often allowed free expression. The cold now forgotten, they lie back against the hard, uneven ground; both of them finding the gentle drumming of the rain against the thin material strangely comforting. The man runs his hand across the soft contours of the woman's pale skin, before pulling the sleeping bag up to gently cover her, as if suddenly aware of their vulnerability in this remote and lonely place.

'I'm taking a lot of risks by doing this,' the woman whispers.

'I know,' the man replies, moving over to find her lips with his once again, this time pulling the sleeping bag over both of their heads; as if the action will hide them indefinitely from the unkindness of the world outside.

Chapter Twenty Five

When the very last of the bags have been carried up the stone steps and placed inside the hallway of the house, Imogen locks the car. She stands for a moment to gaze out at the pretty countryside that surrounds their property and feels glad they are home. Imogen abruptly senses that any dangers which may lie in store for their family will not come from this place; where they have known nothing but peace and happiness for the best part of a decade.

'Mum! The T.Vs not working!' Bridie calls down impatiently.

'I haven't had time to plug everything back in yet!' she replies, jogging up the steep flight to join her daughter. 'Give me a chance, sweetheart.'

Imogen makes her way into the living room, where the new window looks sparklingly clear in the bright morning light. Her eyes automatically drop down to observe the deep scratches which were gouged into the wooden floor by the weight of the fallen brick.

She and Hugh haven't had an opportunity yet to get a quote to replace the damaged boards. So, for the time being, the marks remain, as a semi-permanent reminder of the whole unpleasant incident. Imogen bends down to untangle the maze of wires and plugs that are coiled up in several bundles behind the television set. She finally manages to get all of the appliances to operate much as they had done before.

'Where's Uncle Allan?' she asks her daughter, before she becomes too absorbed in the game show which has just begun to provide her mother with an intelligent reply.

'He's with Ian, I think,' Bridie responds, without shifting her eyes from the screen.

'Thanks. Don't forget you've got that History project to get finished today, darling,' she adds, this time receiving no acknowledgement.

Imogen finds her brother and son propped up, sitting side by side on Ian's narrow bed. They both have joysticks gripped firmly in their hands. The pained expressions on their faces as they stare at the madly flickering screen in the corner of the room makes her immediately burst out laughing.

'Mum! We're at a really important bit in the game- don't put me off!' Ian exclaims in frustration.

'Okay, okay, I'm leaving. Just checking you were both still alive.' Imogen backs out of the room, with her hands held up in a gesture of surrender, still chuckling quietly to herself.

On an impulse, she scoops up her mobile phone from the coffee table in the lounge and takes it through to her bedroom. Imogen stands by the window and looks out across the calm waters of the creek. She carefully scrolls down her contacts list and punches the call button.

'Hi Mum,' Ewan's voice quickly replies. 'How's Dad? Any problems?'

'He's fine, don't worry. They'll keep him at the hospital for another week or so. Your dad's injuries will soon heal.'

'Are you sure you don't want me to come and see him?'

'No, Ewan. Dad insisted you stay in Manchester and complete the end of term exams. You don't want to get yourself behind with your studies and have to catch up after Christmas - you've got enough work to do as it is. How are things? Is Chloe well?'

'Yep, Chloe's fine; she was upset about Dad's accident. Other than that it's been the same old stuff. Are you coping alright, Mum? Being at home without Dad, I mean - I hope Ian's behaving himself.'

'Well, he's been very quiet actually, especially since the fire. But this Blackwater Boys Club seems to have been good for him. He's helping out more around the house and he's made some nice friends.'

Ewan is silent for a moment. 'You know how I feel about it, Mum. When I was Ian's age 'The Blackwater Boys' was full of bullies and drop-outs. To be a member was like a badge of honour to show you were a right 'hard case'. If you tell me it's all changed now, then I'll just have to take your word for it.'

'That's what I wanted to ask you about. Did you know Matt Carlow or Darren Beck particularly well when you were at school? They seem to be the leading lights in the club right now. Beck was involved with this Langley Farm burglary. He provided the police with valuable evidence which showed that Langley was under threat when he fired the gun. He also tried to stop Carlow from striking Thomas. Beck's gone on to complete the community service sentence for his part in it all.' Imogen waits for her elder son's response.

'They were both a couple of years younger than me. Darren and I used to play football together for the 'B' team. If I remember rightly, he was a nice kid. His folks didn't have much money so he had to borrow the school's boots and had free school meals. Darren got a lot of stick for that from some of the other kids. Maybe joining The Blackwater Boys helped to protect him against the bullying - you know - by providing him a group to belong to. I never really knew Matt Carlow, though. Excuse my language Mum, but his older brother was a total bastard.'

'Yes, I know. I remember what he was like. How about Mr Gilbert? Did you have much to do with him at all?'

'He coached our football team. He was alright. Mr Gilbert was the one who finally got Danny Carlow off my case. He threatened to remove him from the football squad if he carried on bullying me and it worked. None of the other teachers had ever managed to have an effect on Carlow's behaviour in any way. He seemed to be totally out of control. I was pretty grateful to the guy, as you can imagine. I was surprised too, because I'd always got the impression Gilbert was a bit too pally with these 'difficult' kids. I know he was trying to be compassionate and see things from their point of view. It's just that I always felt those 'bad lads' were taking the mick' out of him. They knew he was a 'bleeding heart' and that they could use his softness to manipulate him. I don't quite know what I mean by that Mum, it was just a feeling I sometimes got.'

'I think I understand. Should I worry about Ian being a part of this club? Only he's seventeen years old now and your dad and I can't really stop him. Plus, it's the first thing - other than sailing - that he's been really keen to get involved with. A part of me is actually quite pleased. But I don't want him getting in with the 'wrong crowd', you know?' Imogen lowers herself down onto the edge of the bed, feeling genuinely torn.

'I wouldn't worry about Darren Beck. He was probably led into taking part in the robbery by Danny Carlow. He's basically a good guy. I wouldn't put much faith in Matt though, just because of what his family is like. Regardless of all that, you're going to have to trust Ian. You're more likely to drive him into the wrong kind of company if you stop him from doing what he wants. Gilbert's still in charge of The Blackwater Boys and he's not going to let anything dodgy go on. Besides, Ian's got the sense to know what's right and what's not. I know he's moody and distant a lot of the time, but he's still capable of making the right decisions. Look, Mum, I've gotta go. Some of the other guys are just heading out to the Trafford Centre...'

'Sure. Have a great time. Say hi to Chloe for us and give your dad a call tonight on his mobile - he'd love to hear from you.'

'Yeah, will do - and Mum, remember, you've got to let Ian make his own mistakes. You should believe in him enough to know that even if he does have a temporary lapse of judgement, it's not going to be a biggie.'

'Thanks, bye then love.'

Imogen places the phone beside her on the quilt. She knows her eldest son is right. She does trust her middle child. It's just that he's not the sweet little boy he used to be. Ewan went through exactly the same phase and came out the other side pretty much unscathed. But it's hard for her to be absolutely confident about Ian right now. He's so withdrawn and uncommunicative. It's been impossible even to pass the time of day with him in recent weeks without receiving a look of pure scorn for your trouble.

Imogen sighs, trying to dismiss these doubts from her mind. Instead, she pictures Ian as a laughing little boy; obsessed with sailing boats and fast cars. With this image placed firmly in her head, Imogen resolves to keep the faith with her son and rely on him to do the right thing.

Chapter Twenty Six

As Imogen is rushing out of the house, running late to pick Ian up from his Blackwater Cadets meeting, the phone in the hall starts to ring.

'Damn,' she mutters quietly to herself, swiftly taking the call. 'Oh, hello Penny - Yes, fine thanks, but this isn't a great time for me to talk, I'm afraid.'

Allan steps out of the lounge and whispers into his sister's ear, 'I'll go and fetch Ian, if you'd like?' He scoops up his coat and plucks the car key ring out of the bowl on the hall table.

Imogen places a hand over the receiver, 'Are you sure? Do you know where you're going?'

Allan nods, 'I need to get some fresh air anyway, so I don't mind at all.'

Imogen smiles absentmindedly and immediately returns to the phone conversation. 'Sorry, Penny - you're going to have to explain that to me all over again.'

*

It is dark when Allan pulls up outside the school. He has been here once before, although he isn't quite as sure about where he is going as he had claimed. Allan figures it isn't a very large site and if he wanders around for a bit then he should be able to locate the classroom his nephew is in.

A few of the night-time security lights are on, but he still finds it pretty difficult to see exactly where he is going. Eventually, Allan spots a demountable classroom block up ahead which is still brightly illuminated. There are clearly some people moving about inside. He strides towards it. As he gets closer, Allan hears the sound of raised voices. Without thinking about it, he stops and ducks into the dusky shadows created by the wall of the main building. He keeps close to the brickwork, edging his way slowly towards the sound of the argument.

When he is almost at the classroom block, he notices the vague outlines of two people; a man and a woman, standing slightly beyond the triangle of light being projected from the prefab's grubby windows. They are positioned down by the ditch; the one which runs alongside the tall fence encircling the school site. Allan stays absolutely still and listens.

'I've not spoken another word to her about it,' the woman's voice says insistently.

'You shouldn't have said anything in the first place,' the man replies.

'I can't change that fact, Mark. Anyway, you've smoothed things over now, so I don't quite see what the problem is.'

'Someone's complained to the Head. In the current atmosphere, with all the government cuts and everything, it could be enough for me to lose my job.'

'Look, that's got absolutely nothing to do with me or anyone else I happen to know. What was the complaint about then?'

'None of your business. I just want to make it clear you are not in any position to start pointing the finger at me. Compared to you, I'm a bloody saint. Everything I do is for the right reasons. Remember that, because I could make life extremely difficult for you.'

She snorts indignantly, but then says, 'I've absolutely no interest in you or the damned club. Rest assured, I won't be uttering another bloody word about your infantile boy-scout exploits to anybody.'

The woman strides out of the shadows and makes her way to the small set of steps leading up to the two classrooms. Allan promptly emerges from his hiding place and follows her.

'Evening, Caroline,' he calls out politely, jogging to catch her up.

She turns around sharply, but a pleasant smile soon spreads across her face. 'Oh, hi, it's Allan, isn't it? Imogen's brother?'

'That's right. We met at a barbeque once, if I remember rightly.' He puts out his hand.

'Yes, lovely to see you again. Are you here for Ian?'

'I am. Imogen was a little tied up and what with Hugh still being in the hospital, I thought I'd offer my services.' Allan watches her reaction closely.

'How is Hugh? Do send him our love. We were dreadfully upset when we found out about his fall. Life's been pretty hard on all of us lately. We've only just got Nikki home ourselves.' Caroline's response seems genuine enough.

'Is she making a good recovery?' Allan enquires.

'Yes, thank you. No lasting damage from the head injury, which is a great relief. My husband has taken it very badly. Rick feels guilty that the accident happened whilst he was just a few doors away.' Caroline looks around for her son.

Will and Ian both emerge from one of the classrooms, pulling on their jackets and chatting animatedly. The adults' conversation abruptly ends as the boys join them and they make their way back to the cars. Allan encourages Ian to sit next to him in the front passenger seat, ensuring that his nephew's headphones remain firmly out of reach.

'How was the club?' Allan asks, slowly negotiating the car out of the school grounds along its long and twisting driveway. The road appears to be punctuated every few metres by a never-ending sequence of speed bumps.

'It was great, thanks. Matt has decided on a shortlist for our latest expedition. We're going to vote on the choices next week. Then we can set a date and start training.' Ian looks really enthusiastic.

'What's your favourite idea?'

'I suggested we should sail out to one of the islands; camp for the night, and then sail back the following day. It's one of the options Matt selected. I hope the others vote for it too.'

'Camping would be extremely chilly at this time of the year, Ian.'

'That's all part of the fun, Uncle Allan. We've got the proper 'all seasons' tents and gear. We can light a fire and gather around it - which should keep us nice and warm.'

'Rather you than me,' Allan replies with a wry smile, thinking of his recent day trip with Imogen to St Peter's and how bitterly cold it was.

Ian turns to look at his uncle. 'I'd like it if Matt would let me plan that trip with him. As it was my idea and everything. We'd need to get permission from the National Trust to visit Northey Island, because it now belongs to them. Did you know the Vikings invaded Northey in 991A.D. and it's the oldest recorded battlefield in Britain?'

'I believe your mother might have mentioned it to me once or twice,' Allan responds dryly.

'You can reach Northey across the causeway at low tide, so it wouldn't be very much of a challenge for us. I'd prefer it if we had a go at Osea or St Peter's. Osea Island also has a causeway, but the sail over to those two would be much more interesting.'

'St Peter's Island is very exposed to the elements, Ian. I think it might be a bit too adventurous to stay overnight out there.'

'Come on, Uncle Allan. You've sailed to all kinds of exciting places. Don't tell me you're becoming boring like all the rest of them.' Ian twists his head round to stare at the total darkness outside.

There is an awkward silence within the car for several minutes, before Allan finally replies. 'I take your point. Perhaps I'm becoming a tad too cautious in my old age. You go for it, Ian. But when you catch pneumonia, just don't expect any sympathy from me.'

Chapter Twenty Seven

Allan chortles heartily as he tosses the newspaper down onto the breakfast bar.

'You could have provided them with a better picture, Im,' he gently rebukes, pouring himself a strong coffee.

'I didn't send a photo at all. Penny must have given it to the editor. Hugh only looks about twenty years old. I didn't even realise Penny had known him that well back then - it looks like a shot taken on holiday somewhere.' Imogen helps herself to a cup and picks up the tabloid to examine it again more closely.

The front page of 'The Daily Informer' is taken up by a large photograph of a very young looking Hugh, beneath the bold headline: 'Langley's psychologist becomes latest victim in campaign of hate.' The article is written by the paper's chief news correspondent and it outlines the fire attack on Thomas Langley's flat in alarming detail. The reporter's sensationalist prose makes it sound as if Hugh is currently fighting for his life in hospital. There are also heavy hints within the text that it was the family of Danny Carlow, or certainly supporters of the family, who were most likely responsible for the arson attack.

'Penny called yesterday to warn me about the article. She told me to be prepared, just in case the press come to the house. She's e-mailed us a statement to parrot to reporters if we are approached. Although she said it was probably best if none of us make any comment at all.'

'This coverage is only going to inflame the situation - especially around here. Couldn't Penny have put the editor off?' Allan enquires.

'She said it was better to get their side of the story in first. Besides, 'The Daily Informer' has always been very sympathetic to Langley. She said it was a good idea to keep public opinion on side.'

'Ah, so the fire turned out to be a handy little piece of PR for the Langley defence team. Every cloud has a silver lining, eh? Except both Hugh and Langley could easily have been killed in the blaze and the 'safe house' set up by Penny and her bosses didn't turn out to be quite so safe after all.' Allan places his mug down hard on the granite worktop and looks uncharacteristically cross.

'What's the matter?' Imogen asks, surprised by her brother's change of mood.

'Well, it was Penny Mills who persuaded Hugh to agree to take on the Langley case in the first place. The result of which has been to bring no end of problems for your family. Then, when she nearly gets Hugh bumped off in a house fire, she has a photo printed in the national press which was very clearly taken back when she and Hugh were some kind of item. She's rubbing your nose in it, Imogen. I've met her, remember - at the book launch - and I know her type.'

'According to Hugh, you weren't sober enough to have noticed terribly much that evening, Allan. What do you mean, 'back when they were an item'? Hugh never told me he and Penny had any romantic history together.' Imogen starts to feel a little uncomfortable.

'I make some of my keenest observations when I've had a few drinks, my dear. I saw them together and I can promise you that at some point there has been a romantic connection between them. I'm not saying it's going on now, but in the past perhaps. Sorry, Imogen, I just think you need to keep an eye on her, that's all.'

Allan leans over and squeezes his sister's arm. This makes her feel even more concerned. Just what does

Allan know that she does not? She decides to forget it for the time being and concentrate on the here and now. There doesn't seem much point in her dwelling on what Hugh might or might not have done over twenty years ago, before they were even married.

Instead she says, 'Tell me again about what Caroline was up to yesterday afternoon.'

'Well, it was that young teacher who she was arguing with. He accused her of telling someone something she shouldn't have about him and his club, from what I could gather. Gilbert said there'd been a complaint to the Headmaster about him. Caroline said it wasn't anything to do with her. The interesting part was when he seemed to be threatening her – not physically or anything. It appears Mark Gilbert knows information he says could 'make her life very difficult'.' Allan pauses here, clearly relishing the drama.

'So, it could have been Mark Gilbert who Caroline was arguing with on the High Street that day I met her for coffee. Do you think she's had an affair with him and now he's threatening to tell Rick?'

'I didn't get that impression. I think you were right when you said there wasn't anything romantic between them - I didn't pick up on that vibe at all. I got the feeling it was about something more prosaic. Although, Gilbert could have known about an affair she'd had with someone else, perhaps.' Allan gets up to brew more coffee, taking the opportunity to run through the conversation again in his mind. 'Gilbert did make a strange comment, though. He said that compared to Caroline, he was a saint.'

'Hmm. Maybe he does know about an affair then. Although it sounds like it could be more serious than that. Was Caroline aware you were listening to them?'

Allan turns round and grins. 'I did run up behind her as soon as the conversation finished. Sorry, Im, I just couldn't resist seeing the look on her face when she thought she'd been caught in the act. I wouldn't make a very good detective, would I? Though I deliberately didn't let on and she didn't seem aware I'd overheard them.'

'On the contrary, I think you've performed a pretty decent piece of detecting there.' Imogen raises her coffee mug as a mark of appreciation.

Allan bows theatrically, before adding, 'well, I thought to myself, if my little sister can manage it, then just how hard could it possibly be?'

It appears rather cramped in Hugh's hospital room with Penny, Rob Langley and Thomas Langley's solicitor, Clifford Maynard, all seated around the bed.

Hugh is propped up against two large pillows and has his notes and Dictaphone laid out on the sheets in front of him. Clifford and Penny received a phone call from the Crown Prosecution Service the previous afternoon regarding the charges against Thomas Langley. Thomas's eldest son had insisted that Hugh be present when they discussed the prosecution's latest offer.

Rob Langley is a large man. He is wearing civilian clothing, but is still clearly identifiable as a life-long soldier. He is sitting rigidly in his seat, stony faced and deadly serious. Tall and muscular, the hospital chair seems ridiculously too small for his bulky form. He presents a dramatic contrast to the plump and diminutive solicitor sat beside him.

'The C.P.S. has suggested we accept a reduced charge of manslaughter on behalf of your father, Rob. They say that rather than having the threat of a future trial hanging over you both, it would end the whole situation once and for all. The prosecution intimated that with Thomas's current health problems he would be unlikely to serve a custodial sentence for the crime. However, they did add that ultimately this would be a decision for the Judge to make.' Clifford removes his glasses and peers carefully at the man next to him, gauging his response.

'What do you think, Hugh?' Rob says unexpectedly.

'I think that without Darren Beck's testimony in court, your father's defence is weakened significantly. I believe Thomas certainly suffered from PTSD in the decade following his imprisonment in Korea and I have mentioned as much in my report. But I can identify no real signs of it now. Under pressure, your father is probably more emotionally fragile than the average person. However, even with a diagnosis of post-traumatic stress, the evidence shows that in only a half of all cases has this led to a reduced sentence for the defendant. I think you should accept this lesser charge and, when he is better, take your father away somewhere. He certainly does not wish to return to live at the farm.'

Rob turns his gaze towards Penny this time.

'There's no doubt in my mind that you should take it,' the lawyer says without any hesitation.

'Dad is aware of what is going on around him and he is able to make a decision. If I put this proposition to him and say it is what I want, then I am quite sure he will accept it. But I must admit I have my reservations. My father is no killer. He acted entirely in self-defence. His shotgun has a fully legal licence and he was on his own property. Dad has also now suffered an attack on his own life and on the life of one of those people making great personal sacrifices to defend him. I believe the majority of the British public are behind us on this. I cannot see any jury agreeing my father is guilty of cold-blooded murder.' Rob crosses his arms stubbornly.

'What does your brother think?' Hugh asks.

'Andy has had very little to do with the whole episode, I'm afraid. He supports our father, don't get me wrong, but Andy has a new life over in France. He had a difficult time of it out in Afghanistan so he tries to avoid stress as much as possible. We can consult him by all means, but Andy has left the decision-making to me.'

'I want you to take some time to consider the offer,' Clifford says. 'The C.P.S. is in no hurry for a response, the trial has been postponed indefinitely as it is.'

Rob Langley slowly nods his head. 'I've been given a couple of weeks leave, so I won't provide an answer straight away. I want to spend some time with Dad first, so I can get an idea of what it is that he really wants. In the meantime, please accept my thanks for the work you have all done to try and clear my father's name. We both appreciate it.'

When the two men have left, Penny lingers on in the room, taking her time to collect together her bags and papers. 'Did you see the article about you in 'The Daily Informer'?' She tentatively enquires.

'Yes, the nurses brought me in a copy as soon as it arrived. They thought it was hilarious that I'd submitted a photo of myself looking twenty years younger. It's all been rather embarrassing.' Hugh shifts about in the bed, looking bad-tempered.

'I'm sorry, Hugh, that was my fault. The editor called me just before they went to press. I dug out the only photo I had and quickly scanned it across; there wasn't time to do anything else.'

'You should have called Imogen - she's got plenty of recent shots. Most of them are online so she could have simply e-mailed them straight to the paper. It would have been far easier than going to the effort of scanning one.'

Penny can tell that Hugh is really quite cross with her.

'I am sorry, Hugh. It was very late and I didn't want to disturb your family, not with everything they've gone through recently.' Penny looks despondently down at her lap.

'Look, don't worry about it. You'll have to excuse the bluster of an old man suffering from hurt pride - it's not an attractive sight, I know.' Hugh smiles a little. 'Now, tell me how the police investigation into the fire is progressing.'

'No prints on the door or the letter-box. They're currently tracing the accelerant used, although it can be bought in pretty much any hardware store. All of the residents have been interviewed. Apparently, the car-park was very busy that morning. There were a lot of cars parked outside which wouldn't usually have been there. The police are trying to identify them all. The Carlows have also been spoken to. Rick Carlow was in the Maldon branch of his D.I.Y stores for the whole day, along with witnesses. Interestingly, the paraffin which was poured through the letter-box was a brand stocked in his shops. The only other person with a cast-iron alibi is Darren Beck, who was in a job interview at the time the fire was started.'

'I suppose, just because they weren't present for the attack, it doesn't necessarily mean they didn't play a part in the planning of it,' Hugh adds.

'That's correct and it does appear the arson was very carefully planned. Someone had to have followed you all the way from Maldon and then kept a close eye on the flat to make sure you had left before they pushed the accelerants through the door.'

'I believe there must have been someone sitting in a vehicle in the main car-park, watching the rear entrance from there. That is why whoever it was didn't see me go back into the building again from the front,' Hugh takes a sip of water. 'I still have a feeling the dog-walker is involved in this. Perhaps there was an accomplice who arrived on foot.'

'Well, nobody has come forward to claim to be the mysterious man walking his dog on that morning, despite a police appeal in the media.'

Hugh lies back against the pillows and stretches his arms above his head.

'I can't wait to get out of here.'

'It shouldn't be long now.'

'It feels wrong for me to be stuck in this room while Imogen and the kids have gone back home to Cooper's End. I can't help but worry they might still be in some kind of danger there.'

'I really wouldn't imagine so. Langley's now in hospital and he was always the target for these people - whoever they are. I'm sure Imogen is perfectly able to take care of the family herself. She sounds like a very capable sort of person.'

'Yes, she is. I'm also very relieved that Allan is there with them. He enjoys making out he's totally useless and impractical, but in fact he's pretty on the ball. It comes from them all having grown up on a farm, I expect. They had to learn the ropes fairly quickly after their dad died, when all three of them were still extremely young.'

'Allan is staying at the house too?' Penny asks lightly.

'Yes, that's Imogen's brother. He's had a hard time of it at work in the last few months and, just between you and me, he's been experiencing some relationship problems. He's staying with us for a few weeks. It was supposed to be a quiet, restful break by the seaside for Allan. Sadly, it hasn't quite turned out as planned.'

Penny smiles sweetly. 'Oh, I'm sure he has enjoyed his visit, nonetheless. It must be a great reassurance for you, knowing Imogen has someone at home you trust, who can be relied upon to take good care of her and the children whilst you are away.'

Walking briskly, the woman keeps her head bowed until she reaches the clearing. Afternoon sunlight is softly illuminating this pretty little oasis in the midst of the dense wood. The heat of the day is beginning to recede, but after her energetic trek, the woman is hot and tired. She removes her light cotton sweater and sits down on a fallen log.

She does not have to wait long.

After a few moments, she hears the crackle of twigs being snapped under foot and then feels two arms encircling her from behind. The woman smiles wistfully and gently leans back into the man's embrace.

'I thought you weren't coming,' he whispers into her ear.

'It isn't easy for me to get away. Something came up. I'm glad you were still here.'

He climbs over to sit next to her on the old log, slipping his arm around her waist. They remain very still and quiet for several minutes, simply enjoying the warmth from the sun on their faces. The man then twists himself around, kissing the base of her neck and pulling the woman towards him.

'Hold on,' she says, temporarily resisting his advances. 'I came to tell you I'm not sure I can do this any longer.'

'What do you mean?'

'We always knew it couldn't last indefinitely.'

The man stands up and turns to look down upon her, obscuring the sunlight and casting a long, menacing shadow. 'You're breaking it off?'

'I don't know what I'm saying. I just know we need to cool it. Look, I'm going on holiday next week. It will be a natural break for us anyway. I think that when I come back we should try and see less of one another, give ourselves a chance to concentrate on our own lives again. I love you. But we can't keep this up forever.'

He stands very still for a second and then suddenly reaches out and grabs her by the shoulders, gripping them firmly and wrenching her up to face him. He places his lips hard on her mouth, leaning his weight forward so that they both topple heavily to the ground. Pinned beneath his body, she struggles to turn her head and take a breath.

'I'm sorry,' she gasps. 'I've upset you and I'm sorry.'

He rolls over to the side, releasing her from the pressure of his bulky form. He burrows his head into her neck and begins to sob. She puts a hand up to smooth his hair and kisses his damp face. They shift together once again, with both of them clutching desperately for the other, the hungry passion restored for just this one, last time.

The sun is dipping into the trees and the glade is darkening. The two bodies lie entwined and peaceful in their bed of leaves and twigs. Until one of them sits bolt upright.

'Did you hear that?' the woman hisses.

'No,' the man replies warily, lifting himself up onto his elbows.

'I heard someone moving about in the wood.'

'Are you sure?'

'Absolutely positive.'

He stands up and jogs over to the trees to take a closer look. The woman comes to join him. That is when they see a tall figure running away through the forest, too distant for them to chase, disappearing swiftly and silently into the thicket.

'Oh my God,' the woman says quietly, 'you don't think it's possible he'd been watching us the whole time, do you?'

Chapter Twenty Nine

'I was wondering if I could possibly help you to plan the trip?' Ian asks tentatively, hovering at the front desk of the classroom, as everyone else is filing out of the door. 'It was my suggestion we visit one of the islands in the first place and I know the waters really well.'

'It's only your first expedition, Ian. We usually like to start off our new recruits nice and slowly.' Mark Gilbert leans back in his chair, carefully surveying the young man standing in front of him.

'Yes, but Mark,' Matt Carlow puts in, 'Ian *has* got particular expertise on the water. He's the only one of the group who has actually sailed out to St Peter's before. It's a first for the rest of us. Perhaps Ian could assist me as my first mate for this voyage. Then there might be a commission in it for him if he does the job well.'

Ian can't prevent himself from smiling shyly at this prospect.

'Well, if you feel you're up to the challenge, young man, then I have no objections.' Mark Gilbert beams broadly and bangs his hands down on the desk to indicate that a final decision has been made.

'Great! Thanks!' Ian exclaims. He grabs his bag and, with a new-found spring in his step, follows his fellow club members out of the door.

'It's exactly like being stuck in quick-sand,' Hugh declares, as he opens the box of chocolates Allan has brought for him. 'The more you struggle against it, the further down you sink. Eventually, it will completely overcome you. The key is to work against your instincts.

You must relax and stop fighting; only then, will you gradually float back to the top.'

'I see what you mean. My counsellor's advice was much the same.' Allan plucks a chocolate out of the box. 'It's a method that's slowly working. The medication also plays an important part in the process.'

'Oh yes. There are some practitioners who believe patients suffering from breakdown can get themselves out of it without drugs, but I do not subscribe to this view. Fatigued nerves play terrible tricks upon tired minds and leave the sufferer trapped in a dreadful vicious circle. Help is definitely needed to bring them out of the condition,' Hugh adds, with his mouth full of chocolate and strawberry cream.

'I haven't returned to London yet. I'm worried when I do it will set me back.'

'There will be plenty of set-backs, Allan. You must face them all in order to fully recover.'

'I know. It just seems odd that I've been so physically well. It's only my mind which appears to have suffered from the stress.'

'For some people, it is their health which deteriorates first when they are under continuous pressure. They begin to experience recurrent illnesses. Yet for others, the first thing to go is their nerves. Everyone responds to stress in different ways.'

'I simply wish I'd had a bit of a prior warning, you know? Then I could have forced myself to slow down.' Allan seems downhearted.

'Look, a breakdown can occasionally be our mind's way of telling us something has to change. Whether this is to do with your job or your relationship, I couldn't say. It doesn't mean making any drastic decisions - maybe simply adjusting your lifestyle a little.'

'Giving up the drink, you mean?' Allan grins.

'Not necessarily. Examine the way you currently deal with stress. Perhaps your first instinct at the end of a hard day at work should be to go for a long run, rather than automatically reaching for the whisky and soda.'

'Advice accepted and taken on board, Professor. Now, how about you? Are you feeling any better?'

'I'm still pretty uncomfortable to be honest. Although I'm not letting the doctors know that. I'm desperate for them to let me go home.' Hugh shifts himself up. 'Is everything okay at the house? Being in this place is making me imagine all kinds of crazy things. Do you think Imogen and the kids are safe there?'

Allan pats his brother-in-law reassuringly on the arm. 'All is fine, Hugh. We had the press hanging around for a few days, but they soon lost interest. Oh, and the police came this morning.'

'What for?'

'They wanted to search the woods again. In case they'd missed anything the first time around. The copper said they're working on the assumption the two attacks might be linked. The investigation's been stepped up; now that people have been hurt.'

'Did they find anything?' Hugh enquires with interest.

'They were still hard at work out there when I left. The one in charge did say they're making good progress with the forensics, but you know what the police are like - they don't want to give too much away.'

'Do you remember when we went for a run in Limbourne Woods, on that Sunday morning?'

Allan nods.

'After you went off on your own, I passed a kind of encampment. A neat little fire had been constructed out of sticks, down at the bottom of a sheltered hollow. Logs had been arranged around it like seats and it looked as if someone was intending to go back to the place at some later stage.'

'There are lots of youngsters who play out in those woods, Hugh. It could have been set up by one of the wardens at the discovery centre, running an activity for the kids. There are plenty of perfectly innocent explanations,' Allan suggests.

'I know, it's just I recalled the police saying they'd found evidence of a similar camp, hidden in the copse of trees opposite our place.'

'Yes, they did. But you'll have to forget about it for now; you can't exactly go and check it out again from here. Just wait and see what the 'bobbies' come up with.'

'Of course, you're right.' Hugh lies back for a moment, before suddenly sitting forwards again and adding, 'perhaps you and Imogen could take a walk out to Limbourne Woods and have a look *for* me? Make sure you go together; take phones and a flashlight with you. I'd be extremely interested to hear what you find.'

Allan chortles good-naturedly. 'The best bit about staying with you guys, is that I never quite know what I'm going to get asked to do next.'

Chapter Thirty

'The police haven't found anything new at our place,' Imogen explains, as they pass through the gate into Limbourne Woods.

'Any progress on the fire at Langley's flat?' Allan asks.

'The detective in charge told Langley's lawyers they're almost certain the paraffin came from Rick's hardware store in Maldon. Rick has admitted himself that there were some bottles missing from the warehouse. It's still circumstantial though, and the police can't absolutely prove it.'

'So it *was* one of the Carlows who set fire to the flat - seems incredible, doesn't it - that any member of the family could be capable of attempting cold-blooded murder?'

Allan leads the way as they stride purposefully along the forestry path.

'I can't quite believe it either. I'm sure Rick and Caroline weren't involved. Perhaps it was Wendy who got hold of the paraffin? Hugh's mum told me she works in the store part-time. She could have passed it on to Steve.'

'It does seem increasingly likely Hugh was followed to the apartment building on the morning of the arson attack.'

'If it was one of the Carlows who was responsible, then yes, that must have been how they found out where Langley was staying.' Imogen sighs heavily, 'poor Hugh.'

They stomp along in silence before reaching the cross-roads; where the path abruptly splits into two.

'Let's have a look at Hugh's map again,' Imogen says.

'We take the right-hand fork, I believe,' Allan supplies.

Holding the crudely drawn diagram in front of her, Imogen paces off down the track. The rain has finally stopped but the sky remains overcast and grey. As the pair walk deeper into the woods, it begins to become dark and gloomy. Luckily, Allan had followed his brother-in-law's advice and brought a torch. As they approach the place where Hugh believes he saw the camp, Allan switches on the flashlight and sweeps the beam over the surrounding forest.

'Hugh's map indicates the encampment is on the western side of the path. Let's have a tramp through the trees over there and see if we can find it,' Imogen suggests.

As they progress further into the wood, the temperature seems to suddenly drop. Moisture cannot evaporate properly through the thick layers of branches and there is a profound dampness in the air. Imogen feels herself shiver.

'I don't know why anyone would want to spend their time out here. There's almost no sunlight coming through the canopy at all, it's giving me the creeps,' she observes.

'I agree. I don't even enjoy walking in these places much. I prefer to run, and even then I'm always rather relieved when I come out the other side into daylight.'

'Look. Is that the camp-fire down there in the dip? Hugh said it's built in the shape of a tiny wigwam.'

They both jog over to a nearby hollow. The ground is very muddy and they have to slide their way down the bank, halting by a group of logs which have been arranged around a wigwam-like structure of sticks and twigs.

'It's quite cleverly done, really. With a fire burning, it might even be cosy.'

Picking up a long, gnarled stick, Allan begins searching around the little settlement. He kicks up the thick blanket of leaves and shifts the logs over to check what's underneath.

'If they used this camp a lot,' he says, 'then they might have left some of their stuff here.'

'Or, they could simply have dropped something,' Imogen adds.

Allan unearths a pile of cigarette butts over by a tree but they dismiss this evidence as useless. They would never get the police to agree to run any forensic tests on them. Allan stalks around the site, tapping his heavy boots against the roots and soil that line the edges of the hollow. Unexpectedly, his foot alights on something soft. He kneels down to take a closer look. An object is half buried underneath a dense covering of leaves and mud.

'Imogen, come and see this!'

Imogen crouches next to her brother and helps him to dig the item out of the ground.

'It's a hooded top, I think,' she suggests, as they try to brush away the worst of the dirt. 'Someone must have taken it off and then left it here. A very long time ago, I'd say.'

'It's got some kind of logo on it,' Allan declares, scrubbing at the front of the jumper with his handkerchief.

His labours have revealed a small circular motif on the right-hand breast pocket of the black hoodie. Imogen leans in to examine it more closely.

'Do you recognise it?' Allan asks with interest.

'Actually, I think I do,' she replies, with surprise in her voice. 'That's the Beeleigh School logo in the centre, and there, wrapped all around it, are the words: 'Young Cadets'.'

Despite the fact it is only midday, Imogen lights the stove as soon as they return to the house. Allan had placed the filthy old hoodie into a plastic bag and he sets it down on the kitchen table before immediately putting the kettle on. They both feel chilled to the bone after their morning ramble in the depths of Limbourne Woods.

Once they have washed up and seated themselves in front of the roaring fire, with steaming mugs of tea cupped in their hands, the pair are finally ready to discuss what they have discovered.

'I'm going to call Hugh,' Imogen announces. 'I'll put him on speakerphone and leave it here on the coffee table.'

Allan nods his assent.

'Hello darling, its Imogen. We've just got back from Limbourne. Allan's with me and we're going to explain to you what we found.'

'Okay, go ahead, I'm listening.'

'We located the encampment, Hugh. It was just where you said it would be. I would suggest that no one has used it in several months at least,' Allan begins.

'It looked as if the camp had been visited quite regularly at some point. There was a big pile of cigarette ends near the fire and enough log seating for at least four or five people.'

'Did you notice anything else?' Hugh chips in.

'Allan was examining the forest floor at the base of the hollow and he found an old hoodie jacket. It was almost buried beneath the mud, but we managed to dig it out,' Imogen explains. 'We think someone must have dropped it there, a long time ago perhaps.'

'It's a large size, which would probably fit a teenage boy or a slim adult. It's black and on the front of it is a motif for The Young Cadets,' Allan finishes.

'Say that name again?' Hugh responds, obviously taken aback.

'The Young Cadets. The motif incorporates the school logo in the centre. So whoever was using the camp, must have had some connection to the club. Didn't you say Langley was involved with it too at one stage?'

'Yes, he was.' Hugh's voice sounds suddenly distant. 'But he told me that none of the boys who broke into the farm had ever been a part of The Young Cadets. Imogen, have you got a piece of paper handy, and a pen?'

'Hang on, yep, fire away.'

'I want you to get in touch with a man called Bill Pickering. He was the Head of P.E at the Beeleigh School up until a couple of years ago and he was in charge of The Young Cadets. He's retired now but I think he still lives in the area. See if you can organise a meeting with him. Find out if Danny Carlow, Darren Beck or Joshua Nash had ever been members. I think whoever had been using that encampment had also been watching Langley Farm. If one of them knew Thomas through The Young Cadets, then it might just provide the connection I've been looking for.'

Chapter Thirty One

Imogen remembers Mr Pickering. He'd been the Games Master at Beeleigh for all of the time Ewan was at school. He was old-fashioned in his methods and quite strict, but very well respected by both students and staff alike.

The Crofts have got to know a reasonable number of the teaching staff at the local secondary school over the years; mostly through their connection to the sailing club at Maylandsea. One of these acquaintances is the former Head of English, Jeremy Stone. When she and Allan have finished speaking with Hugh, Imogen gives him a call. She informs Mr Stone there are plans in the pipeline to host a get-together for retired teaching staff in the spring of the following year. Imogen claims she has been given the task of putting together a mailing list for the invitations.

Now she is furnished with Pickering's address, Imogen comforts herself by resolving to present the idea of a reunion dinner to the chairman of the P.T.A., as early as possible in the New Year. For the time being, she has other, more pressing things on her mind. She glances at her watch, wondering if she has time to give the retired teacher a ring now. Imogen looks out of the window at the grey drizzle which is misting up the glass. For some reason, she suddenly decides it would be best not to give Pickering any prior warning of her visit. Imogen senses she might get more from him if she simply pops by unannounced.

'Allan!' She calls into the lounge. 'Could you go and pick Bridie and Ian up from school for me? I've got the address of the Games teacher and I want to go and check it out.'

Allan sticks his head around the door, looking surprised. 'Oh, okay,' he replies, without much enthusiasm.

'If you're busy I could ask Kath and Gerry to go?'

'It's not that. I just thought I would be coming with you to interrogate the old man.' Allan's face adopts the countenance of a petulant toddler.

Imogen tries not to laugh. 'Sorry, Al. It's going to look suspicious if we both go together. It will be more natural if I'm on my own when I drop in.'

'Fine,' he says, with a theatrical sigh of disappointment. 'Do you want me to start fixing dinner after we get back?'

'Thanks. That would be great. And don't worry – I'll let you know absolutely everything I manage to find out.'

To reach the Pickering's home, Imogen must drive through the centre of Maldon and out towards the neighbouring village of Heybridge. The retired couple live in one of the small lanes leading away from the Heybridge Basin, where the Chelmer and Blackwater Navigation Canal merges into the Blackwater Estuary.

When she arrives, Imogen pulls up at the small circular car-park which sits just below the sea-wall. She climbs the steps and looks out over the still waters of the canal. Old wooden boats line the quay here and Imogen takes a stroll down the coastal path to the pretty lock gate. She passes the quaint, white-washed stone pub, which will be thronging with visitors come springtime and stops when she reaches the shingle covered lane that runs alongside the marina.

The houses here are fairly eclectic in style. Some are modern; designed with large elevated windows to make the most of the views, whilst others are traditional little Victorian cottages, where immaculately tended front gardens stretch out almost as far as the waterfront. It is in one of these charming period dwellings that the Pickerings live. When Imogen reaches the right house, she notices a light in one of the downstairs windows. Imogen has learnt through her amateur investigating that once you have developed a half-decent cover story, it is best to stick to it.

When a man of average height with thin, iron-grey wisps of hair answers the door, Imogen says, 'Hello. Mr Pickering isn't it? You probably don't remember me. My son, Ewan, was taught by you at the Beeleigh School, several years back.'

'I remember Ewan,' he replies, after a moment's consideration. 'Mad on sailing, wasn't he? There was a Scottish connection, I seem to recall. Now, what can I do for you? Would you like to come in?'

Bill Pickering stands back from the entrance and allows Imogen to step inside. The cottage is lovely and warm. Pickering leads her into a rustic old kitchen, which just about has room for the wooden table positioned in the centre of it.

'Take a seat, Mrs Croft. Would you like a coffee or a tea?'

Surprised that the man has remembered her name she replies, 'call me Imogen, please, and I'd love a tea, thank you.'

'My wife is in bed upstairs with a nasty bout of the flu, so things are a little chaotic I'm afraid.' The man shuffles about the room, searching through various cupboards for the correct cups and saucers.

'Oh, I'm really sorry to intrude.'

'Not a problem. It will give me something to tell Iris about later on.' He smiles kindly and sets the beautifully decorated china crockery out on the table.

'I'm a member of the school's P.T.A, Mr Pickering. They've asked me to organise a reunion dinner for retired staff,' Imogen begins. 'I had your address, so I thought I'd pop in and see if you would like to come. We will use the sailing club as a venue and hope to set a date sometime in early spring – if we get enough interest, of course. Your wife is very welcome to come too.'

'That sounds a very pleasant idea, and do please call me Bill. I'd like to meet up with my erstwhile colleagues again. I had many happy years at the school. How unusual for the new management team to consider us 'old-timers' in this way. It is really most out of character,' he says quite pointedly, in a way that makes Imogen worry he is on to her subterfuge.

'It was the parents more than the senior staff who came up with the plan. We just thought it would be fitting,' she adds quickly.

'Well, that is certainly heartening to hear.' He brings over the freshly filled pot and places it down with great care. 'You know, this visit is a real coincidence, Mrs Croft. I have been thinking about your family rather a lot in recent weeks. Ever since I heard your husband was profiling Tom Langley. That is why I recalled your son so easily. You have been on my mind, you see.'

'Yes, we have made ourselves conspicuous by getting involved in such a highly contentious case.'

'I knew Tom really quite well at one point. We still exchange Christmas cards and a brief note each year about what we have been up to. I was completely shocked by what happened to Daniel Carlow. I feel sorry for Langley; he will absolutely hate all of the publicity. Do you know how he is - after the fire, I mean?' Pickering pours out the teas.

'He suffered badly from the smoke and is still on a ventilator, I'm afraid. Did you know Danny Carlow very well, Bill?'

'My goodness, those of us who taught at Beeleigh during those years could hardly have avoided him. Daniel was a very troubled boy. He was one of those children for whom organised education never works. Once he was within those gates he turned into a monster; bullying other students and the staff too. He was pretty much unteachable most of the time. But if you encountered him outside of school hours, he could actually be reasonably pleasant, difficult enough as that may be to believe.'

Imogen *did* find it hard to believe.

'I think the aspect which shocked me the most when I heard about the burglary and shooting back in the summer, was the fact that Langley had always got on fairly well with Daniel. It seemed to make his death at Tom's hands all the more tragic.'

Imogen coughs hard to prevent herself from choking on the sip of tea she has just taken. When she has regained sufficient composure she says, 'how did Thomas know Danny?'

'From The Young Cadets. Daniel was one of our earliest recruits. Isn't it odd how those boys who find discipline so impossible to handle at school, often choose careers in the army or join the T.A.? I've always thought it a very strange contradiction.'

'Perhaps their problem with school is that there isn't *enough* discipline for them,' Imogen muses.

'An extremely interesting point, Mrs Croft. Daniel certainly seemed to enjoy the Cadets. He flourished in those first couple of years. Langley came on board in 2010 and by then Carlow was one of our junior leaders. I wouldn't say they had a wonderful relationship, but it was certainly workable. We probably used the fields at the Langley Farm for drill practice maybe two of three times in total whilst Daniel was still with us.'

'Danny must have left The Young Cadets at some point then?'

'It would have been towards the end of 2011, because that was when Mark Gilbert came onto the scene. He was young and dynamic and took over the running of 'The Blackwater Cadets'. That club was always more traditionally river-based, hence the name. They put more of an emphasis on sailing and water sports. Of course, Gilbert poached a few of my best students back then.'

'What was the appeal?' Imogen asks.

'Gilbert extended the scope of the club. In fact, I don't think they do very much sailing at all any longer. He introduced all of these outward bound weekends and bungee jumping and that sort of caper, which certainly made the group popular. He also took a more relaxed approach with the students than Tom and I did.' Bill pauses to drink his tea.

'What do you mean by that?'

'Well, I suppose you know he brought in a system of military ranks for the members and allowed the older boys to take charge over the newer recruits. It was more democratic than The Young Cadets and Daniel certainly liked the idea of that. Personally, I felt Mark was letting them run rings around him. The boys called the shots and Gilbert let them do as they pleased. Sorry, that's a little unfair. Anyway, Carlow left to join The Blackwater Cadets towards the end of 2011.'

'Were Darren Beck or Joshua Nash ever in your Cadet group, Bill?'

'Not that I recall. I'd never heard of Joshua Nash until I read the reports about the break-in in the newspapers.'

Imogen is quiet for a moment. 'Thomas Langley never told the police he knew Danny Carlow. In fact, he claimed he'd never set eyes on any of the three boys until the night of the shooting. Can you think of a reason why he would have denied knowing Danny?'

Bill Pickering looks surprised and then says, 'I'm not sure why he would have said that, Mrs Croft. But he might have been trying to simplify things. Tom didn't know Daniel particularly well and it was a few years ago now that he left The Young Cadets – so he might genuinely have forgotten.'

'I've kept you for long enough, Bill. Thank you so much for the tea and the chat,' Imogen says, rising from her seat.

'Yes, I'd better go and see how Iris is feeling. She'll be looking for her dinner soon.'

They walk down the narrow corridor and pause briefly at the front door.

'The only other explanation I can think of,' Pickering abruptly adds, 'is that Tom was trying to keep Andy out of the whole thing.'

'Andy?' Imogen interjects.

'Yes, his son. Andy had left the army at around the same time Tom started to help us out at The Young Cadets. He was living at the farm with his father for a while and Andy took our students out for a few training exercises. The youngsters loved it because he was good fun and, of course, they respected him because of his impressive war record. Andy had served in Northern Ireland and in Iraq. Daniel in particular looked up to him. They became quite good friends. Well, Andy was more like a father-figure to Daniel. Perhaps Tom didn't mention knowing the boy because he didn't want the police to go bothering Andy with questions. He's happily settled out in France now, I hear.'

Imogen shakes the retired teacher by the hand.

'It's been a great privilege to meet you, Bill. I do hope our paths will cross again at the reunion dinner. I will be in touch,' she says with heart-felt sincerity and then is gone.

Chapter Thirty Two

Ian hovers next to his father as he climbs out of the car and makes his way, slowly and cautiously, up the stairs to the house.

'I'm alright son,' Hugh says. 'Just a bit stiff from spending two weeks stuck in bed.'

'Let me take your arm for this last section, Dad. You're looking tired.'

Hugh actually feels quite well, but he allows Ian to escort him through the front door and along the hallway to the lounge, where they find Imogen. She is busily plumping up cushions on the sofa and hesitantly shifting the position of a small padded footstool on the carpet in front of it.

'How high should we elevate your legs, darling? What did the doctors at the hospital recommend?' Imogen enquires as Hugh gingerly lowers himself down onto the sofa.

'This is fine. I'm desperate to be upright again. I've been staring at cracks in the ceiling for far too long as it is.'

Imogen slips into the place next to her husband and leans into his embrace.

'I'm glad you're back.'

Hugh buries his face into Imogen's dark hair and mutters, 'God, so am I.'

'Allan's been pretty amazing actually, but it's not quite the same.'

'Is he here?'

'No, he's gone for a run before dinner.'

'Is he trying to rub my nose in it?' Hugh asks dryly.

'He's taking your advice. You did tell him to exercise away his stress rather than reach for the whisky bottle,' Imogen retorts.

'Oh yes, so I did. I can be a pompous old git sometimes, can't I?' he observes.

Imogen laughs and retreats to the kitchen to prepare the evening meal.

After dinner, Hugh, Imogen and Allan take their half-finished glasses of wine into the lounge, where they seat themselves in the armchairs by the new picture window.

'Great to see you up and about again,' Allan declares, lifting his glass in a toast.

'I'll certainly drink to that,' Hugh replies, taking a long sip of the blood-red Claret.

'Have you got any more work to do for Penny and her team?' Imogen asks.

'Not for the time being,' Hugh says. 'I've completed my profile and there's no date yet for the trial. The Langley's are still discussing whether or not to accept a reduced plea of manslaughter.'

'So, have you decided what to do about Bill Pickering's revelation?' She probes. 'How much does it change the case against Thomas?'

'I think it shows he's been lying; although if he has, the lies have been extremely convincing.'

'How come the police and the prosecution lawyers never picked up on this connection between Danny Carlow and Thomas Langley?' Allan enquires.

'Well, Langley never mentioned his involvement with The Young Cadets to the police. He told me he didn't think it had any bearing on the case and hadn't even crossed his mind. It may just be possible that Thomas didn't remember Carlow from back then. But the fact remains, that if he did recall the lad, he didn't alert anyone to it.' Hugh explains.

'Also,' Imogen adds, 'the focus in this case has been on the events which took place on the night of the burglary itself. It has always been a question of whether or not Langley was legitimately defending himself when he let off the shot-gun and injured the boys. The question of whether or not Langley had come into contact with the young men *before* that night is in many ways irrelevant.'

'Wouldn't Danny's parents have known their son already had a link to Langley? Why didn't they tell the authorities about it?' Allan says.

'I believe Danny had used the knowledge he gained of the farm from his time in The Young Cadets, to help plan the burglary. I also think he'd been staking out the place from the woods for several months beforehand. Perhaps Steve and Wendy realised that too. They might have thought it better not to alert the police to the fact that Danny had worked out a premeditated scheme to do over the Langley property. He may even have always intended to attack Thomas whilst he was there.' Hugh sits back and cradles the now empty glass in his hands.

'Bill Pickering told me Danny left The Young Cadets quite abruptly towards the end of 2011. His reason for going was to join The Backwater Boys; which had a young and dynamic leader and ran new and exhilarating expeditions. We certainly know ourselves that Ian has been incredibly enthusiastic about it. But what if there was *another* reason for Danny leaving? He might have fallen out with Thomas or Andy and that's why he didn't want to be a part of it anymore.' Imogen leans forward, her dark brown eyes sparkling in the firelight.

'It would certainly explain why Danny went on to target the Langley Farm for his robbery. He was most definitely interested in stealing the expensive lead sheeting, but he may also have been settling an old score at the same time.' Hugh sits up, becoming alert once again.

'It might account for Carlow's violent behaviour towards Langley - if it wasn't simply a random burglary, but something more personal instead.' Allan drains his glass.

'You're going to have to tell Penny about this, Hugh. It changes the whole complexion of the case,' Imogen urges.

'Penny is going to take a short holiday. Now the trial has stalled, she says it gives her an opportunity to get away for a week or so. When she returns I'll tell her everything. In the meantime, I'd like to try and discover some more. Thomas and Rob seemed very keen to keep Andy out of the investigation. I'd be interested to know why. I think it's worth doing a little digging into the background of Andy Langley. Let's find out why the family are so eager to protect him.'

Allan yawns. 'All of this sleuthing with the Crofts has worn me out. You two continue the debate, I'm going to bed. I've got a feeling I'll need my rest, as no doubt you'll have something suitably dangerous and exciting planned for me tomorrow.'

Chapter Thirty Three

Hugh's mobility improves greatly over the following days. He has been performing his exercises religiously and trying to get his wasted muscles working again. Hugh still needs crutches to walk any great distance, but he is hoping to be able to ditch those soon.

As November draws to a close, the skies over Cooper's Creek have become cold and clear. The trees in the wood opposite the Croft's house are completely bare. Hugh is drawn to gaze out of the large window in the living room and across to the water. Imagining he sees a brief glimmer of movement amongst the exposed branches of the little copse, he stares closely at the barren, flat landscape. He identifies nothing out of the ordinary and forces himself to turn away. Hugh walks falteringly back to his study. A laptop sits open on the desk and several pieces of paper, filled with scrawled notations, lie scattered around it.

Hugh has been trying to find out what he can about the military career of Lieutenant Andrew David Langley. He does not have access to the man's army records, but Hugh has managed to scrape together a few scant details on-line. He has added this information to what he had already been given by Langley's solicitor.

Andrew was born in Ipswich Hospital in March 1963. He joined the army in 1981; a year after the family had returned from West Germany to Essex. Andy was 18 years old when he signed up and had not continued into higher education like his brother, Rob. When the family returned from Germany, Rob had already left home to study Chemistry at Southampton University.

Thomas seems to have provided his solicitor with far more information about Major Robert Langley's education and career than he had about his younger son's. Hugh has been compelled to work backwards to find out anything at all about Andy. He knows the man left the forces in 2009, because that much Thomas Langley had already told him.

Through an internet search, Hugh has discovered Andy had been a part of the 18th Air Assault Brigade and was stationed at Colchester Barracks at the time of his retirement. Hugh is aware of the Brigade. He had interviewed a number of their men for one of his research projects a couple of years back. He even knows the Commanding Officer. Hugh pauses for a moment and then fires off an e-mail to Lieutenant Colonel Barry Anders, who he has met at several University dinners and recalls as being an affable sort of chap. Realising there is nothing for him to do now but wait, he hobbles out of the room and goes to find his son.

Hugh locates Ian in the dining room. The boy has spread a couple of the maps Gerry lent him across the table and is leaning over them in rapt concentration.

'What are you up to?' Hugh asks with interest.

'I'm planning the route to St Peter's Island. Matt's given me the job of skippering the boat,' Ian replies.

'Whose boat are you taking?'

'Will's dad is letting us use his. It's a 22 footer, so it should be large enough for us and all our equipment. If it's not, then we might rent another one.'

'Are you able to handle a vessel of that size single-handed, Ian?' Hugh says with concern.

'Matt and Will can help, they're both good sailors.' Ian looks downhearted.

'I'm just checking you're prepared for what will be required of you, Ian. I know what a great sea-farer you are. Matt's made an inspired choice by giving you the job.' Hugh places a hand on his son's shoulder and a proud smile flickers across the boy's face.

'I promise I'll take my injections regularly, Dad. I do really appreciate you and Mum letting me go on this trip – especially after everything that's happened over the past few weeks.' Ian glances downwards, avoiding his father's gaze.

'Your mother and I trust you, Ian. We only nag you so much about managing the diabetes properly because we love you.'

Unexpectedly, Ian turns around and embraces his father. Hugh puts his arms tightly around his son, a memory of his middle child as a spindly little boy with curly dark hair, always wanting to sit on Daddy's lap, abruptly forms in his head. For some reason, he finds the image oddly comforting.

It has been a quiet weekend. Allan spent the day making endless pots of coffee and working his way, forensically, through the Sunday papers. Imogen is surrounded by several piles of ironing. The expression on her face indicates that any attempt by members of the family to interrupt her mammoth task, would be extremely unwise.

Hugh shuffles into his study and closes the door behind him.

He powers up the laptop, checks his e-mails. Just as he'd hoped - there it is - a reply from Lieutenant Colonel Anders. Hugh is touched he found the time to respond so swiftly. He clicks on the message and runs his eyes down the page.

There is quite a lot of information here. Anders explains that he did not know Andy Langley personally, but he took a look at his record and is providing Hugh with a précis of the man's career. As he carefully scans through the text, a realisation begins to dawn on the psychologist.

Andy was a member of the Royal Artillery; which means, essentially, that he is an expert on guns.

He was part of the 8th Parachute Regiment Royal Horse Artillery, which became integrated into the 18th Air Assault Brigade when they moved to Colchester in 2003. Andy started his career with the Parachute Regiment in the early 1980s when he was posted to Northern Ireland. The Regiment spent a few years deployed as ordinary infantry soldiers; at the forefront of the very worst era of the 'troubles'.

The Regiment regained its airborne status in the 1990s and saw action in numerous theatres of war. Andy took part in a UN mission to Cyprus in 1994 and then in NATO operations in Bosnia in '96 and Kosovo in '99. He was also deployed in Iraq in 2003 when the 8th PARAs fired the first shots of the conflict.

From 2006 onwards, Andy Langley joined the first of the Regiment's three tours of Afghanistan. Ironically, Hugh notes how Anders describes the combat of this first tour as the most intense since the Korean War of the 1950s. It seems that the 8th PARAs played a crucial role in the break into Helmand Province.

During the Regiment's second tour of Afghanistan, they took part in an operation to move a turbine along a heavily mined and strongly defended road leading from Kandahar to the Kajaki Dam. The jeep that Andy was travelling in came under heavy fire. He was shot in the arm and left leg. Dragged to safety by a fellow soldier, he was airlifted back to Britain within 12 hours of sustaining his injuries.

Andy recovered well, but accepted the army's offer of a retirement package. Barry Anders adds that Langley was given a very good send-off and was well-known and highly regarded at the barracks. The Lieutenant Colonel goes on to ask some questions about Hugh's current research project. The psychologist closes down the message for now and chews over the details he has just read.

Andy was a highly experienced soldier. Hugh is not surprised the Young Cadets enjoyed being trained by him. He could certainly imagine Danny Carlow looking up to Thomas's younger son and being in awe of his achievements.

Hugh looks down at the pile of papers he received from Clifford Maynard. Andy runs a pension in the town of Limoux, in the Pyrenees. He has been living there for three years now. His partner - business or otherwise, is named here as Carlotta Ruiz. Hugh knows the place a little. They have holidayed in Carcassonne and the Languedoc region of France many times as a family, often driving down to visit the towns and villages located in the stunning foothills of the Pyrenees mountains. It is Cathar country and the area is dotted with ruined Chateaux. Perched perilously upon the cliff tops, these medieval strongholds tower over the tiny settlements which lie below. It is a stunning setting for a guest house.

Hugh flexes his legs, trying to get the blood flowing again after sitting at the computer for so long. He ignores the immediate flash of pain he feels in his lower back, reaching instead for a packet of ibuprofen in the desk drawer next to him. After swallowing a couple of tablets he logs on to the computer once again. This time around, Hugh is searching for websites dedicated to finding cheap, last-minute flights.

Chapter Thirty Four

The gears on Hugh's hire-car are incredibly stiff. He has to crank the lever hard to make every change. The countryside he is driving through is so beautiful that he has almost stopped noticing. The winter has been mild here. The only snow to be seen is on the highest peaks of the southern Pyrenees, many kilometres in the distance.

Hugh is staying at a cheap and cheerful hotel in Carcassonne. He only has three days in France to find out the information he is seeking, having flown in from Stansted Airport late yesterday evening. Imogen was furious when Hugh told her of his plans. She even suggested flying out to France herself, rather than allow her husband to travel in his condition.

He had to work extremely hard to persuade her around to his way of thinking. The flight itself was only a little over two hours and he promised Imogen he would be using the car for the rest of the time. She was still not entirely convinced. Hugh had sat her down at the desk in his study and carefully shown her Andy Langley's war record. He had explained that Thomas Langley's son was a lifelong soldier, with a particular expertise in the use of guns.

Hugh told her how he is quite sure Andy knows something about his father's relationship with Danny Carlow which will prove crucial to the case. Finally, his wife could not contain her natural curiosity any longer and conceded that Thomas's youngest son could very well hold the key. She eventually allowed him just one long weekend to find out whatever he could from Andy Langley.

Hugh has told no one outside the family about his trip. Penny is currently on leave and the case itself is in limbo whilst Rob decides what further action to take. The Major is still hoping Danny Carlow's death will be judged lawful. If they can ever manage to get the case to court, Hugh thinks they may have a reasonable chance of success. He simply fears the physical and mental toll on Thomas would be too high a price to pay.

The route between Carcassonne and Limoux takes about forty minutes to drive. Once Hugh has turned off the A61, the journey is extremely pleasant. He is used to this landscape in the height of summer, when the fields are full of sunflowers and the heat burning down onto the terracotta stone villages is intense. The climate today is a little like England in early springtime. The rolling hills are covered in freshly ploughed soil, with just the occasional glimpse of a dark green shoot, protruding optimistically from out of the barren ground.

What Hugh immediately recalls about this area of France, is the sheer vastness of it. The grey outlines of the tallest peaks of the Pyrenees appear to be hundreds of miles away, far beyond the undulating countryside. Even the sky itself seems bigger here than it does back home. Hugh is reminded of when he visited the American mid-west about a decade ago, where he experienced a similar sensation. The huge skies there had been beautiful too, but at the same time daunting. Standing beneath them made you feel small and a little insignificant.

Hugh crosses the Canal du Midi and not long after leaving the Languedoc region, he arrives in the small town of Limoux. He parks opposite the banks of the Aude River. The water levels are high and Hugh imagines they must have had some very wet weather here recently. He walks towards an attractive stone bridge, which seems to mark the entrance to the céntre vîlle.

Hugh has a tourist map upon which he has marked the address of Langley's chambres d'hôtes. He passes under an archway in the town's defensive walls and strolls casually towards the main square. It is obviously not a market day and the area is very quiet. There is a fountain to the north of the square and cafés and restaurants are plentiful, some of them even venturing to place a few tables and chairs outside in the cool afternoon air.

Langley's guest house is situated along one of the narrower streets which lead off the market place. The buildings here are a little shabbier than those that face the square. Most of the shutters are firmly closed. About halfway along, Hugh finds the three storey building owned by Thomas's son. The wooden front door is painted in a faded butterscotch yellow and a rustic sign hanging next to it bears the name: Hôtel Tournesol.

There is a large buzzer beneath the sign, which Hugh presses. He hears no corresponding sound from within but decides to wait patiently by the entrance just the same. He pushes the bell a couple more times. When he receives no response, he turns back towards the centre of the town, it now being clear no one is at home.

He chooses a table at one of the cafés on the square. Ordering an espresso and making sure that his seat is angled to gain a good view of the Hôtel Tournesol, he watches the yellow door for a while. If he were twenty years younger Hugh would have taken this opportunity to smoke some cigarettes - the strong French ones that you can't get back at home. Instead, he orders another coffee and a bottle of water, trying to enjoy the ambience of the place, steadfastly ignoring the niggling pain which has just started up in his groin area.

He sees the yellow door begin to open. Sitting forward in his chair, he watches closely as a tall man dressed in chinos and a leather jacket steps out of the building. He pauses to light a cigarette before making his way into the market square. He moves rapidly, but there is something about his gait which isn't quite right. Hugh senses that his legs are not really operating in sync with one another, but only by the tiniest margin. The man chooses the café-bar opposite Hugh's and takes a seat outside. He chats expressively to the waiter before ordering.

It is clear to Hugh this man is Thomas Langley's son. He has the same muscular build and a certain ageless quality to his features. After about ten minutes, a woman approaches Andy's café from the other side of the square. She is of medium height and is wearing a type of woollen cape which she has wrapped firmly around her. The woman's hair is streaked blond but her skin is deeply bronzed by the sun. When she reaches him, Andy immediately stands up. She presses her body into his, kissing him deeply on the lips.

Hugh waits for Carlotta to place her order. Then he leaves some money on the table and makes his way across the square to join them. When he gets to within few feet of the couple he introduces himself.

'Lieutenant Langley? My name is Professor Hugh Croft. For the last few weeks I've been working very closely with your father.' He puts out his hand.

Andy looks completely taken aback. After several seconds, he seems to regain his poise and stiffly returns the handshake. He pulls out one of the cushion covered rattan chairs next to him, gesturing for Hugh to join them.

'Can I get you a drink, Professor Croft?' He asks. 'We both have cognac.'

'I'll have the same,' Hugh replies, trying desperately to remember how many pain-killers he has taken so far today.

'How is my dad?' Andy enquires. A thought seems to suddenly strike him and he adds, 'weren't you the one who was in the flat too? When the fire broke out?'

Hugh nods. 'Your father is stable, but he still can't breathe on his own, not without the help of a ventilator.'

Andy makes no attempt to explain why he has not been to visit his father. Saying instead, 'I knew that eventually someone would come and speak to me.'

Hugh glances towards the woman sitting opposite them. She has her cape swept over one shoulder. Her tanned face is totally impassive.

'This is my partner, Lotta Ruiz. She and I run the hotel together.'

The woman nods towards Hugh, but the action is not a welcoming one.

'Pleased to meet you, Ms Ruiz,' he responds, immediately wondering if Andy's girlfriend has ever met the rest of the Langley family.

Hugh takes a sip of his cognac. He feels the liquid gently warming his body; slowly deadening the nagging pain which up to now has been interfering with his concentration.

'Were you aware that your father has been offered a reduced plea of manslaughter? Your brother is debating whether or not to accept it.'

Andy swirls the golden liquid around his glass. 'Rob didn't tell me. For what it's worth, I think he should take it. When he's better, and he's served his sentence, he could come here for a while. The climate is very healing. It has done me the world of good, Professor.'

'You must tell your brother that, Andy. He is determined to have your father fight on to clear his name.' Hugh leans forward in his seat.

'Rob wouldn't take any notice of what I said and *I* wouldn't dream of questioning the decision of a superior officer.' There is a humourless smile on the man's face.

Hugh finds Andy's answer odd. He presses on, 'you knew Danny Carlow when he was a member of The Young Cadets. What did you think of him back then?'

Andy appears surprised by the question. For the first time since the conversation began, he looks Hugh straight in the eye. 'I liked him. He was a quick learner with bags of potential. Danny wanted to hear every single detail of my army career. He was fascinated by mechanics and engineering. I was very sad to learn of his death.' He makes this statement as if he has no connection to the boy's shooting at all.

'Have the British police asked you any questions about what happened at your father's farm last summer, Andy?'

'No.' He replies firmly. 'But there's no reason why they should, is there? I was hundreds of miles away when it happened.'

Emboldened by the drink, Hugh asks, 'did you know your father owned a gun?'

'Of course, he's had it for over twenty years. We're a forces family, Mr Croft. We respect firearms, because we understand what terrible damage they can do. My father is a responsible gun owner.'

Suddenly, Lotta interrupts their discussion. She places a hand on her boyfriend's knee and says, in a thick Spanish accent, 'Andy, I'm getting cold.'

Expecting Lotta to leave them to it, Hugh is startled when Andy stands up with her and declares, 'it was a pleasure to meet you, Professor Croft. Thank you for helping my father.'

Thinking quickly, Hugh says, 'I'd like us to meet again. I feel our conversation has been too brief. I want to be able to take a message back to Thomas.'

It is Lotta Ruiz who replies. 'Come to the hotel tomorrow night. I will cook you dinner. Knock on the door at about eight and we will let you in.'

'Thank you, Lotta,' Hugh responds, 'I'll be there.'

Chapter Thirty Five

The following day is sunny but colder. Hugh stays in his room for most of the morning, catching up on his university work and resting. He feels physically exhausted and hasn't any desire to end up back in hospital. He stretches out on the king-size bed, with his papers and files placed in a neat pile beside him.

It is after midday before he ventures down into the hotel's lobby. It is such a lovely day that he longs to take a walk into the old medieval Cité, with its breath-taking views out across the countryside of Languedoc. But he knows it is a long walk from the newer part of the town and realises he is simply not up to it. Instead, Hugh thinks he might just about manage a stroll along the banks of the Canal du Midi, where he can at least catch a glimpse of Carcassonne's mighty fortress.

He decides to have his lunch first, in the hotel's characterless restaurant. The waiter shows him to a table by a set of double doors which lead to the garden. Hugh glances out at the swimming pool and terrace area, now closed for the winter. He thinks absent-mindedly about where he and Imogen will take the kids on holiday in the forthcoming year and whether or not the whole Langley Farm business will be over and done with by then.

Taking his time to read through the menu, he suddenly feels a hand rest itself gently on his shoulder. Then a voice whispers softly into his ear, 'hello, Hugh.'

He keeps his eyes focussed on the card in front of him. The owner of the voice walks around the table and sits down in the seat opposite.

'Penny. What the *hell* are you doing here?' Hugh hisses.

'I was just about to ask you the same thing,' she says calmly, shaking out a napkin and gesturing for the waiter to bring her a drink.

'I don't have to inform you of all my movements, Penny.'

'When they so obviously involve the Langley case, I actually think you do.'

'How did you know where to find me?'

'I called your house to clarify some of the details in your report. Imogen told me you'd flown out here for the weekend. She blustered for a while, but finally decided upon honesty. I think I must have taken her by surprise.' Penny smiles sweetly, savouring a long sip from the glass of white wine which has been placed in front of her.

'You told me you were going on holiday,' Hugh retaliates.

'I was still deciding where I should go when I spoke to your wife. My parents have a place near Montpellier, so I thought I'd come and visit them.'

'Montpellier isn't very close to here,' Hugh points out.

'It's close enough.' Penny grins. 'I don't want us to fall out over this, Hugh. I'm here to help you. It's crazy to imagine you're in any fit state to be investigating Andy Langley on your own.'

'I've been doing pretty well, as it happens. I'm going there for dinner tonight and I've already established that Andy knew Danny quite well.' Hugh orders his lunch, making a point of not asking his companion if she would like to join him.

'That's terrific news. I'm glad I packed my little black dress.'

'The invitation was for *me*, Penny. I don't want to frighten them by turning up mob handed.'

'This is France, Hugh. I'll bring a large bottle of Armagnac and introduce myself as your mistress. Don't worry about a thing. There'll think it's all completely natural.'

*

'You don't need to support me. I can walk perfectly well on my own,' Hugh says, as Penny slips her arm through his.

'I'm sure you can. But I need some help staying upright on these cobblestones,' she complains, wobbling in her high heels as they make their way along the narrow street towards the Hôtel Tournesol.

When they reach the faded yellow door, Hugh knocks loudly. Penny whispers to him, 'this place has definitely seen better days.'

After a few moments, Andy lets them in, raising his eyebrows when he sees that Hugh has brought a companion.

'My name is Penny Mills. I'm your father's barrister and an old friend of Hugh's.' She leaves the explanation there and leans forward to place a kiss on each of his cheeks.

'I'm sorry there's an extra person for dinner. I didn't know Penny was in town until today and I had no way of letting you know,' Hugh gushes.

Lotta steps out of a small galley kitchen, rubbing her hands down a pretty floral apron. Her hair is piled up on top of her head. She is wearing a figure-hugging black dress, not dissimilar to the one that Penny has on.

'Don't worry, Hugh,' she says, 'I have made enough.'

Penny hands over the Armagnac and introduces herself to Andy's girlfriend. They are then shown into a large sitting room with two tall windows, both of which have their shutters wide open to display the cloudless, starlit night.

'It's a lovely house,' Penny comments.

'We are always full in the summer,' Andy responds. 'The guests use the rooms upstairs; where most of the suites have views of the river.'

'Do you miss England, at all?' She asks.

'I never actually lived there for very long. I spent most of my career abroad. England doesn't really feel like home to me.'

They sit down on an antique looking sofa and Andy pours them both a drink.

'It must be very quiet in Limoux, especially outside of the tourist season.' Hugh shifts around in his seat, trying to discover a position he finds comfortable.

'Not as quiet as the farm in Essex. We've got good neighbours here and Lotta's family aren't too far away.'

'How did you meet?' Penny enquires.

'I was in Barcelona for a few months and we met there. Lotta's family are Catalonian and live near the French border.'

The meal is a pork, vegetable and bean stew. Lotta informs them it is a Spanish variation on the region's famous cassoulet dish. Hugh finds it delicious, particularly after the bland food he has been eating at his hotel.

Penny accepts another drink but Hugh declines. He is driving back to Carcassonne tonight and needs to keep his wits about him. He also wants to be able to listen closely to what Andy is saying. He has no intention of missing something significant.

Loosened up by the French brandy, Andy is telling them about the underground river in Foix, which meanders through a network of caves under the mountains.

'Did you know?' he adds, 'that the oldest cave paintings in France were discovered by a couple of young boys out looking for their lost dog. It's amazing to think what else might be lying undiscovered in the hills. Those carvings had been there for thousands of years.'

'Did they find the dog?' Penny quips, falling silent when her hosts appear totally unamused.

'It is not for everyone,' Lotta says gravely, 'the caves, I mean. Andy and I were there in the summer. A guide took our group down into the deepest catacombs, far beneath the mountain. The American man in front of us found that he began gasping violently and could not breathe – what do you call it?'

'Hyperventilation,' Penny adds.

'His wife had to lead him out into the sunlight again. When we came back up a little later, the lady told us her husband had never suffered from anything like it before. She said that something about being down there must have triggered the attack.'

'The fact he was on holiday and away from familiar surroundings could have brought it on; turning a sense of unease, which he could usually tolerate, into a moment of sheer terror,' Hugh explains. 'We don't realise how comforted we are simply by being in our normal environment.'

Hugh turns towards Andy. 'Has your father ever suffered from respiratory problems in the past? One of the medics who attended the fire said Thomas was wheezing badly in the ambulance, almost as if he had asthma.'

The man's response to this query is not at all what the psychologist was expecting. Andy seems shocked and uncomfortable. He even looks like he may start hyperventilating himself. He begins coughing, and sweat is pouring down his face. Lotta jumps up and rubs his back in a gentle, circular motion while Hugh rushes out to get Andy a glass of water.

'I'm sorry,' Hugh says when he returns. 'I didn't mean to upset you.'

After taking several large gulps he replies, 'it's not that, Hugh. I just get these episodes every so often. Since I left the forces, it's become harder to keep a lid on my memories. Too much time to think, eh?'

'You should see a counsellor about it. They could really help.'

Andy nods, but makes no comment on the possibility of receiving therapy. Instead, he says, 'I don't know of Dad ever having had asthma. It's strange you should mention it, because our mother suffered quite badly from the condition when she was a girl. Apparently, she nearly died from an attack once. But not my father, no.'

The ladies gather up the empty plates and take them into the kitchen.

When they are alone, Hugh asks of his host, 'why did Danny leave The Young Cadets? Bill Pickering said the two of you were good friends, so I don't understand why he left so suddenly.'

Andy looks tired. Just hearing the question seems to have physically exhausted him. It looks as if he needs to make a monumental effort simply to form the words of reply. 'Dad didn't like it. He wasn't happy that Danny and I had become so close. Because of the nature of my career, I was never able to settle down and have children. Dan was becoming like a son to me and it made my father uncomfortable. I don't know for certain, but I think Dad must have told Danny to go. It's what I always suspected. It is one of the reasons I decided to move away. I was angry with him for doing it.'

'Why did Thomas not want you to develop a friendship with Danny? Why did it matter so much to him?'

Andy doesn't get a chance to explain. The ladies have come into the room carrying two large bowls filled with meringues along with several dessert dishes. They are both laughing raucously and Penny is clearly drunk. When they sit back at the table, handing round the plates, Hugh senses that the fleeting opportunity he had to get any more information out of Andy Langley, is now gone.

Chapter Thirty Six

Penny dozes for most of the journey back to the hotel in Carcassonne. The concentration required to stay on the right-hand side of the twisting roads at night, has left Hugh feeling very tired. But his mind is still busily ticking over the information Andy has provided him with.

Hugh wakes Penny up and helps her out of the car. She sleepily leans her athletic body into his. As they walk towards the reception desk, she deftly slips an arm around his waist. Just as swiftly, Hugh removes it, gently pushing her away and feeling in his coat pocket for the key card.

'It isn't going to happen, Pen,' he mutters impatiently.

'That's very dismissive,' Penny retorts. 'It's not as if we haven't done it before. Rather a lot if I remember rightly.'

'I'm not going to argue with you, Penny. We had a relationship a long time ago and now I'm married. That's all there is to it. If you were honest with yourself, you would admit that you only really enjoy the excitement of the chase.'

Penny pulls a plastic card out of her handbag and begins to make her way up the wide staircase. Pausing for a second, she suddenly turns back. Hugh sees there is a watery sheen across her bright green eyes.

'Do you know what? For such a brilliant psychologist, you can be incredibly dense about people sometimes.'

She spins around and strides purposefully in the direction of her room.

*

Imogen gets up from her seat and goes to stand by the window. She stares out at the sky, which is dominated by thick swirls of dark grey cloud.

'So, she just turned up at your hotel unannounced? She must have taken a flight within hours of speaking to me on the phone. Now that's what I'd call fast work.'

'I'm sorry I didn't tell you about it while I was away. To be honest, I didn't have the time. I was too busy trying to get what information I could out of Andy Langley. Also, I didn't want you to worry – I thought it would be best to speak to you face-to-face.'

Hugh moves across the room and places his arms around his wife's waist, resting his head on her shoulder.

'You do know that I love you? I would never have chosen to go away for a weekend with another woman.'

Imogen is quiet for a few seconds, leaning back into her husband's embrace.

'You don't think Penny has got anything to do with this Langley business, do you? Other than being Thomas's barrister, I mean? Because why on earth would she travel all the way to the South of France just to see what you had found out from Andy?' Imogen finally says, twisting around to look Hugh squarely in the eye.

Allan enters the room with a tray of coffees and declares, 'Penny was there because she desperately wants to have an affair with Hugh. I know her type intimately. She saw her opportunity and went for it.'

'Is that true?'

'Yes, I think so – of course, she's wasting her time.' Hugh selects a mug and sits down in one of the armchairs. 'Penny made a pass at me last night. But I told her it wasn't ever going to happen.'

'What gave her the impression that it might?' Imogen takes the seat opposite Hugh.

'Should I leave you guys alone?' Allan asks warily.

'No, you can stay,' Imogen replies, with her gaze still fixed steadily upon her husband. 'You're our guest.'

'I used to go out with Penny, back when we were both in the sixth form. It was such a long time ago, Im. That's why I never mentioned it. *She* seems to think there could still be something between us.'

Imogen relaxes into the chair and stares up at the ceiling. 'Or, she's been manipulating you.'

'What do you mean?' Hugh demands, looking a little insulted.

'Ah, I see where you're going with this,' Allan interjects. 'Penny plays to Hugh's ego a bit, in order to soften him up. Meanwhile, she pumps him for everything he knows about the Langley case.'

'Why would she want to do that? It doesn't make any sense.' Hugh's expression is petulant.

'Of course!' Imogen suddenly remarks. 'What if *you* weren't followed to Langley's place on the day of the fire after all? What if it was *Penny* who told them where the safe house was?'

'Let's just think this through rationally for a second. Firstly, Penny had nothing obvious to gain from killing Langley. He is her client, for heaven's sake. Secondly, I have known Penny Mills and her family for a long time. I genuinely don't think she's capable of murdering anybody. Penny is simply a middle aged woman who recently split from her husband. She is confused about what the future holds for her and is trying to cling to the past, although, she would never admit that to herself.'

'I have to concede, Imogen, that I think Hugh might be right. I'd just like to point out she *is* a particularly hot middle-aged woman.'

'Okay. Let's be on the safe side and assume Penny can't be completed trusted. This means that anything we find out in relation to the shooting stays purely between ourselves – and the police, when the time comes.'

Hugh nods.

'Did Penny hear what Andy Langley told you about his father and Danny Carlow?' Imogen enquires.

'No, she was in the kitchen with Andy's girlfriend when we were talking and I didn't get the chance to discuss it with her later on.'

'Too busy fighting off her advances,' Allan chips in.

Hugh is relieved to see Imogen laugh at this.

'Good,' she says, her voice adopting a steely edge, 'Let's keep it that way.'

Chapter Thirty Seven

Mark Gilbert unfolds the diagram and lays it out across the desk.

'Looks pretty good, doesn't it?' Matt Carlow says proudly.

'Yes, Ian's done an excellent job.'

Matt perches on the edge of the desk adding, 'I just need to double check with Uncle Rick that we can use the boat. Then, it's simply a case of getting hold of all the camping equipment and gaining permission from the St Peter's Foundation to stay overnight on the island. Do I need parents to sign slips for the boys who are still at school?'

Mark sighs heavily. 'Yes. I need to speak with the Headmaster first. He isn't going to be too keen, not after the letter of complaint he received from Mrs Nash.'

'Joshua isn't even a member of The Blackwater Boys any longer, what's her problem?' Matt appears incredulous.

'No, but he was at the time of the break-in at the Langley Farm. Mrs Nash told the Head she was convinced we were somehow involved in it. I know, it's totally ridiculous, however the allegation has placed a seed of doubt in Bob's mind.'

Matt gives the impression of considering this for a moment. 'Do we need to involve the school at all? Couldn't we approach parents directly for their consent? There are only a couple of kids who are still under eighteen anyway.'

Mark says nothing.

'I mean, the Crofts are definitely on board and I would have said they were potentially our only problem.'

Mark looks a little puzzled by Matt's choice of words but replies, 'I suppose we aren't actually affiliated to the school. The Boy Scouts don't have to square their expeditions with Bob bloody Clark.'

'Exactly,' Matt adds triumphantly. 'I'll get some slips printed up this weekend so we can give them out at the next meeting.'

'Okay, but listen, Matt,' Mark says firmly. 'I will have to accompany you on this one. I'm feeling the heat from my superiors and I've got to run this trip exactly by the book.' The teacher gazes almost pleadingly at the young man before him.

'Sure thing, Mark. You come along for the sail and make sure our camp is ship-shape. After that, Darren will take you back to the mainland. You know how the lovely Rachel doesn't like you to be away overnight. I'll be in charge. We'll be back the following day and no one will be any the wiser.'

Matt breaks into a broad smile and pats his downcast teacher on the back. Then he packs the plans into a neat blue folder and strides confidently out of the door.

The Christmas decorations have just gone up around the Croft household. Imogen has positioned an enormous spruce beside the picture window, so the lights can twinkle out over the surrounding countryside.

Bridie is still at an age where she enjoys dressing the tree. Many of the decorations were handmade by her daughter and mother-in-law, both of whom enjoy fabric crafts. Imogen herself has not got the patience for it, but she absolutely loves the results. The house looks very jolly and there are some unique little touches here and there.

'Are you absolutely sure you're ready to go back to work?' She asks her husband with concern, as they sit at the breakfast bar and drink tea.

'Yes. The doctor said it's good for me to be moving about again. I won't overdo it. I'll give tomorrow a try and if I'm in any pain then I'll come straight home.'

'Okay, darling.' Imogen smiles and lightly touches Hugh's face.

'What's that for?'

'I'm just glad you're getting better.'

He gives her a kiss.

'Thank you for being so understanding about the whole Penny thing,' he adds awkwardly.

'I trust you. Although I do wish you'd told me before that you and Penny had a history. I don't really know why you didn't.'

'Well, I hadn't told you back when we first got together. Mainly because I didn't want you worrying about her when I was at home in Essex during the university holidays and you were on Garansay with your mum. Since then it really hasn't seemed relevant to mention it. We're talking about nearly 25 years ago.'

'I can see that. But if there are any other skeletons lurking in the Croft closet, please disclose them immediately.'

Hugh puts his hands in the air and grins. 'That's it, I promise.'

'Now, I've been thinking,' she says, in a change of direction. 'What we need to discover, is why Thomas Langley was so worried about Danny Carlow becoming friendly with his son. Perhaps there is a connection between the Carlows and the Langleys that we don't already know about.'

Hugh considers this for a moment.

'It's got to be something the police and the prosecution team weren't able to uncover,' he suggests.

'Okay. The police are concentrating on the night of the burglary, right? They will have checked to see if Langley has any previous criminal record, which he hasn't. They will also have examined the testimony of the two boys who helped steal the lead flashing. The police didn't find out that Danny had actually *known* Langley *before* the break-in and had most likely targeted him specifically.'

'This was because Thomas lied about it and the Carlows didn't mention it to the police either,' Hugh supplies.

'Exactly. Both families were keen to dissociate themselves from each other. Now, why would that be the case, do you think?' Imogen sips her tea and looks at Hugh carefully, gauging his response.

'Because whatever connects the two families, is detrimental to them both. It is something that neither the Carlows nor the Langleys want to come out.'

Imogen nods. 'That's the conclusion I've reached too.'

'So, there's a secret which involves all of these people – Danny and his parents, Andy and Thomas.' Hugh seems lost in his thoughts for a few moments before suddenly declaring, 'I don't believe Danny knew about it.'

'What do you mean?' Imogen asks.

'Well, Danny quite happily befriended Andy Langley. He saw no problem in it at all. It was *Thomas* who was unhappy about the relationship.'

'And it was Danny's *parents* who never mentioned to the police that Langley had previously been a part of The Young Cadets, along with their son,' Imogen adds.

'This secret may be something only the older generation knew about. Andy could have been aware of it, I'm not sure yet. He was definitely holding something back from me when we spoke in France.'

'If this secret is known only by the senior family members, then it must be something that happened quite a long time ago - which could be the reason why the police haven't picked up on it.' She becomes instantly alert.

'What we need to do, Imogen, is to start digging into the past of the Langleys and the Carlows. I'm starting to think Thomas has been leading me a merry dance. I'm pretty certain the majority of the facts he told me about his life were true. It's just that I now believe there are certain crucial elements he has deliberately left out.'

Chapter Thirty Eight

Imogen signs the slip and hands it back to her son.

'You're going to be completely up to date with your homework, yes? And Mr Gilbert is *definitely* going with you?'

'Of course, Mum.' Ian sighs heavily.

'The forecast for next weekend says it's going to be mild but wet. Are you *sure* your equipment is waterproof?'

'We've planned for everything, Mum. At least it won't be cold.' Ian hesitates for a moment and then places a kiss on his mother's cheek. 'Thanks for letting me do this. I'm really excited about it.'

Imogen is embarrassed to discover she is blinking back tears. 'That's okay. Just take care of yourself. You know how much we worry about you.'

Ian smiles and takes the scrap of paper off to his room.

Imogen returns to Hugh's study. She has spent the morning taking a look through her husband's notes on Thomas Langley. So far, she hasn't noticed anything out of the ordinary. Hugh asked her to see if she could spot a detail he might have missed.

What *has* caught her interest is the mention in Thomas's police statement of Rose Langley's brother. Thomas had been visiting him on the day of the burglary. Imogen is wondering if he might have some more information about the family's past.

There is an address for him in Clifford Maynard's pack. Rose's brother is in his eighties and lives in Ipswich. The police had interviewed him about Thomas's movements on that fateful August day. Their questions had been fairly short and perfunctory; mere formalities to confirm the times of his arrival and departure.

Imogen finds the number. She grabs a notepad and pen and goes out into the hall to make the phone call. It is a woman's voice that answers and she sounds stressed. 'I'm sorry to bother you,' Imogen begins, 'I was wondering if Joseph Palmer was available, please.'

'Who's calling?' The voice demands.

'My name is Imogen Croft and I'm working with Thomas Langley's defence team. I'd just like to ask Mr Palmer a few more questions if that's possible.'

A charged silence follows.

'My Dad's having his afternoon nap. I'm not prepared to disturb him, I'm afraid.'

There is a challenge in the woman's tone.

'Perhaps *you* could help me then? Do you know your uncle very well, er, Ms Palmer?' Imogen persists.

'It's Mrs Bailey, actually, and I've not seen Tom Langley for a good few years. I doubt if I can be of any assistance to you. Listen, Dad's very upset about the shooting. He doesn't want any of his bowling pals to find out he's linked to it. I'd rather you didn't call back.' It seems as if she is about to slam the phone down.

'Mrs Bailey, please wait a minute. Could you just tell me what you recall about the Langleys as a family? Did you ever visit them at the farm, after they returned from Germany?' Imogen fully expects to be greeted by the sound of a dialling tone. Instead, there is a brief period of silence.

'You're talking about a very long time ago. I was quite close to my Aunty Rose but never knew my cousins very well. They'd joined the army almost as soon as the family moved to Essex. My Aunt never really recovered from the death of little Joe - Mrs Croft, was it? It was a terrible tragedy and it destroyed her. I just thank God she's not alive now, to have to deal with yet another death. At least with Rose not around, it means we can wash our hands of the Langleys, once and for all.'

'What do you mean? Who was little Joe?' Imogen blurts out in desperation, but the line is already dead.

Imogen immediately returns to the file of papers. She searches through every sheet but cannot find any reference in the pack to a Joe or Joseph Langley. She turns her attention to the laptop. Imogen logs onto the appropriate genealogy site and does a search on the name. She finds the registered births of Robert and Andrew, with parents Thomas and Rose Langley (née Palmer). Not anyone called Joe.

She decides to leave it there for the moment. Imogen has invited Caroline and Nikki for lunch and is already way behind with the preparations. Nikki has finally returned to school and seems to be well on the road to recovery. Imogen swiftly prepares a mixed salad and sticks a couple of shop bought quiches into the oven. Just minutes later, she hears the Carlows' 4x4 pull up onto the driveway.

Caroline is looking unusually glamorous. She is an attractive woman, but most of the time she tends to play down her good looks with neutral make-up and casual clothing. Today, Imogen notices her carefully applied cosmetics and elegant red silk blouse, immediately wishing she had made more of an effort herself.

'Wow, you look terrific,' she states and embraces her friend warmly.

'Thanks. I Thought I'd brighten myself up for a change.' Caroline smiles a little wistfully.

Imogen steps towards Nikki and pulls the child into her arms. She runs her hand along the girl's soft, honey brown ponytail and declares, 'I'm so glad to see you up and about again, Nikki. I can't tell you how worried we all were.'

The youngster grins shyly and immediately runs off giggling with Bridie to her room.

Imogen leads Caroline into the kitchen and offers her a drink.

'I've got wine if you'd like?'

'Yes, please, Im.'

She pours them both a glass of chilled Sauvignon Blanc and they sit up at the breakfast bar. The rain is streaming down the window and Imogen decides to switch on the light to combat the dreary dullness of the scene outside.

'You must be glad Nikki is looking so well,' Imogen says.

'Oh, words can't describe how relieved we are. If she hadn't fully recovered – just between you and me – I don't think Rick would have been able to carry on. He feels so guilty about the hit and run. Rick thinks he should have prevented it from happening somehow.' Caroline appears pre-occupied and takes a healthy swig from her glass.

'Thank Goodness she's better then. Of course, there wasn't anything he could have done to prevent it, but as parents we are consigned to shouldering guilt. Nothing anybody else says can ever alleviate it.'

'So true. Rick dismissed everything I said to try and make him feel better. He seemed so distant for those few weeks she was in the hospital. It was as if his mind was off somewhere else entirely.' Caroline looks thoughtful. 'Do you know? He very nearly told Will he couldn't go away next weekend with The Blackwater Boys. He's got himself completely worked up about it – thinking that Will might have an accident. It's totally out of character. Rick is usually dead keen on Will taking part in outward bound stuff; he says it toughens him up.'

'Rick's had a fright. We all did when we saw Nikki lying in the road. None of us will ever forget it.' Imogen stands up and begins to search in the cupboard for plates.

'But you and Hugh are okay with Ian going to St Peters?'

'Funnily enough, yes.' Imogen twists around and places her hands on her hips. 'Ian has shown a great deal of initiative in planning the route and organising the equipment. He is really enthusiastic about the entire adventure. My son is almost back to his old self again.' Imogen feels the tears prickling at her eyes once more and swiftly turns her attention back to the jobs.

The girls decide to eat their lunch in the sitting room, watching a movie. Caroline and Imogen remain in the kitchen. Caroline has progressed onto sparkling water. Her companion is still on the wine, although the hot meal is helping her to sober up a little.

'Rick's been questioned a lot by the police,' Caroline confides. 'They seem convinced he supplied the paraffin which was used to set fire to Langley's flat. They've got no real evidence. They just keep pestering him about it.'

'Do you think someone could have taken it from the shop, without Rick's knowledge?'

'It's possible, I suppose. You do know Rick wasn't involved, Imogen? I'd hate it if that's what Hugh thought.' Caroline's face seems genuinely troubled.

'Come on, Caroline. We are perfectly aware that Rick isn't capable of attempting to commit murder.' Imogen pauses for a second. 'But somebody did, and it must have been an individual or group who felt they were avenging the shooting of Danny Carlow.'

Neither of them says a word for several minutes, until Imogen suddenly asks, 'how well did you actually know Danny?'

Her friend jolts backwards in her seat - as if she has been slapped in the face. 'What exactly do you mean by that?' She snaps.

'I simply meant; was the boy as lawless as we all think? I've heard some conflicting accounts of him. One of his ex-teachers told me that outside of school he could be quite a different person.'

Caroline seems uncomfortable with the direction the conversation has taken. She replies all the same. 'Well, he gave his parents a great deal of grief, that's for sure. Although, I believe I know what his teacher was driving at. Danny was hot-headed and had a short fuse. But he was totally loyal to the people he loved. The only problem for him was that there just weren't very many of those.'

222

Chapter Thirty Nine

Allan surprises his sister by announcing he will be leaving them for a couple of days. He has decided to go and stay with his ex-wife in Fort William. From there, he is planning to visit his two grown-up children from that marriage.

'I think it's a great idea,' Imogen responds. 'Do give my love to Suz and the kids.'

'I've offered to take them all out for a slap-up meal. Suz says Alice and Dan are becoming really quite serious. She thinks they might get engaged soon.' Allan seems a little saddened by this idea.

'Alice is still young, but they already live together. Our children have to fly the nest some time.' Imogen goes across to her brother and places a hand on his shoulder. She shies away from adding that it'll be babies next. The concept of Allan as a grandad is just too bizarre for her to contemplate at this time in the morning.

Imogen gives her brother a lift to Stansted airport. She notes with interest how Allan's visits to Suz always appear to be last minute affairs. It almost suggests that if he allowed himself any longer to think about it, he might decide against seeing her. Imogen has a hunch this is because Allan and Suz were once such a dynamic couple. They had in the past so obviously adored each other it must be painful for them both now; knowing they will never experience that kind of intimacy again.

Imogen drives straight home to Cooper's End. She is keen to get back onto the Registrar General's website. Hugh advised her, late last evening, that as they don't know what relationship 'little Joe' was to Rose Langley, she should try to locate the register of his *death*, rather than his birth. From what Mrs Bailey had said, it certainly sounded as if he had died whilst the family were living in Essex.

After logging on and paying her fee, Imogen attempts the search once again. She is still assuming his name would have been Joseph *Langley*. Imogen realises that if he possessed a different surname, she doesn't have any hope of tracking the boy down.

She is in luck. There is a death certificate which seems to match the names and dates. Joseph Henry Langley died on the 24th August 1981. He was 16 years old and his parents are listed as Thomas and Rose Langley. The death was registered at County Hall in Chelmsford a few days later. Imogen squints carefully at the spidery handwriting. She manages to decipher that the cause of death was asphyxiation due to a severe attack of asthma.

She prints off the document and sits back in the swivel chair to digest the words for a second time. Hadn't Andy Langley mentioned to Hugh that his mother suffered very badly from asthma as a child? Perhaps this boy had inherited the condition from her. Could that be correct? Because if Joseph was Thomas and Rose's biological son, then where was his birth certificate?

Suddenly, like misty clouds being burnt away by the bright morning sun, Imogen begins to see the picture with greater clarity. She scoops up the solicitor's bundle yet again. Sifting impatiently through the sheaths of thick white paper, this time Imogen knows exactly what it is she is looking for: Hugh's notes about the Langley's move to New Zealand.

If Joseph Langley was sixteen years old in the summer of 1981 then he must have been born in either 1966 or '67. She quickly scans through Hugh's report.

Thomas Langley told him they arrived in Christchurch during the Christmas of 1964. Andy and Rob had both been born by that time. The family then returned to the UK in 1968. What Thomas had failed to mention, was that they had brought a young baby back with them.

Imogen reclines in the seat and stares up at the ceiling. She allows her mind to process this new piece of information. She imagines Rose giving birth to a healthy little boy whilst they are living in New Zealand. She names the baby after her brother, because she is homesick and desperately misses her family back in Suffolk.

Imogen sits forward again. She considers why 'little Joe's' birth certificate wasn't sent back with them to the UK. Imogen immediately realises she has absolutely no idea what the procedure is in these circumstances; when one member of the family is born in a different country from all the rest. She tries the internet again. This time to search for birth certificates from New Zealand's centralized government system.

To her astonishment, she finds the database is almost identical to the one she has just used for England. Within seconds, the document appears on the screen in front of her. Joseph Henry Langley was born on the 8th October 1966, at Christchurch Hospital, South Island, New Zealand. Imogen thinks of Christchurch now, a few years on from the devastating earthquake. She wonders if the same hospital building still stands.

Despite the evidence being displayed before her, Imogen feels that she still needs clarification. She takes a look at the website for the New Zealand High Commission. Quickly realising her questions are not going to be easily answered here, she locates a phone number for their offices in London's Haymarket.

Before she makes the call, Imogen notes down the relevant information she has about Joseph and his family. Then she writes out each of the queries she would like answered, with the most important underlined at the top. Imogen is determined to get her facts completely straight. Only then, will she attempt to piece together what all of this could possibly mean.

Chapter Forty

As Hugh's car pulls onto the driveway, Imogen is waiting for him.

For a rare treat, she has ordered in a Chinese takeaway. Ian and Bridie are unusually talkative about their exploits at school. As they sit around the dining table and share news, it makes for an impressive domestic tableau. In reality, Hugh and Imogen are dying for the meal to be over so they can analyse this new evidence in peace. When the youngsters declare they are too full for dessert, Imogen almost cries out in relief.

The kids quickly disappear off to their rooms. Hugh and Imogen remain in their seats. Not even making a move to clear away the jumble of plates and aluminium containers; the bright, greasy contents of which are spread out garishly before them.

'Why on earth did Thomas not tell me he had another child?' Hugh questions, as he pours out two more glasses of Merlot.

'Because the boy died 33 years ago, perhaps? I spoke to a very helpful chap at the New Zealand High Commission. He told me that when families repatriate to their country of origin, the birth certificates of all children born in New Zealand are automatically transferred to the relevant authorities. These days it's all done electronically. Back in the 1960s, the documents would have been sent half-way around the world by post. Unfortunately, many certificates were lost in transit. He looked up Joseph's details for me and pointed out that his government are currently in the process of integrating their records with those of UK residents who have at one time possessed a New

Zealand working visa. This means in a couple of months, Joseph's birth details will be linked to Thomas Langley's and therefore show up on the English system.'

'Even without records, Joseph had surely not been forgotten by his parents. I specifically asked Thomas to talk about the traumatic events which had occurred in his life. The death of a child must rank as the worst of them all.' Hugh takes a large gulp of Merlot. 'This guy has really taken me for a ride.'

'I wouldn't be so certain. I've read through your notes and I think he told you more than he had intended.'

'Like what?'

'Well, he intimates they went through a very difficult patch in the late seventies and early eighties. He actually admitted to having another breakdown during that time. It must have been following Joseph's death. Remember, he said he became very depressed.'

'That's right. He also said that Rose really beat herself up about making them come home from New Zealand. Thomas mentioned something about not being able to go back and change things – about God having a plan. I thought it was a sign Thomas had a particularly fatalistic view on life. Now I'm wondering if Rose had blamed herself for Joseph's death. Perhaps she thought if they'd stayed on in New Zealand he wouldn't have died. Thomas had obviously got used to trying to comfort her by suggesting that nothing she could have done would have changed anything. He probably had to keep telling her over and over again - to help her regain some peace of mind. It's heart-breaking.'

'I can't see how living in New Zealand would have prevented Joseph having a fatal asthma attack. Unless Rose thought the air was cleaner over there. It sounds as if she was torturing herself for no reason,' Imogen adds.

'Sadly, that is the lot for many bereaved parents. They imagine if they had only acted differently, the child would still be with them.'

Imogen sighs heavily. 'Poor Rose. She lost her youngest son and then her other two boys went straight off to join the army. Her niece said she never got over it. I wonder if Thomas ever has either.'

Hugh suddenly sits forward. 'Do you remember when I went to check out the Langley Farm – the day I was running with Allan?'

Imogen nods.

'I peered through the living room window and everything was exactly as Thomas had left it. There were photographs on the mantelpiece. One of them was of two boys. At the time I believed it was Andy and Rob. I did think it was a little unusual, because the younger one was sitting on the older boy's lap and he seemed very small - like a toddler. There was certainly a larger age gap between those children than there should have been. The wee one must have been Joseph.'

'If Thomas has pictures of the boy out on display he's not making any attempt to hide the fact Joseph existed,' Imogen supplies.

'No, but he's mentioned nothing about him to the police or to his defence team.'

'And Rob and Andy haven't spoken of him either. Although I'm not sure there's any reason why they would.'

'Wait a minute,' Hugh declares, placing his glass down firmly on the table. 'When I asked Andy at dinner, if his father had ever suffered from asthma, he went as white as a sheet. I thought he was going to have a panic attack. He only just about managed to compose himself. That was when Andy mentioned how his mother had suffered from the condition as a child. He didn't utter a single word about what had happened to his younger brother. I think that is very odd.'

'Hmm, I agree. So is there a connection here to the Carlows, or is the death of Joseph Langley another issue entirely?' Imogen looks at her husband expectantly.

'At this precise moment, I really don't know. But I'm absolutely determined to find out.'

'Should we inform the police about the boy? Does it have any bearing on the case, do you think?'

Hugh considers this for a moment. 'Penny is still in Montpellier with her parents. A new date for the trial seems a long way off. I say we keep this to ourselves for the time being. We can do some more digging and see if we can discover why the Langleys have been keeping Joseph's existence a secret. There's no evidence at this stage to suggest it's a police matter.'

Imogen nods her agreement. She doesn't want to disclose what they've discovered just yet. Her plan is to wheedle some more information out of the Carlows. In order to do this she is determined to keep her cards very close to her chest.

Three young men sit comfortably around a roaring fire of sticks and kindling. They have worked hard to make this camp hospitable. The smooth logs which they use as benches were shifted here from locations deep within the forest. Their efforts certainly proved worthwhile. The boys have had numerous meetings and even the odd party in this sheltered hollow. It's a place their teachers and parents know nothing about. A few of the lads bring their girlfriends down here too. It must be a half-decent hideaway, as none of them has so far complained.

The tallest of the three men absent-mindedly kicks at a thick root protruding from the ground next to his feet. 'Are we absolutely clear about what needs to be done?' He demands.

The other two nod their heads.

'We'll meet by the gate to Limbourne Woods at midnight. There'll be a full moon, so we shouldn't need a flashlight. It will be dark in the woods themselves, but if you stick to the path and bear right, it will bring you straight out the other side.'

'Should we bring anything along with us?' asks the youngest of the group.

'Just a rucksack. Make sure it's dark in colour and doesn't have any identifiable markings. Wear the khaki gear I got for you and I'll paint your faces after we meet. Any problems getting out of the house unnoticed, text me and we'll go ahead without you.'

'Are you sure the barn will be open, Dan?' asks the other lad; the one with the long, shaggy hair. 'It seems unlikely he would store such valuable stuff in there without securing the doors.'

'Is that right, Daz? Well, I've been watching the place for months and I happen to know old Langley doesn't give a shit about his farm or what's in it. He barely ever goes out to the sheds at all. He can't wait to get shot of the old dump.'

Joshua Nash looks as if he might ask another question, but seems to think better of it.

'Now, whatever money we get for the sheeting will go towards funding our next expedition. I'm getting pretty sick and tired of Gilbert whining about government cuts. He should show a bit of initiative and make things happen for himself. But it's not really about the money. It's about you, Josh. If you can show me you've got the balls for an operation like this one then you're definitely in. I think it might even warrant a reward. I reckon that Corporal Nash has got a very good ring to it? What do you think?'

Joshua grins broadly. 'Thanks, Dan.'

'Until Saturday night I want you all to keep your traps shut. If Gutless Gilbert gets wind of this then it's all over, understood? No more Blackwater Boys. That goes for you, too, Dazza. Ever since you've been going out with that geek, Sarah Linwood, you've turned into a real boy scout. Toughen up mate, or you lose a stripe – simple as that, okay?'

'Sure, Dan,' the blond lad responds without enthusiasm. 'I get the message.'

'Great. Now push off home for now and don't either of you even consider bottling out of this - it's going to be an absolute blast.'

Chapter Forty One

The Christmas lights strung across Maldon High Street make the timber-framed buildings look almost Dickensian.

As the man from the Rotary Club flicks the giant switch, a muted cheer rises from the crowd. The Crofts have gathered to observe this ritual every year since they moved to Essex. Imogen suspects that even Bridie's interest is finally beginning to wane. Her daughter looks cold and bored. Then she spots a group of girls she knows from school and her expression immediately brightens.

'Can I go and talk to Claire, Mum? She asks.

'Of course. Meet me in front of Clarkewells in half an hour. Don't be late darling, because it's freezing.'

Hugh and Ian have already gone off to the camping shop to buy a new sleeping bag for the trip on Saturday. Imogen hadn't been totally convinced his old one would be warm enough. Hugh had inherited it from Kath and Gerry decades ago. It was about time they replaced it.

Imogen wanders up the High Road and glances into the shop windows as she passes. The seasonal displays in some of the more old-fashioned stores are very beautifully done; especially in the toy shop; where an intricately painted doll's house dominates the impressive frontage. It makes Imogen nostalgic for the Christmases they had when the children were little. She laments how the magic of those years has long since faded.

'Is that what you've asked Santa for?' A voice behind her enquires.

Imogen turns round. 'Hi, Caroline.' She chuckles good-naturedly and gestures towards the display.

'Something I always wanted as a child but never had. Pretty sad, eh?'

'I think it's probably better if these things remain a dream. If you'd actually been given the house, it would have been loved and played with for a while. As the years went by, it would simply have become neglected and ignored. That's far more depressing than never receiving one in the first place.' Caroline smiles kindly. 'So as you gaze at it now, the thrill is just the same as it was when you were a little girl.'

'An interesting way of looking at it,' Imogen replies.

'Have you got time for a quick drink?'

'Sure, but I need to meet Bridie in twenty minutes.'

They duck into a wine bar across the street from the toy shop. It is fairly empty this early in the evening, but a few people have obviously found their way inside after watching the switching on of the Christmas lights, creating a reasonably jolly atmosphere.

Once they are settled at a table by the window, Imogen says, 'did you happen to know Thomas Langley – before the shooting at the farm? He didn't get out much, but you grew up around here and his boys were a similar age to you.'

Caroline considers the question for a moment. 'No, I didn't. But then I went to school in Burnham, not Maldon. It was the closest town to my parents' house. I met Rick through the Sailing Club.'

Imogen ponders this for a moment. 'Has Rick ever talked to you about Langley? Did you ever get the sense that he and Steve already knew him – from before Danny was killed?'

'No. Rick had never uttered a word about the man, not before the burglary, that is. What is this all about, Imogen? Have you found out something?' Caroline fixes her friend with an enquiring look.

She pauses for a second and then responds. 'I believe Danny's death wasn't as random as we first thought. I think Langley already had a connection to Danny – he had a history with him prior to the break-in. There are certain facts about this case which up to now we've all missed.'

Caroline is silent. She maintains her composure for a while, and then crumples. Tears start to roll down her cheeks.

'Oh God, Caroline, I'm so sorry. I didn't want to upset you.' Imogen leans forward and embraces her.

Caroline glances up at her friend, mascara is smudging her eyes and she appears totally anguished. 'You know about it, don't you?' She entreats.

'What do you mean?' Imogen is genuinely confused.

Caroline lowers her voice to a whisper. 'Me and Danny.'

Imogen automatically recoils, almost knocking over a glass of wine with her elbow. She cannot disguise the look of revulsion which has formed on her face.

'I beg your pardon?'

'I nearly told you about it the other day at your house. I thought you'd worked it out already. I just couldn't bear to witness your disgust. Well, I've seen it now.'

'Hang on a minute.' Imogen gets out her phone and calls Hugh. She tells him to pick up Bridie from Clarkewells and then drive the kids home. She adds that he shouldn't worry; she'll get a cab back later.

During this time, Caroline has begun to pull herself together. She is dabbing at her eyes with a handkerchief and has taken a large gulp of white wine.

'Tell me what happened, Caroline. When did it start?'

'I'm not trying to make excuses, so please just hear me out. A couple of years ago, Rick and I were having real problems. He had completely clammed up and withdrawn from me. Rick's not the most talkative man at the best of times and this was even worse. I suggested we go for some counselling but he refused. Then, one of the work vans had broken down, and Rick asked me to get it sorted out. I called up Steve and he sent Danny round to look at it.' Caroline sighs. 'We chatted for a while and there was a kind of spark between us. I suppose we were both pretty lost at that point in our lives. Although, that doesn't really cover it – I loved him, Imogen, and he loved me.'

'Where did the two of you meet up? It must have been very difficult to keep it a secret.'

Caroline seems embarrassed by the question. 'Danny and his mates had created a sort of encampment out in Limbourne Woods. We used to meet there. We pitched a tent in the colder months. You are right, though. It was difficult to keep it a secret. Last summer, somebody saw us.'

'Mark Gilbert,' Imogen adds.

Caroline looks surprised.

'I saw you both arguing, that day we met for coffee, and Allan overheard your conversation at the school a few weeks ago.'

'Mark was angry because I had told you how he sometimes leaves The Blackwater Boys on their own for expeditions. Well, he certainly had done during Danny's time. He assures me it's not the case now.'

'Did Gilbert threaten to tell people about the affair?'

Caroline lets out a humourless laugh. 'Well, he certainly didn't dare while Danny was still alive. Mark Gilbert did whatever Danny told him. But after he was killed, I didn't feel quite so comfortable. I've been living in dread that Mark would inform Rick.'

'Were you still together at the time Danny was shot?' Imogen asks.

'No. We weren't complete fools. We both knew our relationship couldn't go on forever. The day Gilbert saw us, in the woods, was the last time we ever met up in secret. I told Dan that very afternoon it had to end. I had too much at stake to ever believe it could carry on.'

'Danny must have been very upset.'

'He was. But he also understood. I thought he had his whole life ahead of him to find someone else.' Caroline gulps down a sob.

'If it turns out the affair had something to do with Danny's death, I'm going to have to tell the police.'

Caroline nods her head slowly. 'It's funny, because since Nikki's accident I've felt much closer to Rick. I believe we can get our marriage back on track. If he finds out about me and Danny then I can't see that ever happening. Of course, I love my children too and would never want to hurt them. I was always running a terrible risk by having the affair. For Danny it wasn't the same. I truly think I was the only person Danny Carlow ever loved. So he had nothing to lose at all.'

'Does it count as incest?' Allan asks luridly, during the drive back from the airport.

'I don't think so. It's not exactly socially acceptable either,' his sister replies.

'Her poor husband. Imagine discovering your wife was up to something like that? It would kill you.' Allan whistles through his teeth.

'Well, he doesn't know about it yet, and hopefully he'll never have to. It's Nikki and Will I'm worried about. I'd hate it if they had to be told. That's what I can't understand right now. I can't comprehend how Caroline could have done it knowing if her children ever found out they would be utterly devastated.' Imogen keeps her eyes on the road ahead.

'It's easy for you to say, Im; with your happy marriage. I mean, no offence, but you don't really appreciate what it must be like for a woman who is living with a man who won't even give her the time of day. I'm not condoning the relationship, but I can see how it might happen. She'd given all of those years to her children and what was left in her life? Nothing but misery and loneliness.' Allan sighs, gazing out of the window as the featureless landscape rushes by.

'Okay, I take your point. But she couldn't have chosen a worse person to turn to for solace. Caroline still had to socialize with Wendy and Steve, whilst pretending everything was carrying on as normal. It must have been incredibly awkward.'

'Hmm, it wasn't any of their business though, really. Danny was an adult. Now Rick's a different matter entirely,' Allan says thoughtfully. 'Do you think it's possible he *did* know about the affair? I can't think of a better motive for murder than the discovery that your wife is sleeping with your nephew.'

'It certainly would provide him with one hell of a motive. But it wasn't Rick who killed Danny, it was Thomas Langley.'

Imogen is appreciating hearing Allan's opinion. He is providing her with a fresh perspective on things. When she told Hugh last night, he was completely appalled. He would not have been able to contemplate the situation from Caroline's point of view. Hugh could only think about Rick and the children. He had no sympathy for Imogen's friend whatsoever. Allan is better at understanding people's faults and shortcomings than her husband. Probably because he's made plenty of mistakes himself.

'How was your visit? Are Suz and the kids well?' Imogen asks, in a change of subject.

Allan's face brightens. 'They're great, thanks. I thought I might struggle with the long journey. On the whole, it was fine. When I caught sight of Suz; all these wonderful feelings just swept over me like a wave. It was so good to see her again.'

'Steady on, Al. You know how the illness can play tricks on you. It can make you feel emotions which actually belong to a past experience. You don't want to mistake them for the real thing. Suz is happily settled with Owen these days.'

'I'm aware of that, Imogen. Don't deny a chap a lovely sensation, will you? I simply enjoyed seeing the mother of my children, that's all.'

'Good, I'm glad.' Imogen does not ask if the trip has helped Allan to make a decision about Abigail. She isn't even sure if that was the reason why he went. Instead, she concentrates on the route back to Cooper's End, trying to ignore the steel grey storm clouds which are gathering with ever increasing pace far above them;

making the inside of the car seem, all of a sudden, depressingly dark and gloomy.

Ian's bag is bulging full of gear. He has his new sleeping bag rolled up and attached with Velcro to the side. The whole family have been rushing about the house, helping him to collect everything on his extensive tick list. Ian is in charge of the first aid box and there was a brief period of mild panic when no one could locate the antiseptic wipes. It is nearly nine o'clock and all the jobs now seem to be done.

The torrential rain which battered the coastline for most of yesterday appears to have passed over. The sun is even making an attempt to break through the cloud. The heavens opened as soon as Imogen and Allan arrived back in Cooper's Creek the previous afternoon and didn't let up until the early hours of this morning.

Hugh is going to drive his son over to the starting point of their expedition in Maylandsea. He is then planning to spend a few hours at the university, catching up on some of the work he has missed in recent weeks.

'Are you ready, Ian? We don't want to hold the others up!' Hugh calls out, whilst he collects together his briefcase and papers.

'Just coming!' Ian hollers back.

Imogen makes sure her middle child has his waterproof jacket and trousers. She double checks the plastic container with his syringes and insulin bottle inside. As Ian finally strides confidently into the hall to collect his luggage, she pulls him into an embrace.

'Take care, sweetheart, and make sure you take your medication. Don't forget in all the excitement. The rain will be coming on again by evening, so get your tent up as soon as you arrive on St Peter's. Oh, and have a lovely time.'

Ian hugs her tightly. 'I won't forget, I promise. I'll give you a buzz when I arrive.'

'Come on,' Hugh urges, 'let's get this stuff into the car. I'll be back in time for dinner, darling. Bye!'

Bridie and Imogen stand at the living room window to watch them depart. Waving madly as the car slowly disappears along the stony track. Imogen is suddenly reminded of the famous recruitment poster from World War One, in which the mother and daughter proudly cheer their menfolk off to war from the bay window of an impressive country house. The comparison makes her feel silly and a little melodramatic. Ian is only going away for one night.

When Imogen finds herself alone, she goes into Hugh's study. She takes out a sheet of blank paper and writes the name Joseph Langley in the centre of it. Underneath, she adds the dates of his birth and death. Joe was sixteen years old when he died from the asthma attack. He was only a couple of months away from his seventeenth birthday. The Langley family had bought the farm in the autumn of the previous year. Andy and Rob had left the education system by this time, but presumably Joe must have still been in Year 11 when they moved to the area.

Imogen writes *school* and then a question mark on the paper. The Langley Farm is definitely in the catchment area for the Beeleigh School, she thinks. Imogen considers the boy's age. Joseph would have been about four years older than her if he had lived, making him a similar age to Steve Carlow. Was that the connection? Did Joseph attend secondary school with Steve and Rick for a brief period during that year? Imogen wonders if they remember him. She writes their names on the page too.

Joseph would also have been the same age as Hugh. But Kath and Gerry had sent their son to a private school over twenty miles away from Maldon; he never even attended his local primary. Imogen doubts if her husband would have ever come into contact with the boy. She cannot think of any retired members of staff that she knows who would be old enough to have been teaching back then. It's just too long ago.

Thomas Langley is still in no condition to answer questions. Although he might very well be the only person who can provide the information she needs. Then Imogen glances back at Hugh's pack of notes. She pulls out the section on Langley's sons. Her husband told her yesterday that Rob has gone back to Afghanistan. They have not yet made a decision about Thomas's plea. She looks at Andy's address. On a whim she takes the sheet out into the hall with her and dials the phone number.

Imogen can hear the unmistakeably lengthy trill of the French dialling tone, filling a distant room somewhere. It goes on for so long she imagines there cannot possibly be anyone at home. The trilling abruptly stops and an English voice says, 'hello?'

'Mr Langley?' Imogen ventures.

'Yes.'

'My name is Imogen, I'm Hugh Croft's wife.'

'Oh, hello there,' Andy replies warily. 'How may I help you?'

'I'm assisting my husband with his research, Mr Langley. Something has come up that we need to ask you about.'

There is silence on the other end of the line.

'Mr Langley, I'd like you to tell me about Joseph.'

Chapter Forty Three

The silence continues for a worrying length of time.

Finally, Imogen receives a reply.

'He died so long ago. Is it really necessary to bring it all up again now?'

'Another boy is dead. We need to know everything, Andy.'

'How did you find out about Joe? Did my dad tell you?'

'No, your aunt mentioned his name when I spoke to her.'

Andy seems to hesitate again. 'Joe was different. He wasn't like me or Rob. I suppose the word you'd use these days is 'bookish'. If he'd lived, he wouldn't have joined the army like us. It was History that Joe was into, if I remember rightly. He was always Mum's child and Rob and I were Dad's – if that makes any sense to you?'

'It does.'

'It didn't mean Dad didn't love him. But he always wanted him to be someone else. He tried to toughen Joe up the whole time - making him join this and that club. Joe always lost interest in the end, because it was never his kind of thing. There was lots of stuff Joe couldn't do because of his asthma, although Dad was funny about that too.'

'In what way?'

'Well, Dad saw it as a weakness. He didn't really like people knowing about it. I think he had an image in his mind; of the plump kid trailing along behind all the rest, clutching his inhaler. Dad didn't want Joe to be seen in that way.'

'What about Joe? How did he want to be viewed by other people?'

Andy is thrown by the question. 'I'm not sure. He wasn't bothered about having a tough guy image, but he wanted Dad to be proud of him.'

'How exactly did Joe die?'

'You'd have to ask Dad about that, Mrs Croft. I wasn't there when it happened.'

'You surely must have spoken about it as a family?'

'Not really. My parents never wished to have it mentioned. They were devastated.' He pauses for a second. 'If you don't mind me saying, Mrs Croft, I thought you were ringing for a totally different reason.'

'Oh yes?' She is immediately intrigued.

'I may have settled out here in France, but I've not entirely adopted the lifestyle. I thought you were calling to ask me about your husband.'

'Ah,' she responds, suddenly realising what Andy is driving at. 'You suspected I was going to ask if my husband had another woman with him when he came to visit you.'

'Yes. So you know about it then?' He sounds surprised.

'I do. They are just work colleagues.'

'Okay. Well, as long as you are aware. I had a girlfriend who cheated on me once. I forgave her in the end, but I never forgave those bastards who knew all about it and never told me. *They* were simply taking the piss.'

The rain starts again about mid-afternoon. Imogen hopes that The Blackwater Boys managed to get their tents up in time. She knows from her own experience of student back-packing, how there is nothing worse than climbing into a soggy sleeping bag. Hugh called earlier to say he would be dropping in on his parents on the way home. He said to go ahead with dinner and not wait for him. Imogen is preparing a meal just for herself, Allan and Bridie. Knowing that Kath would never send her son away unfed.

Imogen pulls down the newly fitted blind at the kitchen window. She hadn't worried about it before, but now that darkness has fallen, the sight of the wind battering the trees out in the woods is making her feel uneasy.

'The boys arrived okay, did they?' Allan asks, as he strolls into the room and takes a couple of glasses out of the cupboard.

'Yes. They got to St Peter's by lunchtime. I just hope they've got decent shelter out there. Look at the weather, Allan.' Imogen pops up the blind a little and points towards the torrent of rain gushing down the glass.

'If they've got the tents up, they should be fine,' Allan gives his sister's shoulder a squeeze. 'The worst case scenario is that they'll get a bit wet.'

Allan opens a bottle of red wine to have with dinner. It seems quiet with only the three of them at home. Bridie says she is tired and after watching a little T.V with her mother, she disappears off to bed. It is getting late, but Imogen is finding it difficult to settle to any task. Allan is reading a novel, seated comfortably by the wood burner. Although he is increasingly finding that his sister's fidgety movements are distracting him.

'What on earth is the matter?' He asks impatiently.

'I don't know. I just feel as if time has suddenly slowed down - like we are waiting for something terrible to happen. Where the *hell* is Hugh?'

'Call him if you want; he's only up the road.'

They hear the sound of wheels pulling onto the grave drive outside.

'There he is,' Imogen announces with considerable relief. 'I hope he's bloody well eaten at his parents' place. I'm not going to start cooking again at this hour.'

But the familiar clink of Hugh's key turning in the lock is not the noise which follows. Instead, the bell starts ringing repeatedly and a fist simultaneously hammers on the wooden panel of the porch.

Allan jumps up. 'I'll go, you stay here.'

As he opens the front door, Imogen is amazed to see a wet and windswept Penny Mills, standing on the step, looking like she has just run a marathon.

'What do *you* want?' Allan enquires rather rudely.

'May I come in?' She asks, between panting breaths.

'Of course,' Imogen says, leading the bedraggled woman through to the warmth of the living room.

Penny removes her sodden jacket and straightens her damp hair. Imogen has never seen her looking so unkempt.

'We haven't got long and I need you to listen to me carefully,' the woman says.

'Why exactly should we do that?' Allan demands. 'When for the past few months all you've been trying to do is steal Hugh away from his wife.'

'I can understand why you don't trust me. But I need you to hear me out, Imogen, because your son's life may very well depend on it.'

Chapter Forty Four

Imogen gestures towards the sofa and they all take a seat. She says nothing at all, simply allowing Penny to continue.

'After I left Hugh in Carcassonne,' she begins.

Allan lets out a grunt.

'I went to visit my parents in Montpellier. I have been very busy at work and haven't seen them in a while. I was feeling guilty about what happened with Hugh, and was cross with myself for not concentrating more on the Langley case. So I decided to interview my parents to see if they remembered anything about Thomas Langley and his family. They lived at Limbourne Green while we were growing up, you see - not that far from the Langleys' property. This was before they moved to Coggeshall in the mid-eighties. I thought they might recall something useful.'

'Did you go to school in Maldon then? Had you known any of the Langley children?' Imogen asks impatiently, knowing they don't have much time.

'No, I didn't. I was at primary school with Steve Carlow, but my parents moved me to Stane Hall when I was of secondary school age,' Penny explains.

'The Langley boys arrived in Maldon a few years after that. So your parents were still in the area in the early eighties?' Imogen presses.

'Yes, because my older brother stayed on at Beeleigh. He enjoyed his schooling there. Alex was always more sporty than academic. He was captain of the football team. Anyway, my parents knew the name Thomas Langley straight away. They hadn't seen any of the coverage of the shooting on television and I'm afraid

I hadn't spoken with them about it sooner. I certainly should have done.'

'What did they remember, Penny?' Imogen demands.

'They recollected the death of the Langleys' son. Rose and Thomas had *another* child, Imogen. A *younger* son.'

'I know this already, Penny. His name was Joseph and he died of an asthma attack in 1981. What has this got to do with Ian?'

'Asthma was the *cause of death* identified in his post-mortem, but it wasn't *how* he actually died.' Penny pauses for breath. 'My mum said the poor boy was literally *frightened* to death. He was sealed up in a hole overnight and the sheer horror of it brought on an asthma attack which killed him.'

'How do your parents know this? There's no record of it anywhere,' Imogen blurts out desperately, with a growing sense of dread.

'Because Alex told them. My brother had said the rumours were flying around the school. There was this group you see, called The Blackwater Boys - or something like that. They went sailing and camping and stuff. This club was run by the worst kids in the school. The most vicious of all the bullies. He said Joseph Langley had joined Beeleigh in the middle of the fifth year and was given a terribly hard time by the other kids. Then, for reasons which seemed inexplicable, he suddenly joined The Blackwater Boys and was hanging around with all the hard cases. He said that 'little Joe' had developed a bit of a swagger, was looking as if he finally fitted in with the rest. It came at a price. The Blackwater Boys operated a system whereby the leaders handed out assignments – like having to perform lots of dares to prove you were tough enough to be a member. These dares would culminate in a kind of final initiation. This would take place during a member's first ever expedition.'

Imogen is staring at Penny in horror.

'Joe's first trip was to somewhere called, St Peter's Island. Everything they did back then had to be linked to the water, Alex said. They'd sailed out there and were planning to camp. As soon as my parents mentioned the name of the place, I remembered Hugh had talked about your son going to that very same island. I was pretty sure he'd referred to the 'Blackwater Boys' too. I knew I had to tell you face to face because you might not believe me otherwise. Imogen, I think Ian could be in real danger.'

Imogen is on her feet. She is grabbing a sweater and madly opening cupboards to find her wellie boots.

'Penny, can you call the police? I don't know what you're going to say to them, but make it convincing. Allan and I will sail over to the island. Can you stay here with Bridie? Hugh should be home soon. Tell him to wait at the house. He's not fit enough to follow us. Penny, I'm relying on you to persuade the police to send a boat out there - just in case Allan and I don't make it in time.'

Penny puts a hand up to her mouth, but nods with understanding.

Allan is already in his sailing gear. He tosses the car keys to his sister and they disappear into the night.

Chapter Forty Five

'I hope you aren't expecting us to sail to St Peter's in your little Skipper?' Allan says warily.

'I've got the keys to the shed at the club. We can take one of the boats with an outboard engine. It will need to have some lights too. The rain seems to be easing off a bit, but I'm worried about that wind.' Imogen is putting her foot down along the narrow lanes which lead to the sailing club at Maylandsea.

'Let's hope it's behind us. I didn't bother to look at the forecast today.' Allan checks his phone to make sure it is charged. 'There's still no reply from Ian. What do you think we're going to find when we get to the island?'

'I'm trying not to think about that, Allan. I just have to focus on getting there as quickly as possible.'

Allan doesn't reply. But in his head, he is trying to work out some kind of plan.

When they arrive at the club, the entire building is in darkness. Imogen strides towards a large shed at the top of one of the steep concrete jetties. She unlocks the doors and Allan switches on his flashlight. They don't waste time in making a decision. The first boat they encounter with a motor and lights is the one they start to bring out of its covering. They shift it onto a trailer and wheel it down to the water's edge.

The tide is very high. Imogen climbs into the boat. Just before he pushes them off, Allan runs back up to the shed and comes back with a pair of wooden oars.

'I hope we won't need to row, Allan!' Imogen shouts above the noise of the wind and rain.

'Just in case,' he calls back, before shoving the vessel into the waves and jumping aboard.

As soon as they are clear of the jetty, Allan starts up the engine. Initially, the wind is propelling them forward and they make good time powering along Lawling Creek towards Mundon Stone Point. The cloud cover is dense and beyond the steady beam produced by the light on the vessel's bow, Imogen can see almost nothing that lies ahead.

Once they have passed the Stone Point, the wind begins to batter them from the north-west. They are motoring directly into the waves and this means the boat is rising and falling at regular intervals. Each time they encounter a larger swell the boat drops violently into the water and Allan worries the engine may cut out.

Finally, they reach the shelter provided by Osea Island to the west of them and Ramsey Island to the east. From here they can follow a direct line towards St Peter's. The rain has come on heavily again and the wind is blowing river spray into their faces. Imogen has lost the feeling in her hands and feet with the terrible cold. She tries to flex them to get the blood flowing once again. She turns around and glances at Allan who is facing dead ahead, keeping a firm hold on the rudder, with a look of pure determination in his eyes.

Now they are getting closer, the lack of visibility is a real problem. They need to maintain a bearing north-north-east to navigate through Goldhanger Creek and reach the landing stage on St Peter's. At this juncture they are struggling to even make out where the island is amongst the sea of blackness. Imogen scans the horizon. After several minutes she spots a distant flickering of light. Imogen gestures to Allan and points towards the faint glow.

He nods his head and then calls over to his sister. 'I'm going to use that marker to lead me around the island to the jetty. I think we need to kill our lights. I can't see any sign of the police launch so we're on our own. We're going to need to surprise them, Imogen; because you and I are totally outnumbered.'

'Okay,' she replies, switching off their guiding beam, immediately plunging the small vessel into pitch darkness.

Imogen takes several deep breaths, trying to keep focussed on the illuminations provided by the string of houses she can just about make out, running along the far shore at Goldhanger. This, along with the indistinct glimmer of the encampment on St Peter's, should hopefully keep them on course.

Allan glides the boat round on a sharp easterly bearing, until Imogen is sure they must be parallel to the Gore Saltings. Then he cuts the outboard engine. Shifting himself to the centre of the boat he grabs the two oars he had brought along with them at the very last moment.

'I'm going to row us into shore. Can you guide me in? I don't want them to hear us approach.'

'Sure,' Imogen replies, manoeuvring down low at the bow so she can get a good view of the route ahead.

As their vessel drifts in closer, Imogen spots Rick's large yacht moored up against the landing stage. She pats her brother on the left arm to indicate he should take them in this direction. With some careful steering, they get the boat near enough to the tiny shingle beach for Imogen to step out into the water and drag the boat up the bank. Allan climbs out to assist her and they tie the vessel up to one of the rotten wooden supports under the old jetty. Allan reaches back into the hull and takes out the flashlight which he hands to his sister and then one of the oars, which he rests over his shoulder.

'What's that for?' Imogen whispers.

'Self-defence,' Allan replies.

They duck into the undergrowth at the top of the beach and survey the landscape. Allan glances at his watch. It is 2am.

'Their encampment is on the other side of the island, I think. It must be next to the ruined chapel.' Imogen declares, 'if the boys have to spend the night in some kind of 'hole' under the ground, then Ian could be *anywhere* around here.' There is desperation in her voice and it sounds as if she is about to cry.

'Wait, it's not that easy to dig a hole in the ground big enough for a grown person to fit inside, let alone seal it up. They must be using a room – like a cellar or something similar. The structure must already be in place.'

'The stone pill-box,' Imogen gasps. 'Remember when we were here before? We nearly went inside to shelter from the wind but it gave me the creeps and I couldn't bring myself to go down there. The steps seemed to descend pretty deep because I couldn't make out what was at the bottom.'

'Let's head in that direction, then. Keep yourself low, Imogen, and don't put on the flashlight just yet. We're going to have to pass quite close to the camp, so quietly does it, okay? No speaking from now on, understood?'

Imogen nods steadily, although her heart is pumping away inside her chest.

Allan goes first. He stalks across the overgrown field which lies between them and the chapel. The pill-box itself is a few hundred yards beyond. As they get nearer, Imogen can see several tents, set out in a circular formation around the remains of a camp fire. There doesn't appear to be any sign of life. A few portable lamps have been dotted about to create a sort of pathway.

They stealthily circumnavigate the boys' camp, heading towards the chapel and aiming for the coastal trail which will lead them to the concrete bunker. Imogen has to concentrate very hard to stop herself from breaking into a run. She suddenly finds her vision is blurring. When she puts a hand up to her face she discovers that tears are streaming down her cheeks.

They pass the crumbling remains of the old chapel, starting to jog when the pill-box comes into sight. Allan stops dead when they reach the steps that lead inside. He turns towards his sister and takes the torch, leaning the oar against the wall of the concrete structure.

Allan points the flashlight into the darkness and begins to descend. Imogen follows on close behind. After only a few metres, Allan finds that his wellie boots are splashing into wetness. He directs the beam at his feet and realises the whole of the ground floor of the pill-box is flooded with a shallow pool of rain-water. The entire cavity is roughly eight foot square. Allan and Imogen wade through the muddy liquid, urgently searching for any indication of an underground room. Imogen nearly pitches over when she kicks her boot hard against a large stone.

Without saying a word to one another, they kneel down. With all their strength they manoeuvre the rock to the foot of the steps.

'There's a catch here!' Allan exclaims when he examines the floor underneath.

He puts both hands through the rusty metal ring and hoists it upwards, the force of the water on top making it incredibly hard to shift. It appears to be a kind of metal hatch. As soon as it begins to rise, Imogen slips her fingers inside and helps Allan to force it back.

When the hatch is finally up, the rain water which has gathered at the base of the pill-box starts to cascade into the opening, splashing onto the ground below with an eerie echo. This is when they hear a noise from within. It sounds like the terrified whimper of a brutalised animal.

'Oh, Dear God!' Imogen mutters under her breath. She quickly shifts herself so that her feet are dangling over the edge of the hole.

'Careful, Im. We don't know how deep it is,' Allan calls over.

'I don't give a shit about that,' she replies, suddenly kicking her legs out and allowing her body to drop silently into the void.

Chapter Forty Six

'**I**'m in!' Imogen shouts to her brother.

'I'll throw down the flashlight, get ready to catch it!' He hollers back.

The heavy object plummets through the air, nearly hitting her on the head before she manages to get a proper grip on it. She didn't fall very far, not more than about four or five feet. So the space she is now occupying is fairly small. Imogen switches on the torch and sweeps it around the subterranean room.

The shaft of light rests upon a bundle of what looks like jumbled up sleeping bags and pillows, shoved right up into one corner.

'Are we finished now?' A voice suddenly asks; drenched in fear but shot through with a pitiful trace of hope. 'I knew you weren't *actually* going to leave us here all night.'

'Ian?'

The bundle immediately starts to move and two figures fight themselves free of the mass of damp bed-clothes. One of the shapes propels itself towards her, almost knocking Imogen over backwards with the strength of its embrace.

'Mum?!' Ian cries, 'is it really you?'

'Of course, sweetheart. Is that Will over there?'

'Yes, Mrs Croft,' comes a timid reply.

'We need to get you two out of this place.'

'There's a box over there by the wall,' Ian says. We used it earlier to see if we could get the hatch open.'

They drag it across so that it lies directly beneath the opening. Imogen climbs onto it.

'Allan?' she hisses into the darkness.

There is no response.

Ian gives his mother a leg-up and Imogen slowly raises herself onto the cold, wet floor above. There is no sign of Allan. She leans back into the hole and offers a hand to Ian and Will who quickly clamber out. When they are all safely positioned on the lower level of the old bunker, Imogen turns towards the boys and puts a finger up to her lips. She walks to the bottom of the concrete steps and listens closely.

Imogen can just make out the faint sound of voices coming from above ground. One of the boys at the camp must have heard them and woken up, she concludes.

Imogen twists around and whispers, 'something's going on up there. You two stay here; I'm going to take a look.'

'We're hardly gonna let you go alone, Mum.' Ian is utterly incredulous.

'Okay. But stay behind me, both of you,' she commands. Feeling there is no time to argue.

Imogen leads them cautiously up the uneven stairs to the surface. She keeps the flashlight switched off, but held firmly in her right hand. When they get back onto ground level, they keep low and duck behind the grassy mound which lies between them and the camp. Imogen edges her way around the little hill, keeping her body pressed tightly into the undergrowth.

When she has reached the half-way point, she sees a group of people up ahead. They are dimly illuminated by the lights of the encampment. Imogen can make out Allan; standing tall and seemingly barring the progress of two other men. He is clasping the long wooden sailing oar in his hands like a weapon.

She sidles forward a little further. From this position she can discern their voices more clearly. The boys in front of Allan appear to be having an argument.

'Christ, Matt. Just let them go!'

'This is an invasion of the camp, Daz. We've got to defend ourselves.'

'The game's up, man. It's time to let Ian and Will out, anyway. They've been in that place long enough as it is.'

'What's happened to you, Dazza?' Matt Carlow spits, turning his head towards Darren for a split second, 'you're as soft as Gutless Gilbert.'

In this moment Allan strikes. He sweeps the oar hard across Matt's legs, sending him sprawling to the ground. Imogen bolts towards them. Allan quickly squats down over Matt Carlow and holds the wooden oar firmly across his body.

As Imogen reaches him, her brother looks up and says, 'have you got the lads?'

'Yes.'

'Then take them back with you on the boat. I'll stay and deal with this lot.'

'I'm not just going to leave you here, Allan.'

During all this commotion, the remainder of the camp has begun to stir. A few of the boys are emerging from their tents in brightly patterned pyjamas, rubbing at their eyes and gazing about them in tired confusion.

Darren Beck steps forward, 'Mrs Croft?'

'Yes, Darren?'

'Are Will and Ian okay?'

'As well as can be expected.' Imogen feels the full strength of her suppressed anger start to bubble up.

'I'm sorry. I had no idea Matt had something like this planned. None of the other lads know anything about it.'

'You still helped him to put the boys down there,' she retorts in disgust.

'Yes, but they went willingly, Mrs Croft. We've all had to do something similar to get our commissions, you know? I wouldn't have let them stay in there all night. I was just about to go and get them out myself when you got here.'

Imogen has to take very deep breaths in order to control her rage. 'Where is Mr Gilbert, Darren? Does he have any part in this?'

'He helped us set up camp then I took him back to the mainland. His girlfriend doesn't like him to stay away overnight.'

Imogen isn't sure if it's delayed shock or simply the effects of the bitter cold and exhaustion, but she begins to laugh. A loud, hysterical laugh which makes Darren look firstly startled and then frightened.

Allan has manoeuvred the now passive Matt Carlow into a sitting position and is securing his hands behind his back with a piece of rope.

'We're going to take Rick's boat and sail home, Darren,' Imogen almost snarls at the boy. 'I suggest you call the police to come and pick up your friend. If anyone else in the camp wants to come back with us, tell them to be at the jetty in five minutes. Any later than that and we will be gone.'

Chapter Forty Seven

Caroline Carlow is sitting on the end of the Croft's sofa. Her expression is pained and Imogen can tell she is terrified her sordid secret is about to be revealed. This is the least of Imogen's worries at the present moment.

Having given up hope of getting any sleep herself, she hustled Allan off to bed about half an hour ago. He was buzzing with adrenaline on the sail back from St Peter's Island. But when they arrived home she could see his hands were badly shaking. Imogen knows her brother will have set back his recovery by helping her tonight. Hopefully, the damage won't be permanent. She will certainly never forget what he did for Ian and Will.

Rick is slumped in one of the armchairs. He has barely spoken a word since they delivered his cold and miserable son back home to him. Hugh is in the kitchen making coffees. As he comes into the room with the tray, Penny Mills emerges from the guest bedroom, wrapped in a full length towelling robe.

'May I join you?' she asks tentatively. 'I can't get a wink of sleep.'

'Actually, that's a good idea,' Imogen says. 'I think you should probably hear this.'

She turns towards Will's father, who looks as if he is trying to shrink himself into the fabric of the seat. 'Did you know this was going to happen, Rick?'

Caroline appears genuinely surprised. 'What does Imogen mean?' She asks, shooting an accusatory glance at her husband.

He clears his throat and fiddles with the buttons on his shirt. 'I wasn't sure.'

Caroline gasps.

'If Danny was still in charge I would never have let Will go. I believed Matt was different. As soon as I knew they were going to St Peter's it brought all those awful memories back to me again, but I thought that was just my problem. I didn't think they were still doing it now. Well, as I say, I couldn't be sure.'

Hugh offers the man a drink adding, 'can you start from the very beginning, Rick? When did you first join The Blackwater Boys?'

'I was one of the youngest members. Steve got me into it. I was only about 12 or 13 when I started hanging about with them. I just ran errands for the boys in the early days and helped build the camps out in the woods. It was good fun at first. Times were different then and we had a lot more freedom. My parents were happy for us to go off all day and never asked where we'd been or what we were up to. Of course, Steve and I loved the water. Anything to do with boats we were dead keen to get involved with. The Blackwater Boys was perfect for us.'

'Was the group properly organised back then? Was it run by a teacher at the school?' Imogen enquires.

Rick considers this for a moment. 'There was a P.E teacher who came along with us every so often. Although I wouldn't say he was in charge. I can't even recall his name. He used to sit in the camp and smoke with us, I remember that much – things have changed a bit now, eh?

Imogen thinks that perhaps they haven't.

'The real leaders were the boys. In those days they were absolute tough nuts. A lad called Nick was the guy they all answered to. Each one of these kids had spent a few years in borstal. None of them had proper homes to go to. They were the ones who introduced the 'assignments'. Nick and Steve would take turns in coming up with an idea. My first task was to steal a pound of sweets from the newsagent at the end of the High Street. The owner chased me about half a mile down the road. I very nearly didn't get away from him. He was a better runner than I'd expected. He'd looked pretty old to me.'

'Why on earth did you do something like that, Rick?' Caroline asks in disbelief.

'Because if you were a member of The Blackwater Boys, you'd made it. You could strut around the school and no one would dare utter a word against you. It was like having immunity from the bullies for life. Imagine how that would feel to a young boy starting out in secondary school? It was hard to resist.' Rick keeps his eyes down, avoiding his wife's gaze.

'Tell us about Joseph Langley,' Imogen says softly.

'He joined Beeleigh half way through the fifth year. That's year 11 these days. It's probably the worst possible time to join a new school. The hormones are flying about and everyone's already got themselves a group to hide amongst. For a newbie, you're like a walking target. Joseph didn't help himself either, he was very thin and a bit *effeminate*, you know? It's all the rage to be that way now, but it wasn't back then. My God, it wasn't. He got terrible stick for a few months. Then Nick and Steve set their sights on him. I'm really not sure why. They invited him to join The Blackwater Boys. By this stage we'd become quite well structured - with the expeditions and everything. The initiations had also started. For mine, I had to sleep out in the open in January. All I had was a sleeping bag. One of those old fashioned ones that's like two scraps of material sewn together. I caught flu and had to take a week off school.'

'Had anyone gone down the 'hole' before?' Imogen says, shuddering at the thought.

'No, that ordeal was dreamt up purely for Joseph. We decided to sail to St Peter's for our summer expedition. We chose the island because we wanted to camp out in the wild and loved messing about on the river. After we arrived, Nick disappeared for a while and when he came back he had a weird look on his face. He'd found the hatch at the bottom of the pill-box and he said he'd got an idea for Joseph's initiation.' Rick stops here and gazes around the room, making sure he catches everyone's eye. 'I swear we did not know the boy had asthma. He had never told us and the school didn't say a word.'

'Fine,' Imogen cuts-in impatiently, 'just tell us what happened.'

'It was a glorious day. The sun was beating down. I'm sorry to admit, we all had a wonderful time. We swam in the sea and played football. Then, as it got dark, we sat around the camp fire and we drank and told stories. It was one of those evenings when the atmosphere is very close, you know? There was almost no breeze whatsoever. It couldn't have been more different than what it's like out there tonight. About midnight, Nick announced it was time for Joe's test.' Rick's face begins to lose its rigidity. His mouth and chin are wobbling uncontrollably. 'He just took him off. The boy didn't know what was going on. His expression was simply one of confusion.'

'Why didn't you stop him?' Caroline says, in almost a whisper.

'I was nothing, Caroline. The lowest of the low. Steve's spotty little brother who fetched the beers out of the cool bag. I'm not making excuses for myself, but I know full well there wasn't anything I could have done to prevent it.'

'What role did Steve play in all of this?' Penny puts in.

Rick sighs heavily. 'He helped Nick to seal up the hatch. I think the plan was to go back and get him a few hours later. But when we'd had a couple more drinks we all fell asleep and the next thing I knew it was dawn. It was pretty cold by then and I had to pull on some more layers. When I climbed out of my tent, it was the first time I'd ever seen Nick look rattled. He said Steve was still asleep and I was going to have to help him get the hatch opened.'

Rick pauses here and nobody in the room attempts to hurry him.

'We couldn't see Joseph at first. It was so quiet that I thought there must have been another way out and he'd escaped. Then Nick shifted round and the light fell on his body. He was curled up into a ball and his eyes were open. Neither of us said a word but we both knew he was dead. It wasn't what Nick had planned. It was a terrible accident.'

'What did you do next?' Hugh asks.

'We brought him up top and laid a blanket over him. There were no mobile phones in those days. We packed up camp and headed back. There wasn't any great plan to it, but we decided we'd say he'd collapsed and wasn't able to breathe – like he had heat stroke or something. It was obvious from his, err - posture, that Joseph had died fighting to catch his breath.'

This is clearly the last straw for Caroline, who rushes off to the bathroom. Imogen hears her retching into the toilet bowl.

'We left him there, on St Peter's. As soon as we got to the mainland we called the police. They went out and picked up the body. There was an inquest and they decided it was 'death by misadventure', or words to that effect. My father made us go along, he said it was the least we could do. What really stuck with me was how the Coroner laid into old Langley. He gave him a hard time for not informing his friends and the school about Joseph's asthma. He pretty much blamed him for the boy's death. Which made Steve and I feel bad, I can tell you.'

'How did people find out what really happened?' Imogen's mind is ticking away fast.

'There were about ten of us on the island that night so we were never going to be able to keep it quiet. Gradually, the story got out. It became more like a myth than anything else, but soon it was all over town. My parents asked us a hundred times or more if it was true. Every time they did we swore blind it wasn't. I believe they both went to their graves knowing in their hearts we'd been lying to them.'

'What happened to Nick?' Hugh enquires.

'He died of a brain haemorrhage in prison about fifteen years ago. Someone struck him on the head with a pool cue. It couldn't have happened to a nicer guy.' Despite the attempt at sarcasm, Rick's expression remains blank.

'Did Langley know about the 'hole'?' Penny sits forward in her seat.

'He must have heard the rumours. But he never took it any further. For a long time I think he was too busy caring for his wife. She took Joseph's death very badly, I heard.' Rick peers down at his stone cold coffee. He hasn't even tasted a drop.

Caroline has come back from the bathroom. She is standing very still, just inside the doorway.

'When we get back to the house, Rick, I want you to pack your bags and leave. You can say goodbye to the kids. After that, I never want to set eyes on you again.'

The man makes no effort to object. He doesn't even glance in his wife's direction. He simply nods his head and, as if he has the weight of the world bearing down upon his shoulders, he slowly rises out of the chair.

Chapter Forty Eight

The moon is so bright you can see all of the contours on its surface. There is such a perfect stillness to the air. It is something Andy knows he would never experience back at home. It's one of the reasons he wanted to stay in this part of France. He hears Carlotta open the door that leads from the garden terrace into their little kitchen.

'What are you doing outside in the dark?' She calls to him.

'It isn't dark. I can see perfectly well in the moonlight.'

She pulls her shawl more tightly around her and steps towards him, resting her head against his broad shoulders.

'I shouldn't have gone back to see him, Lotta,' he murmurs quietly. 'We were happy.'

'You can't run away from the past. There wasn't anything else you could have done. I'll wait for you, Andy.'

He looks up at the sky once again, but the vision before him has blurred. The view is spoilt. He breathes in deeply and allows the shuddering tears to fall, knowing this peaceful life is gone forever and that it's entirely his own fault.

*

'Who could have guessed that Rick had actually done something worse than Caroline? I can't get my head around the idea she's now occupying the moral high ground.' Allan carefully selects another croissant, whilst he considers this remarkable turn of events.

'I wouldn't say she's come up smelling of roses either,' Hugh adds.

'I don't know how you've got the appetite, Allan. I'm absolutely shattered and I feel like hell.' Imogen sits impassively in front of a steaming mug of black coffee.

The phone in the hall starts to ring. Hugh goes to answer it.

He comes back into the kitchen a few minutes later. 'Allan. It's the police. They want to talk to you.'

When he has left the room, Hugh steps towards his wife and wraps his arms around her. 'I'm sorry I wasn't here for you guys last night. What you and Allan did was truly incredible.'

'We didn't have much of a choice under the circumstances; I couldn't have left Ian at the mercy of those people. By the way, why did the police patrol boat never arrive?'

'Penny wasn't able to persuade them there was anything wrong. A rumour about something which might have happened 33 years ago didn't seem compelling enough to risk sending their men out in that awful weather. She did try her best.'

'I can see why they were sceptical. I suppose it's our own fault anyway. We should never have let Ian go with them. My instincts told me something was wrong about that club. I'm kicking myself that I gave in to outside pressure.' Imogen finally takes a sip of the bitter liquid.

'There was no stopping Ian, darling. Let's face it – the boy's learnt one heck of a lesson.' Hugh smiles wryly.

'I'm not ready to see the funny side of this just yet. Not after what we heard last night.'

'Penny's brother lives in the Midlands these days. It would be interesting to find out exactly what he remembers from back then. My parents didn't move to Maldon until '83 so I don't suppose they can tell us anything. We had a house just outside Colchester before that.'

Allan comes striding back in. He picks up the *cafétiere* and pours himself a fresh cup before proudly announcing, 'Matt Carlow's got a broken leg.'

'Don't tell me they're going to arrest *you*?' Imogen exclaims.

'No. Matt's not pressing charges. But the police want us both to go into the station in Maldon this morning to provide a statement about what happened on the island. Darren Beck's already given them chapter and verse. They want to hear it from us, too.'

'God, it's going to be all round the school by Monday morning. I hope Ian's ready for this.'

'I think Ian's still getting over the sight of his mother, swinging to the rescue like the parent-teacher division of the SAS.' Allan laughs heartily.

'Those boys were utterly traumatized, it's no joking matter,' Imogen says stonily.

'They'd only been down there for an hour,' Allan retorts. 'I think the lad's more embarrassed than anything else; for letting Matt and Darren push him around. He totally fell for their pseudo-military crap: hook, line and sinker.'

'How come all this stuff about dares and initiations is still going on within The Blackwater Boys after all these years?' Imogen suddenly asks.

'It gets passed on between the members,' Hugh explains. 'They'll be nothing written down, but over time it simply becomes a part of the culture; like the expeditions and the camping. Gilbert interpreted it as a system of actions and rewards. Plenty of organisations utilise the same concept to a certain degree.'

'What about the use of that horrible underground room?' Imogen persists. 'How did Matt know about it and why on earth would he use it again? After what happened with Joseph Langley you'd have thought Steve would have warned him off it.'

'Perhaps Steve wasn't as devastated by Joseph's death as Rick said he was,' Allan suggests thoughtfully. 'Maybe he saw the boy's fate as a sign of his weakness. He didn't turn out to be the right material for The Blackwater Boys after all - he wasn't tough enough. Joseph didn't pass the test.'

'So Steve told his boys about it. The ultimate initiation for new members. I wonder if they've used it on anyone else in the intervening years,' Hugh muses.

'If that's true, then it shows Joseph's death in a new light. It doesn't seem quite so much of a tragic accident after all. It suggests there was something premeditated about it.'

Imogen abruptly ends the discussion when her son enters the room. Ian looks tired and troubled. His eyes are puffy and his face is blotched with reddish patches.

'Would you like me to make you some breakfast, sweetheart?' She asks.

The boy remains frozen to the spot and doesn't respond for a moment.

'I've got something to tell you,' he finally declares.

Imogen feels her heart sink into her stomach. There is something about the boy's desolate expression which fills her with dread. The room is silent. Clearly no one present wishes to encourage this confession.

Ian gazes down at the flagstones beneath his feet and continues. 'The day of the fire. When you thought someone must have followed you to Mr Langley's flat, Dad. They did - and it was all because of me. *I* told Matt Carlow when you were about to leave the house. It was my first assignment for The Blackwater Boys. I knew you were going to interview Langley - I overheard you talking on the phone. So I told Matt. He said to call him in the morning when you were ready to set off. I've been such an idiot. For some reason I didn't think about why he wanted to know where Langley lived. I thought it was just a dare – to find out a secret nobody else was supposed to know. Only later did I discover what I'd done. Since then I've tried to pretend it never happened. I'm so sorry – is it my fault Mr Langley is in the hospital?' He looks desperate.

Imogen and Hugh are speechless. The news hangs ominously in the air between them.

Allan decides to intervene. 'Ian. You're going to have to come to the police station with me and your mum this morning. You will need to tell them what you've just told us, okay? You've made a pretty bad mistake, mate, so you need to try and make it good. You didn't start the fire, pal. But you've been what the lawyers call an *accessory* to the crime. You assisted them to do it. I don't know how the police are going to respond to this information, so you need to prepare yourself. At least you've done the right thing now.'

Imogen manages a nod of agreement and forces herself to place a reassuring hand on her son's arm.

Chapter Forty Nine

Hugh barely uttered a word before the others left the house. Imogen could tell he was really struggling to comprehend what Ian had done.

It was Hugh who had experienced the horror of the fire and truly understood its potentially devastating consequences. Imogen, too, is finding it hard. She just keeps thinking how her son is not a child any longer – he is seventeen years old. Should he still be making this kind of mistake? Have they failed to instil the right sort of values in him? What did they do wrong?

Fortunately, D.S. Edwards, at the Maldon police station, proves to be more understanding. She is a pretty, plumpish woman in her late thirties. Imogen gets the feeling she has children of her own, although she cannot be certain of this. Edwards listens calmly to Ian's statement and asks him a few questions. The whole interview is taped and a duty solicitor is called in to be present for the entire procedure.

After he has told them everything he knows, they go into what appears to be a family room. Imogen and Ian are directed towards a colourfully upholstered sofa while the Detective Sergeant lowers herself into the soft chair opposite.

'Now we've got Ian's testimony,' she begins. 'We will be passing his statement on to the team at the Met who are investigating the arson attack on Mr Langley. They will no doubt be interviewing Matthew Carlow again. They may also have to check your phone records, Mrs Croft; to verify Ian's story.'

'Of course,' she replies.

Edwards turns towards Ian. 'Now, I hear you had a very unpleasant experience on Saturday night, young man.'

He nods his head and the tears start to roll down his face. Imogen takes hold of his hand.

'I work with these kinds of cases a lot, Ian. You see, there are gangs in existence which set out to befriend young people and provide them with a sense of belonging. They make you feel loyal towards them and encourage you to believe that their members are your friends. In actual fact, Ian, they are clever people who are trying to manipulate you. They want to make you do things for them which are illegal. They are extremely skilled at doing this, so you mustn't be ashamed of having been taken in by them. I come across these individuals a great deal in my line of work. It's very rare to find someone who will speak up against them. You should be proud that you have come to see us today.'

Ian is sobbing by this point and Imogen hugs him tight.

'What will happen now?' She asks the policewoman.

'It depends on what action the Met decide to take, Mrs Croft. But it is very unlikely that Ian will be charged with an offence. I will recommend the issuing of a caution with no criminal record. The police are slowly getting better at recognising the all too common scenario of young people being groomed to commit crimes. Recent high profile cases have forced us to be.' The D.S. smiles kindly. 'Take your son home, Mrs Croft, and don't be too hard on him. He's actually had a very lucky escape.'

Allan takes Ian and Bridie out to a burger restaurant for lunch. He quite perceptively realises that his sister and brother-in-law need some time to talk.

As so often occurs after a period of persistent wet weather, the skies have suddenly cleared and the sun appears piercingly bright. It is almost an affront to eyes grown so accustomed to the gloom.

'I wish you'd come with us to the police station,' Imogen says to her husband, as they watch them drive away. 'The D.S. put the whole thing into perspective for me. We really shouldn't be too tough on him.'

Hugh sighs. 'I might just require a little more time to consider this, Im. People could have been killed by that fire.'

'I know, but Ian didn't realise what they were planning to do. He trusted Matt. Ian's been very silly, but he's not a monster - he's still our little boy.'

'Yes, of course. Only I can't help thinking that Bridie or Ewan would never have made a decision which was so bloody idiotic. Then I feel bad for making the comparison.'

'They are their own people, Hugh. We can't expect Ian to be like anyone else. I'll tell you something – he's never going to do anything like this again. Going into that police station shook him up badly.'

'Good. He needs to learn a lesson.'

'Now, Hugh. Sit down and listen for a minute. Ian's confession has got me thinking.'

Hugh takes one of the armchairs by the window and looks at his wife with interest.

'If Ian had to perform some kind of 'dare' straight after joining The Blackwater Boys, then Will Carlow must have had to do the same. What if it was *Will* who threw the brick through our window? The police found evidence of an abandoned encampment over in the copse - so it's got The Blackwater Boys written all over it. Your mum always said she felt it was the act of a youngster who didn't fully comprehend the consequences of their actions.'

'Then why was Matt targeting us. Was it to do with me profiling Langley?' Hugh is intrigued.

'No, I don't believe it was. Just a couple of days before, I'd been rude about The Blackwater Boys to Mark Gilbert on the phone. He caught me at a bad moment. I asked him if he left the kids on their own - without supervision. He really took offence and now I realise it was because I'd touched a raw nerve. Perhaps he told Matt Carlow about it. He was possibly just having a moan and letting off steam. But Matt decided to teach me a lesson. He made it Will's first assignment, and killed two birds with one stone.'

'It certainly makes sense. Should we tell the police?'

'I'd rather not, Hugh. Will's got enough going on at the moment with his parents splitting up. I think the broken window was an isolated incident. It doesn't have anything to do with the Langley case or the death of Joseph.'

'Agreed. What implications does Ian's confession have for the investigation into the fire at Langley's place?'

'Well, I don't believe Matt could have set the fire by himself. Someone must have been waiting there for him. Ian told the policewoman he knew Langley's safe house was somewhere in Buckhurst Hill, because he'd heard you talking with Penny about it. The Carlows already knew the general area he lived in. They simply needed to find out the exact address. They could only achieve this by following you there.'

'I suspect it was Steve who I saw walking his dog by Palmerston Road. I reckon Matt must have called ahead and told him I was making my way in his direction. He followed me to the door. They both waited until they thought I'd left and then one or both of them stuck the paraffin through the letter box.'

'Was Rick involved too?' Imogen suddenly asks.

'I expect Steve simply took the bottle of accelerant out of his brother's store room. He probably had no greater involvement than that.' Hugh sits back in quiet contemplation. '*Why* did they want to kill Langley? It seems so extreme. It's such a step-up from chucking bricks through windows and stealing a pound of sweets from the corner shop. Thomas Langley had been responsible for the death of Danny, but it *was* an accident, wasn't it? Is there a part of this puzzle we aren't seeing here, Imogen? Do the Carlows know something we do not?'

When Bridie and Ian return to school on Monday, they discover that Mark Gilbert tendered his resignation over the weekend. They are informed he will not be working out his notice, but has been given a wonderful opportunity to coach professional football overseas and decided to start straight away.

The rumour mill is already hard at work. By lunchtime, most of the students know about the camping weekend on St Peter's Island, although the exact details of Ian and Will's ordeal in 'the hole' have not yet been disclosed. The entire incident is rapidly becoming the stuff of adolescent legend.

Hugh is back in his little office along one of the labyrinthine corridors which make up the university's humanities faculty. His mind has not been fully focussed on his lectures. He is too busy revisiting the conversation he had with Imogen the previous day. In his head, Hugh is running through all his meetings with Thomas Langley. He is hoping to detect something out of place. A comment or an action he should have picked up on earlier.

He sets aside the essay he is currently marking and picks up his file on the Langley case. He flicks through the endless pages of spidery notations until he reaches the entry he is looking for. There was just one occasion when Langley hadn't behaved as he normally would have done. It sticks in Hugh's memory because on that particular day it was evident the old man had been out. He recalls the muddy boots and the umbrella lying discarded by the front door when he arrived.

Thomas had offered him an explanation before Hugh had even enquired. He'd been out walking in the park.

He missed the open space of the farm. Hugh reads through his comments again to invoke that particular morning more clearly. Thomas had been agitated. He had lost his customary calm. For the first time, Hugh thought he had identified the farmer's remorse for Danny's death. The fatalistic attitude had gone. Hugh checks the date on the entry. Then he makes a grab for the phone.

'Penny?' He demands.

'Yes, what's wrong?'

'Nothing. Look, I just wanted to ask you a question. Did the police ever check out Thomas Langley - in connection with the hit and run on Nikki Carlow?

'I know they examined his car. They wanted to ensure Langley didn't have a dark blue hatchback and it turned out he'd never owned one. I don't think it went any further than that.' Penny sounds alarmed. 'Have you found out something, Hugh?'

'I'm just trying to pin down a solid motive for the Carlows to want Thomas dead. When I looked through my records, I had logged how Langley was acting oddly in the days following Nikki's accident. It might be nothing. I thought it was worth establishing if the old man had an alibi for the afternoon she was knocked over.'

'I will give the D.I. a call and see how the investigation is progressing. I'll get straight back to you when I've got a result.'

Hugh gazes at the pile of essays. Deciding he has no hope of concentrating on them today he jumps to his feet. He grabs his coat and briefcase. Knowing he has a few hours to spare before his next tutorial, Hugh resolves to pay an old friend a surprise visit.

Thomas Langley was moved to Colchester Hospital a couple of weeks ago. Rob decided it would be easier for him to visit his father there when he is home on leave. Hugh needs to take a cab to reach the hospital building from the university. When he arrives, Hugh informs the receptionist he is Langley's psychologist and is allowed to enter the ICU without any fuss. As he walks towards Thomas's room, he suddenly realises he has brought nothing with him; no flowers or fruit. He simply shrugs his shoulders and pushes through the door.

Thomas Langley is lying perfectly still in the centre of the crisp white sheets. Although he is completely helpless, Hugh observes how the man remains sturdily built. His injuries have not depleted him in any way. The twisted plastic ventilator tube is attached by a mask taped onto his mouth. Hugh has to come very near to the bedside to see him properly. He pulls up the visitors' chair and leans in close. Then he notices that Thomas's eyes are open.

He recalls how Rob said his father was perfectly aware of what was going on around him. He intimated that he would be able to get a valid answer out of him if necessary.

Hugh smiles at the patient. 'Hello, Thomas. I'm sorry I haven't been in to see you sooner.'

The man's eyes flicker back and forth.

'You seem comfortable. The doctors say you are getting stronger every day. They hope to have you off the ventilator in time for Christmas.'

Thomas blinks.

Hugh moves in nearer. 'I know about Joseph,' he whispers.

The old man stares straight ahead.

'I was wondering why you never mentioned him to me before.'

No response.

'I'm sorry about what happened to Joseph. It might have helped if you had spoken to someone about your son, Thomas. It must have been very difficult to carry that burden for all those years.'

Thomas's eyes turn to rest upon Hugh's face.

'For a long time you had Rose to think about. Her grief was all that mattered to you. When she was gone the pain came flooding back. Finally, you managed to find some peace though, didn't you, Thomas? The peace came as soon as you heard Danny Carlow was dead. At last there'd been some kind of justice for Joseph. A son for a son. Although, after a little while, you discovered the feeling didn't last - was that when you decided the others had to pay, too?'

Thomas succeeds in shifting his head very slightly away from Hugh's gaze. He closes his eyes tight shut - showing his visitor their conversation is now over.

Hugh decides to walk back to his office. It takes him about 45 minutes, but he needs to clear his head. It was only as he had looked closely into Thomas's eyes that he recognised his anguish. The man had hidden it so well during their interviews. Hugh believes it had been temporarily forced aside by the old man's misguided conviction that he'd finally done something positive to avenge his youngest son's death.

Hugh has seen this syndrome many times in his own patients. They would throw all of their energies into pursuing a civil claim against a company or an individual who they believed were responsible for the death of a loved one. When victory finally came they would feel elation and convince themselves that grief itself had been vanquished. But then it would slowly creep its way back into their hearts. The return of that awful despair made all the worse for the fact the patient had persuaded themselves they were getting better. They thought that by taking revenge, an obstacle had been overcome.

For Hugh, the passage of time along with a genuine attempt to find some kind of acceptance is the only true healer. He can see now that Thomas never achieved this. He would not have actively sought psychiatric help - he hadn't even done so when he returned from the Chinese prisoner of war camp, back in the fifties. What saddens Hugh the most, is how he can clearly see the good man Thomas Langley should have been. It was purely the tragic circumstances of life which had taken that away from him.

Chapter Fifty One

It is only a week until Christmas and Imogen has nothing prepared. A handful of gifts have been bought but no cards written or sent. The previous few weeks have simply been too fraught for her to even think about the festive season.

Allan is still living with them. His sister would like to ask him if he is going to invite Abigail to spend the holidays at the Croft household. She feels terribly sorry for the girl, who is surely sitting at home in their flat simply waiting for word from him. Imogen never ceases to be amazed at how men can leave relationship issues hanging indefinitely in this way. The lack of clarity in the situation just doesn't seem to bother them quite so much.

Ian has been quiet for the past week. But it has not been the surly reticence they have become used to. It has been a thoughtful reserve. Imogen has found he is willing to help her around the house more and that her son is withdrawing less into his headphones and his computer games.

Imogen desperately needs to get some of her Christmas shopping done. Usually, she would set aside a day, perhaps catching the train into London and visiting Oxford Street, taking in the lights at the same time. This year, she has left it too late. Imogen is going to have to purchase her presents locally; out of necessity rather than on principle.

As she is about to leave the house, she has a thought. Imogen gets out her mobile and calls up Caroline. The woman sounds surprised to hear from her but seems keen for them to meet. They arrange to have a coffee at Lucio's in half an hour.

There has been no rain for the past few days and the water levels of the rivers and creeks have gradually returned to normal. It is cold and clear and the forecast hints at the possibility of snow. Imogen cannot imagine anyone being out at the little encampment in the woods at this time of the year; in the absolute depths of mid-winter.

She doesn't know what has happened to The Blackwater Boys and whether or not they are still meeting up without Mark Gilbert and Matt Carlow. Hugh said last evening he believes they will be back. There may be a brief hiatus in the leadership, but they will slowly drift together again and reform. He suggested they had too much shared history for the group to simply disappear without trace.

Lucio's is looking extremely festive. The dark wooden panels are festooned with burgundy-red decorations and Imogen chooses a booth near to the counter. This time deciding to avoid the window seats, although she couldn't really say why.

When Caroline enters the café, she spots her friend straight away and breaks into a broad smile. She is well dressed; in her silky red blouse and a pair of dark jeans. She appears well. Imogen makes a point of standing up to greet her properly, pulling the woman into a warm embrace. They order their lattes and sit down.

'How are things?' Imogen asks tentatively.

Caroline creases up her face. 'Rick's moved out. I think he's staying with Steve and Wendy. I haven't asked him. When he comes to see the kids he always takes them somewhere; like the movies or for a pizza. He doesn't ask to have them overnight.'

'How are the twins coping with it?'

'They are confused. Although they do know we haven't been getting along for a while now, despite the fact our marriage had recently improved.' She sighs.

'Do you think there's any chance you could forgive him?' Imogen takes a sip of her milky drink and adds, 'I mean, you *have* made some mistakes too.'

'I'm very aware of that, Imogen. I have been living with the guilt for several months. When I think about what Danny and I did, it makes me realise we never set out to hurt anyone. Nobody else in the world may ever accept it, but our relationship was built on love. We ended it so my children wouldn't find out. It was a big sacrifice. I know Danny was no angel, but he loved me very much. That made him a different person.'

Imogen smiles. 'I think I'm beginning to understand, Caroline.'

'Rick, on the other hand, has been a coward. He allowed those bullies to put that poor boy under the ground. Then, worst of all, he permitted *our son* to go off to the island knowing the same thing might happen to him. He simply sat back and let it go ahead. I can't forgive him for it, Imogen. I just can't.'

'Perhaps with time you will feel differently?' Imogen suggests weakly, but her friend has turned her face away.

'Matt and Steve have been questioned again about the fire,' Caroline then says, glancing nervously towards the door.

'It looks pretty certain they were the ones who tried to kill Thomas Langley,' Imogen explains.

Caroline twists her head back. 'I think I might know why.'

'What do you mean?'

'After we had been at your place the other night, I told Rick to go for a drive. I didn't want to be around him. I needed some time on my own. While he was out, I went up to our room and started to pack up his things. I laid out the big case and began to chuck his clothes in. As I was rummaging around his side of the wardrobe I found a letter. It was addressed to Rick and had been sent to the hardware store.'

'He hadn't shown it to you before?'

Caroline shakes her head. 'It was anonymous, as far as I could tell.'

'What did it say?'

'It was typewritten and short. It simply read; I'm going to kill your child, like you killed mine.'

Imogen unsteadily places her cup on the table. 'You need to show it to the police, Caroline. When was it sent?'

'The post mark was a couple of days before Nikki's accident.'

'Do you think Steve received a letter too?'

'I've no idea. But I think when Nikki got run over Rick must have told Steve about the note, because he was really angry about Nikki's accident. Steve and Wendy were hanging around the hospital a lot and Steve kept complaining about how the police couldn't protect us. I hadn't seen him so upset since Danny died.'

'So Steve decided to handle things himself. To protect his family,' Imogen mutters.

Caroline leans in closer to her companion. 'If I go to the police with this, it's all going to come out. Everything that Steve and Rick did to the Langley boy all those years ago *and* my affair with Danny. It will tear our family apart.'

Imogen is quiet for a moment. 'I know, Caroline. But surely you must realise there isn't any choice?'

As they sit around the table after dinner, everyone is unusually quiet. Allan has seemed lost in his thoughts for most of the day. It is Hugh who breaks the silence.

'Is Caroline going to take the letter to the police?'

'Yes. I told her it wasn't inevitable that her affair with Danny will have to come out. The only people who know about it are us and Mark Gilbert – I don't think we'll be seeing much of him in the near future. I said we were all happy to keep her secret. I don't believe it had anything at all to do with Danny's death.'

Hugh considers this. 'I agree. There's no point in upsetting Will and Nikki now. Not when their parents are separating anyway and Danny is gone. It would be pointless.'

'I've made a decision,' Allan announces, as if the previous exchange had never taken place.

'Oh?' Imogen remarks, hardly daring to hope her brother has finally grasped the nettle.

'I've been going over things a lot in my head the past few days. I had decided to let Abigail off the hook. You know, tell her she was too good for me and would be better served finding a nice young bloke who she could have a family with. It seemed to be the right thing to do.' He takes a sip of wine. 'But when I was out running today, through the woods, down by the creek, it suddenly struck me. It became crystal clear that I've been looking at everything the wrong way round.'

Imogen adopts a puzzled expression.

'Well, I've been trying to spare Abigail the pain of finding out about my affair with Alison by giving her the anguish of breaking up altogether. I simply realised today that perhaps I should give *her* the choice. I'm going to tell Abigail everything about Alison Dickson – right from the very beginning. Then I'm going to give her some time to think about it. She needs to make a decision based upon all of the facts. Up to now I've been treating her like a child. Running off to my ex-wife and sharing secrets with her, instead. It's time I moved on, guys. If Abigail is prepared to forgive my mistakes, I will ask her to marry me.'

Chapter Fifty Two

Imogen slips an arm around her husband's waist and nuzzles her face into his neck. She looks back towards the carriage window and gives her brother another wave before the train pulls jerkily out of the station and slowly disappears down the track.

'I'm really sorry to see him go.'

'Me, too,' says Hugh. 'I'd grown quite used to his company.'

'He hardly seemed interested in the Langley case at all before he left,' Imogen points out a little wistfully.

'Why should he be?' her husband responds. 'It was an interesting diversion for him for a while, but he's got his own life to lead now. Let's hope Abigail is prepared to take him back.'

'Oh, I think she will. Although in my heart I'm not actually sure it's the best thing for her. I know it's disloyal to say so, but Allan hasn't really treated her very well. If Abigail were a friend of mine I would tell her to steer well clear.'

'And she would completely ignore the advice because she loves him.'

Imogen smiles warmly and gives Hugh a tight squeeze.

'You're absolutely right.'

When they arrive home, Ian informs his father he received an urgent phone message from Penny Mills while they were out. He tells his dad he needs to call her straight away.

Hugh removes his coat and lifts the receiver.

'I'm glad you got back to me,' Penny immediately responds.

'Have you heard from the Met?' Hugh enquires.

'I certainly have.'

'Hang on a minute,' Hugh says, and he gestures for his wife to come over and listen in. 'Carry on, Penny. Imogen's here too.'

'The Detective Inspector told me at first that they had hit something of a brick wall with the investigation. Absolutely no witnesses had come forward to identify the driver of the vehicle, so they focussed on identifying the car itself. They had no registration number so they weren't holding out much hope. All they could do was to circulate the description and perform a search on the police database. Apparently, a couple of days ago they had a result. The anti-terrorist unit were doing spot checks on vehicle hire companies. One of their men noticed that a dark blue Vauxhall Astra had been reported damaged on the day of Nikki's accident. He'd seen the bulletin about the hit-and-run and made the connection. The car hire people said the guy who brought the vehicle back had paid in cash for the damage *and* for the hire of the car. The name and address he gave turned out to be false. They did manage to provide a rough description of the chap, though.'

'It sounds like another dead-end,' Imogen adds.

'Perhaps not,' Penny replies. 'The reason the anti-terrorist unit stumbled upon this car-hire place is because it operates out of Stansted.'

'The airport?' Imogen interjects.

'Yep,' says Penny.

'Andy Langley,' Hugh mutters softly.

*

Penny is joining the team from the Metropolitan Police who are flying out to France in order to interview Thomas Langley's son. Penny said she told the D.I to check all flights out of Stansted bound for Carcassonne airport on the day the hire car was returned. They found Andrew Langley on the passenger list. It isn't quite so easy to give a false name when you book a plane ticket. Usually, it has to match the details on your passport.

Imogen and Hugh recline in the two armchairs placed beneath their lovely picture window and gaze out at the bright white sky. It looks as if the forecast may be right for once and snow is on the way. Hugh has fixed them both a neat brandy, even though it is only mid-afternoon. They feel slightly shaken by Penny's news. It provides a kind of closure to the case, but it is unsettling just the same.

'I thought Andy hadn't been to visit his father at all since the shooting,' Imogen says.

'Obviously, he had.'

'Andy Langley had nothing against the Carlows, did he? Andy had been friends with Danny and was very upset when his father told him he wasn't able to continue their relationship. I don't understand why on earth he would have tried to kill Nikki on his father's say so.'

'The attack on the girl was pretty half-hearted, Imogen. I hope the police can see that too. I believe Andy simply made the terrible mistake of going to visit his dad. He probably felt guilty and sensed he should show him some moral support. It was during this visit Thomas told his son what had really happened to Joseph. I don't think Andy knew the details properly before. He and Rob were already away in army training when the boy died.'

'After that, Andy finally knew exactly why his father hadn't wanted him to pursue a friendship with Danny,' Imogen states.

'Yes, because Danny's father had killed his younger brother.'

'I still can't see how that knowledge would turn Andy into a potential child-killer. He was a man who dedicated his life to serving his country.'

'Oh, I'm sure he didn't want to do it. He probably thought his father had gone stark-raving mad. To start taking vengeance on the people who caused Joseph's death after all those years had passed. In a sense, Thomas *had* entered into a kind of madness. He was beside himself with grief and anger and desperately needed an end point to it all. Andy didn't hire the car and try to run down Nikki because he wanted justice for his brother. He didn't even believe it would help his dad to overcome his anguish. He did it because Thomas asked him to and he is his father. Thomas must have told him he had to kill one of Rick's children for the sake of the family. For some people, an appeal to family loyalty is a request it's not possible for them to refuse.'

'How would Andy have known how to identify her?' Imogen suddenly asks.

'We'll have to wait for him to give us the details,' Hugh says. 'I suspect he was tailing the Carlows for a while, watching their routines and habits. When Nikki stepped out into the road, he saw his chance. It must have been awful for him when the car hit her.'

'Are we feeling sorry for Andy, then?'

'When I met the man, I have to confess that I liked him. Despite the fact it was clear he wasn't telling me everything. I do pity him, yes. If he had stayed in France and followed his instinct to get as far away from Langley Farm as possible, he would still be happy now. In his 'sunflower' hotel, with the woman he so clearly loves.'

Imogen sits impassively, sipping the soothing liquid and savouring the way it deliciously burns the inside of her mouth. 'What will happen to Thomas now?'

'I think he's got away with it. There's no way of proving he killed Danny deliberately and he may not have done. But the feeling of release it gave him was intoxicating. I don't think Andy will implicate his father in the attack on Nikki. He will take the blame for that himself and serve whatever sentence is meted out to him.'

'So Langley gets off scot free?' Imogen's unconscious choice of words immediately calls to mind the heated conversation she had with Wendy Carlow in the High Street all those weeks ago.

'He'll never see the inside of a prison cell, if that's what you mean.' Hugh looks out towards the water, where tiny white flakes have begun to sprinkle themselves across its calm surface.

'Are you going to write a book about the Langley case for Martin?'

Hugh turns back to his wife and smiles. 'I think I'll just live quietly with my family for a while. Concentrate properly on my students and my research. The next time I'm asked to help out with a high profile case, I may very well say no.' He reaches forward and takes Imogen gently by the hand, absent-mindedly twisting her wedding ring around between his thumb and forefinger.

They remain like this for some time until Imogen disturbs their peace by saying, 'the night when Allan and I went out to St Peter's Island, Penny said something odd to me.'

Hugh's face goes blank.

'When we had returned, she took me aside and apologised for having made a pass at you in France. She said it was wrong of her and unfair on me and the kids. Then she muttered something else - it was almost like an afterthought. Penny added that she should have learnt her lesson by now, because this was the second time you had chosen me over her. Since that night, I haven't been able to get those words out of my head.

Hugh, just what exactly did Penny mean when she said it was the *second* time?

The moon is so bright and clear that Thomas Langley doesn't bother to switch on the light. Instead, he allows the pale bluish glow to illuminate the room through the curtain-less window. Thomas is very tired and it is getting late, but he is suddenly drawn to the photographs on the mantelpiece. He picks up one of the studio shots which is mounted in a heavy silver frame. It is a picture of his middle child, Andrew, with his younger son, Joseph, seated on his lap.

The little boy is only a toddler here. Thomas recalls it was taken a few years after they had returned from New Zealand. Joseph looks so small and spindly but his blue eyes are full of life. He was very much like his mother, Thomas thinks to himself. It is strange how he never recognised that fact when the boy was still alive.

Thomas makes his way up the stairs to bed. He is so tired after driving all the way to Ipswich and back that he falls straight to sleep. Abruptly, a noise wakes him. He goes to the grubby window which looks out over the farm's courtyard. Thomas imagines he sees figures moving around down there.

He wastes no time and pulls on his dressing gown. He goes straight to the gun cabinet in the hall. Finding the key in the drawer he takes out the shot gun and checks the ammunition. Then he stuffs his feet into a pair of wellie boots and strides out into the night.

Langley may be in his seventies, but he likes to think he is still pretty strong. He stripped all the lead flashing off the cottage roof single-handed and it wasn't an easy job. It would have exhausted a man half his age, he firmly believes. Langley is certainly fit enough to defend his own farm.

When he reaches the courtyard he can see the barn doors have been forced open. Immediately, he suspects they must be after the lead. How did they know it was in there, he wonders? Is it those bloody kids who've been watching him from the woods again? He thought he'd scared them off the last time. Little buggers.

Langley steps inside. It is pitch black within the barn and he can't make out a thing, but he can hear them. They're rummaging about at the back somewhere. Like filthy rats in a rubbish dump.

'Who's there?' He calls into the darkness.

There is absolute silence for a moment and then Thomas hears the sound of heavy footfalls. Before he has a chance to react, he is violently knocked to the ground. He's temporarily winded, but quickly regains composure. As he begins to right himself he senses a dark shadow fall across his body. He glances upwards just in time to see a tall figure bringing down a hard metal object against the side of his face.

When he comes to again, Thomas feels a surge of adrenaline. He knows those lads have got his lead and he's damned if he'll let them get away with it. Langley puts a hand up to his forehead and feels the blood. He shifts himself onto his feet and cocks the gun. Pointing it purposefully ahead of him, he allows his aim to rest briefly on the back of one of the rapidly retreating figures in the distance.

Then he starts to run. He was a champion sprinter in his early army career, so he'll have no trouble catching up to this rabble of good-for-nothings, who no doubt spend their days sat in front of computer screens and games consoles.

Thomas thinks he must be in a bad way, because they're getting away from him. One of the lads has nearly reached the copse of trees. He'll never be able to track them down in there. So he stops for a moment and lets off a shot. A friendly warning, if you like.

Thomas is immediately reminded of his army days because the three boys ahead of him abruptly drop to the ground. He'd be quite impressed if they were his cadets. They've got pretty fast reflexes. Thomas moves in a little closer and then he shouts out to them. He tells these lads to give him back his stuff and he'll let them go.

For a little while none of them answers. The full moon is making it as light as day, but he can't see those boys lying in the undergrowth. Their camouflage gear is too effective. Thomas is beginning to feel a bit unsettled. If they don't respond to this he'll have to up the ante. Maybe fire a few shots into the grass. See how they like that.

Finally, one of them lifts himself up off the ground and Thomas can identify his position. The farmer lets him go after he throws him the rucksack. He's not an unreasonable man. His word is good.

After this boy disappears into the woods, Thomas calls out again. He tells them to show themselves or he'll start shooting at the ground. He thinks that utilizing some scare tactics should speed things up a little. He's got the gun, for heaven's sake, they must be absolutely terrified out there.

The silence continues for too long. Thomas begins to get anxious. If these lads call his bluff then he's got no more cards up his sleeve. He's damned if they're going to take off with all that lead sheeting. Thomas sweated blood to remove it.

He is just deciding what to do next when the old man feels his legs go out from under him. He falls flat on his back, and the breath is forced out of his body. What the bloody hell's going on?

Thomas's mind races. He holds the shotgun tight. He must have instinctively kept a firm grip on it as he went down.

In an instant, the same tall figure is looming over him again. This time, the light of the moon isn't behind him but is glowing directly onto his face.

Thomas sees the menacing grin and the yellow-stained, crooked teeth. Those small, terrier-like eyes.

Danny Carlow.

Before the lad can deliver a second blow with his crow-bar, he is momentarily distracted. The other boy has come up behind him and makes a grab for Carlow's right arm. He shouts at him to stop and this buys Thomas a few precious seconds.

In that time, an image floats into his head. He sees that spindly little nipper again. This time he's riding on his bike; going up and down the lane in front of their cottage. His mother stands at one end and he at the other. The boy is shrieking with laughter.

Thomas raises the shotgun as far as he is able, carefully aims, and then gently squeezes the trigger.

■■

Acknowledgements:

My thanks go once again to my editorial team; Bob, Sue
and Anne. Without whose continual guidance and
patient care, my books would not see the light of day.
Thanks, as ever, to Rakesh, Shona and Jamie, who have
to live with my plot lines and characters for months at a
time. Yet are always ready with excellent advice and
eager encouragement.
I also need to extend my gratitude to the late Dr Claire
Weekes, whose books and case-studies about the
overcoming of nervous illness were an invaluable source
of information for me when writing of Allan's breakdown.
Her timeless work really is the definitive guide to this
subject.
Finally, I would like to thank all those people who have
read my books so far. Your wonderful words of support
have given me the confidence to keep writing. Every
comment is truly appreciated.

K.
February 2014

Imogen and Hugh will return in:
'The Woman Who Vanished'

THE GARANSAY PRESS

298

Printed in Great Britain
by Amazon.co.uk, Ltd.,
Marston Gate.